ALSO BY FRANCIS DUNCAN

In the Mordecai Tremaine Series

Murder Has a Motive

So Pretty a Problem

Behold a Fair Woman

In at the Death

MURDER for CHRISTMAS

WITHDRAWN

FRANCIS DUNCAN

sourcebooks
landmark

Published by Sourcebooks Landmark, an imprint of Sourcebooks, Inc.
P.O. Box 4410, Naperville, Illinois 60567-4410
(630) 961-3900
Fax: (630) 961-2168
www.sourcebooks.com

Originally published in 1949 in the United Kingdom by John Long. This edition issued based on the paperback edition published in 2015 in the United Kingdom by Vintage Books, an imprint of Penguin Random House UK.

Library of Congress Cataloging-in-Publication Data

Names: Duncan, Francis, author.
Title: Murder for Christmas / Francis Duncan.
Description: Naperville, Illinois : Sourcebooks Landmark, [2017] |
  "Originally published in 1949 in the United Kingdom by John Long."
Identifiers: LCCN 2017002597 | (softcover : acid-free
  paper)
Subjects: LCSH: Murder--Investigation--Fiction. | Christmas stories. | GSAFD:
  Mystery fiction.
Classification: LCC PR6007.U527 M87 2017 | DDC 823/.914--dc23 LC record
available at https://lccn.loc.gov/2017002597

Printed and bound in the United States of America.
VP 10 9 8 7 6 5 4 3 2 1

PROLOGUE

No one could have foretold how it was going to end. Not even the murderer.

It is not to say that the crime was hastily conceived and clumsily executed. The majority of murderers are anxious to live to savor the fruits of their villainies. They realize that one slip may deliver them to the hangman. They know that to be careless is to be lost. And in this case, the murderer possessed both desire to profit and the knowledge of how perilously thin the dividing line is between safety and disaster.

But no human plan, however devilish its ingenuity, can be depended upon to follow in practice the exact lines of its careful theory. Somewhere along the route, incalculable and unforeseeable will lie the unexpected, the unknown factor.

The moon was like a spotlight playing over the stage of a theater. Or, like a camera tracking over a studio floor and alternately presenting its audience with close-ups and long shots, sharply outlined image and somber obscurity.

The snow had stopped, but the sky had not yet cleared.

The clouds were drifting sullenly, as if reluctant to leave a prey freed only with difficulty from their grip. Sometimes they would gather menacingly upon one another and would crowd over an earth grown dark and full of fear; and then it would seem that they were thrust impotently apart and the white light would flood down, cold and revealing, and not to be turned aside.

And in the moonlight, every detail would be there in hard relief. The black-and-white roofs of the village under the hill; the thin, bare arms of the trees along the roadway; the smooth white downs rolling up to the sky; the big house with its old gray stones; and the white tracery where the snow clung to the creeper.

From the village came the sound of a bell. When the darkness was triumphant, it was a strange and mournful echo that could not be located and that held a note of menace. Imagination needed little encouragement to liken the sound to the tolling of doom.

But when the scene lay exposed under the moon, the fear and the mystery were driven back. The bell was no longer sinister. It was a glad sound of music that carried triumphantly across the snow, ringing out from the square tower of the ancient church.

The landscape was a Christmas card in three dimensions. There would have been no incongruity if a sleigh drawn by reindeer had come sweeping over the brow of the downs. It did not, in fact, seem fantastic that the red-robed figure of Father Christmas was outlined in the moonlight, moving quickly along the terrace of the big house. It was, after all, Christmas Eve, when such things—particularly in such a setting—were to be expected.

Although it was late, the occupants of the house were not all in their beds. High up in one wing, a light still burned. At intervals, a figure crossed the illuminated frame that was the window.

There were other signs of activity that were not quite so apparent. But if one watched carefully, it was sometimes possible, especially when the moon was obscured, to see a faint glow behind the windows of the ground floor. It was a glow that changed its position, as though it owed its origin to a flashlight carried by someone who moved stealthily within the house.

And outside in the snow and the shadows there were muffled, hidden figures. Concealed from the house and from each other, they watched intently—and waited upon opportunity.

The atmosphere was brooding, tense with foreboding. Fantasy and mystery, violence and death were abroad. It seemed that time was moving reluctantly and with an ever more tightly coiled dread toward some terrible climax.

And at last the climax came.

It came when the bell had stopped. It came when the moonlight, searching again through the clouds, swept softly across the white lawns, revealing the ragged line of footprints. It came when the cold light flooded up to the half-open french doors and, tracing the moisture on the polished floor, came to rest upon the red thing of horror that was Father Christmas, stark and sprawled upon its face in front of the despoiled Christmas tree.

It came with a woman's scream—desperate, high-pitched, and raw with terror.

1

"I believe," said Denys excitedly, "it really is!"

From the depths of the big, round-backed chair facing the log fire there issued an inquiring voice.

"Really is what?"

"Going to be an old-fashioned Christmas!" Denys switched her attention from the leaden sky and gave a cry of delight as she caught sight of the first flake revealed in its gentle descent against the dark background of the laurels flanking the drive. "Here it comes, Roger! Real, delicious, sugar-icing snow!"

The big chair groaned.

"Horrible!" it stated. "Wet, beastly, uncomfortable stuff. I suppose we'll have to run the gauntlet of all the uninhibited little urchins in the village. Snowballs in the back of the neck every time we step outside the grounds. *Brr!*"

Denys Arden laughed happily. It was a laugh that did disturbing things to Roger Wynton's self-control.

He was, of course, in love with her. He had been ever since

he had swung his car a little recklessly around one of the many corners in the narrow lanes that meandered through the lush countryside about the deep-rooted village of Sherbroome to startle her horse and become the admiring victim of her fury.

That had been early in the preceding year on a day when the roads had rung hard under the frost and a keen wind had whipped the roses into Denys Arden's cheeks and tumbled her chestnut curls into an attractive confusion. Oblivious of her stormy indignation, Roger had stared up at the trim figure in the riding habit with an admiration so open that the color in her cheeks had ceased to owe its presence entirely to the wind. And, feeling her mastery of the situation endangered, she had tossed her head in one last indignant gesture and edged past him.

When he had reached home, Wynton had made inquiries concerning her. He came of a family whose name (if in varying spellings) had recurred many times in the records of Sherbroome, but his professional training as an architect, and a tour abroad, had caused him to lose touch with the social life of the district. Certainly he could not recollect any of the gawky schoolgirls he had once known who was likely to have emerged from her freckled chrysalis into such a spirited vision as the girl he had just encountered.

The solution to the mystery had proved to lie in the fact that Sherbroome House was occupied. The dignified gray house, which stood aloof from and yet seemed to dominate the huddled little village of mossy roofs and half-timbered cottages, had entranced him as a boy. Its neglected orchards and derelict outbuildings had been his paradise of adventure, peopled with brave figures from his imagination.

The Melvins had come to Sherbroome when the first Sir Hugo, who had braved the Channel with William of Normandy, had ridden into the West Country. Sherbroome House had been the seat of authority in the surrounding countryside. Elizabeth of England had graced it with her presence for a whole five days not long after Sir Reginald Melvin, fighting his own ship, had helped to disperse the Armada along the hostile length of that awesome virgin's rocky coasts. Her stay had played havoc with Sir Reginald's treasury, but it had gained him a barony.

Great days they had been for the Melvins, Barons of Sherbroome. But they had paid in the end for their allegiance to the throne. Royalist in an area held by the Parliament during the civil war, they had returned to power with Charles the Second, only to make the fatal mistake of adhering to the Jacobites when George of Hanover crossed the water. And when Culloden was a bloody defeat and Charles Stuart had accepted the end of the gamble and gone back to France and exile, the head of the sixth Lord Sherbroome had fallen from the block on Tower Hill and the barony had been proscribed.

Somehow the family had managed to retain the house and a shrunken estate, but the sinews of war were gone, and there were no more scenes of splendor. And late in the nineteenth century the old tree had been stripped so bare of fruit that what was left had passed into the hands of a distant cousin who could not afford even to live in his inheritance, and Sherbroome House had become a shuttered, decaying home of ghosts and memories.

As long as Roger Wynton could recall, there had been rumors. The village still regarded the big, gray house with respect, and there were always old men to swear that one day the Melvins would return, and the lights would blaze again along the terrace.

But the years had gone by, and the impoverished descendants of the proud family that had once entertained a queen had shown no sign that they were coming back. And now it did not seem that they ever would come back, for Sherbroome House had been sold.

The new owner, Roger learned, was Benedict Grame. While it was likely that he had bought the house for a purely nominal figure—it had been no more than a white elephant— Grame had spent a great deal on putting the place in order. Which meant that he must be a comfortingly wealthy man.

The girl, Roger had insisted gently. Who was the girl? Grame's daughter?

No, not Grame's daughter. In fact, nobody's daughter. At least, she had no living parent. She was in the care of Jeremy Rainer, who was one of Grame's closest friends. Rainer had brought her up and had, apparently, provided for her since the death of her father who had been his partner.

Did she spend much time at Sherbroome? The answer was that she did. Rainer and Grame were on intimate terms, and Grame seemed very fond of Denys. That was her name. Denys Arden. She was often to be seen riding in the neighborhood. Roger Wynton had needed no more than that. As often as he could get away from his London practice, he, too, was to be seen riding in the neighborhood.

On the fourth carefully planned occasion, he had managed to meet her by chance and had recalled their original encounter. Her sense of humor had been equal to the situation—he had imagined it would be—and from then on, as the French say with such charm, the affair had marched.

Wynton had become a very frequent visitor to the ancient gray house where he had passed so many boyish hours. He had sat again in its mellow rooms and heard the ring of his footsteps upon its wide stone terraces, and it had grown very dear to him now that it spoke to him of Denys. In high summer, with the sunlight warming the polished oak, and now in the deep winter with the grayness softened by the leaping flames of a log fire, he had found a new magic in it because of her presence.

He rose from his chair, deliberately slowly so that he should not betray himself, turning so that he could see her framed against the window, her head held back and the firelight playing on the white grace of her throat.

"Don't look like that, Denys," he said. "I can't bear it. I'm so mad about you."

She smiled at him. "I like you when you make pretty speeches, Roger," she said softly.

He went to meet her and caught her hands. "Denys… darling…you do care?"

She nodded seriously. "Yes, Roger," she said.

"Then say you'll marry me—soon!"

"No," she said firmly. "Jeremy—"

"Jeremy!" he exploded. "Jeremy! Why should he come between us? I know what he's done for you, but there's a limit to what he has a right to expect!"

The shadows of a troubled mind were in the girl's brown eyes, but her resolution was unchanged. "It's old ground, Roger. We don't need to travel it again. I've got to make him see it our way."

"It would be easier if we knew a little more of his reasons. *Why* does he keep objecting? I'm not so infernally ugly that I scare children!"

"You're really quite a nice ugly duckling," she said.

Her fingers ruffled his hair in a manner that was both possessive and tender and traced the familiar line of his cheek. There was something solidly reassuring about Roger Wynton's rugged features.

"If I'm not exactly a rich man," he went on, "he knows that you wouldn't have to worry about money. And he knows I'm in love with you. It must be plain enough!"

"It is," she told him with a flash of mischief she could not suppress, and he smiled wryly.

"Isn't there anything we can do?"

"I've tried everything," she said. "It's no good hiding from it. He just doesn't like you."

"But why? What's it all about? If he'd say what was in his mind, it would give us something to go on, but this is just sheer blind prejudice. The truth is that he's scared of losing you. It isn't just me he's up against. He'd find objections to anyone who wanted to marry you."

He put his hands on her shoulders. She could feel the strong, nervous pressure of his fingers.

"What about Grame? He's obviously fond of you, and he seems to have influence with your guardian. Couldn't you get him on our side?"

Denys shook her head. "I told you I've tried everything, Roger, and one of the first was Uncle Benedict. It's no good.

He said that when he spoke to Jeremy about it, he might just as well have waved a red flag at him. Whatever influence Uncle Benedict has, it evidently doesn't go that far."

Wynton was silent for a moment or two and then replied: "I've got to say this, Denys." His voice held a note of determination. "There's something odd about Rainer. It's true," he added quickly, as he saw her instinctive movement of protest. "There's something queer about this whole place. The sooner I can get you away from it, the happier I'll be."

He was so serious that her indignation withered before it had been allowed to take vigorous root. "What on earth do you mean, Roger?" she asked.

"I mean that I don't like to think of your being here with all these strange relatives of yours. I know they're not really your relatives, of course. Maybe that's why I'm being so frank about them. They're not normal. You can never tell when they're going to stop behaving like ordinary people and do something completely irrational."

"You mean like Uncle Gerald turning up at the flower show last year dressed as a schoolboy in short trousers and scandalizing all the dear old ladies in the sewing circle?"

"And having himself pushed through the village street in a perambulator with a baby's dummy in his mouth and the local band in front!"

"You're surely not going to find anything sinister in that,

Roger! You know how Gerald loves practical jokes. He's just an overgrown boy."

"I can appreciate a practical joke, but it seems to me that his knees are the wrong shape for that sort of Peter Pan act."

"Now you're throwing your sense of proportion overboard!"

"Perhaps I am," he admitted. "But it's certainly a peculiar household. Gerald with his periodic outbursts of schoolboy humor and alternately soaking himself in whiskey and swearing to reform, and Charlotte shutting herself up in her room for hours at a time and behaving like a soured old maid with a dark secret. It amazes me that Grame manages to put up with them. A month of it would send me crazy, but he seems to take it all cheerfully enough."

"When you put it like that," said the girl slowly, "it does seem a rather somber picture. But they've always been nice to me. I can't suddenly turn on them."

"I'm not suggesting that you're the victim of any evil designs on their part," said Wynton hastily. "But the atmosphere of the place is unhealthy. I can't understand Rainer allowing you to spend so much time here."

"He encourages me to come," Denys told him. "I didn't think," she added slyly, "that *you* had any objection to that."

"I haven't. But I'm curious. Why did he decide to spend Christmas here?"

"We always spend Christmas with Uncle Benedict. It's a sort of tradition."

"I know that Grame likes to go in for this Christmas family gathering kind of thing and that you've always been members of the party. But I thought that this year Rainer was going to America and that all the arrangements had been made for him to sail last week. What made him change his mind?"

The girl was frowning now. It was evident that the question had touched a matter over which she had already been puzzled.

"I don't know, Roger," she admitted. "It *was* rather strange. He canceled all his plans quite suddenly. It wasn't like him at all."

"He didn't give you any reason?"

"No."

"And that wasn't like him either, was it?"

"He doesn't keep many things from me. I did wonder why he hadn't made at least some comment. I thought—" She broke off as they heard the sound of the opening door. Instinctively, they drew apart, turning to face it. A tall figure loomed upon the threshold. Saturnine in the gloom, it stood motionless.

Denys found her mind behaving idiotically. *Thunder Without*, it said. *Enter a Conspirator*. She wanted to giggle nervously.

And then Nicholas Blaise saw them standing at the deep window, behind which was now a whirling curtain of softly falling snow. He came into the room. "Hullo," he said and added, as he came toward them. "Cheering on the weather? It looks as though we're going to have the traditional setting for the Christmas festivities."

His manner was easy, but his dark, questing eyes missed nothing. They did not know whether he had overheard any of their conversation, and he gave them no hint.

It was seldom possible to tell what Nicholas Blaise was thinking. Nor was it certain how much he knew. But he had been Benedict Grame's secretary and intimate companion for many years, and undoubtedly he knew a great deal about every guest who came to Sherbroome House.

It was difficult to assess his age. He had the air of a young man at first glance, but when one studied him more closely, the slightly receding hair, the shadowed experience in the dark-brown eyes deep set against the long, thin nose, and the expression in the finely drawn intelligent face all revealed him to be older than he had seemed. His hands were long-fingered, artistic, and expressive. He might be an unobtrusive background figure, but there was little that escaped him.

There was a faint air of amusement about him now. He had the look of a man who was fully aware that an attempt was being made to keep something from him, and who was savoring the irony of the fact that he knew quite well what that something was.

It was a little disturbing. Denys Arden found herself waiting for him to speak with a feeling of tension. It was absurd, of course. Nick was perfectly normal and was behaving in a perfectly ordinary way. It was her imagination that was making her think there was something vaguely mysterious in his manner. It was Roger's fault. His ridiculous fancies about the house and the people in it were making her see things that did not exist.

"I hope it will pitch." Blaise was peering out of the window. "If we have a good fall, Benedict will be in his element."

It was so much the ordinary kind of remark he might have been expected to make that Denys felt security returning.

"Uncle Benedict certainly likes to have all the Christmas trimmings," she said with relief. "I suppose he'll be playing his usual part?"

Blaise turned back from the window with a smile.

"I think he looks forward to Christmas Eve all the year. He was sorting out his costume this morning, and he's been hiding mysterious parcels for days past!"

Christmas with Benedict Grame followed an orthodox and unvarying course. A house full of people, a large Christmas tree, and Grame himself taking a child's natural delight in appearing late on Christmas Eve in full regalia of long, red cloak and white beard, making what he imagined to be an unobserved visit to the tree for the purpose of loading it with presents for his guests.

He was a bachelor, and it seemed that having no children upon whom to expend his enthusiasms, he had chosen this method of finding enjoyment. The very nature of his idiosyncrasy ensured its being regarded tolerantly, and since Grame was a rich man whose generosity was well known amongst his acquaintances, he was able to indulge in his annual play-acting without ridicule. As a rule, his guests knew of his custom before their arrival. If they didn't, they soon learned their cues from their more-experienced companions.

If any cynics, stripped of sentiment by contact with a harshly materialistic world, thought that it was an odd kind of foible for a man like Grame to possess, they kept their counsel. Courtesy and the Christmas atmosphere had a great deal to do with their attitude, of course, but it must be admitted that the fact that Benedict Grame was not the sort of man whom it was politic to cross was not without its own significance.

The blue eyes sheltered beneath the bushy gray eyebrows were normally calmly philosophic, but there were times when they could flash a spark to kindle his anger. And on those occasions the big, raw-boned frame would seem to expand to dominating size, and one would realize that the slow-moving man who regarded life with such amused detachment—and who could derive youthful pleasure from disporting himself as Father Christmas—had fire within him.

Denys Arden had made the discovery when she was a

small girl, and the respect it had engendered when the man she had always termed her uncle had found her engaged in a wild abandon of infant scribbling among the papers in the forbidden territory of his study—and had taken her to task—had remained with her through the years.

For some inexplicable reason, that ages-old but still-remembered incident came fleetingly back into her mind as she stood looking at Nicholas Blaise. He wondered what was in her thoughts, but she did not tell him the reason for the flicker of amusement in her eyes. Instead she said, "Who's going to be here, Nick?"

"The usual crowd," he told her. "Rosalind Marsh, Austin Delamere—all of us, of course. The Napiers are coming. They'll be bringing Mrs. Tristam."

"Oh!" said Denys.

"Yes," said Nicholas Blaise.

Lucia Tristam was becoming a frequent visitor. Her age was indeterminate. She was over thirty, but beyond that, speculation was difficult. Undeniably, she was a good-looking woman. Her dark-red hair, luxuriant and with a myriad subtle glints of flame in it when she tossed her head against the light with studied carelessness, would have saved her from being ignored in any gathering. Possessing in addition a colorful personality and a figure of tawny grace, she was in no danger of languishing unadmired.

"She's a widow, isn't she?" asked Wynton.

"So she says," observed the girl. "We don't know that she's a widow, any more than we know that her name really is Lucia."

"You mean they're both attributes acquired for effect? I gather you're not fond of the lady?"

"I'm not," said Denys bluntly.

"Of course, you haven't met Mrs. Tristam yet," interposed Blaise, obviously sensing danger and addressing himself to Wynton before the girl could elaborate. "You haven't been over a great deal since she's been down here, and so far your visits and hers haven't managed to coincide. She came to stay with the Napiers last September."

"For a month," said the girl.

"I don't think any definite time limit was set," remarked Blaise tactfully, "although she does seem to be extending her stay."

It was obvious that there was more to be told. "She seems to like the air in these parts," Wynton said exploringly.

Blaise gave him a shrewd glance. There was a glimmer of humor in his brown eyes.

"I don't think," he said, "it's altogether the air."

"*I'll* tell you," said Denys. "Nick is too polite. The Tristam woman is a man hunter. At the moment, she doesn't seem to be able to make up her mind which man she wants. The odds are pretty even on Jeremy and Uncle Benedict."

Roger Wynton raised his eyebrows.

"So that's it."

"That," she told him, "is it."

"What do the victims think about it?"

"She's clever," said Denys. "She has a good figure. And you know what men are."

Nicholas Blaise had the wary look of a man who could see troubled waters ahead and had no wish to be lured into them.

"I'll continue my tour," he said. "I really came in to see if Benedict was here. You haven't any idea where he is?"

"Sorry," said Wynton. "I haven't seen him this afternoon."

Blaise was turning when Denys said, "Just a moment, Nick, before we lose you again. Had you finished telling us about the festivities? Is anyone coming whom we don't know?"

"Well, there's Professor Lorring. I expect you know him by reputation at least. He's the scientist. Oh, and there's Mordecai Tremaine."

"Tremaine?" said Wynton, and Blaise nodded.

"Yes. It's his first visit."

"Old or young?" said Denys.

"Elderly. Something in the sixties, I should imagine. He's an interesting character. On the sentimental side. I think you'll like him."

Blaise looked from one to the other of his companions as

he spoke. They were not certain whether there was anything significant in his manner or not, and he took advantage of their hesitant silence to make his exit.

"Sounds like the same mixture as before," observed Wynton, as the door closed upon Blaise's dark figure. "Apart from Lorring and Tremaine. And I don't suppose they'll make any violent difference."

"You must admit, Roger," said the girl, "that Uncle Benedict's Christmas parties are usually very jolly affairs. He does his best to make things go with a swing."

"Yes," returned Wynton slowly. "Yes, he does."

He seemed to be preoccupied, having replied to her in a mechanical fashion. But before she could make any comment, the door opened again.

Wynton sensed the dislike in Jeremy Rainer's gray eyes even before the older man had crossed the room. He reacted instinctively, and antagonism crackled between them.

"I didn't know you were here, Wynton." The words were calm enough, but the frost of enmity was on them.

"Roger came over to take me out, but I didn't think the weather was very promising, so we decided not to bother after all," Denys said hastily.

"You were very wise, my dear. It looks as if we're in for a heavy fall."

"We were just saying to Nick that Uncle Benedict

will be delighted. Snow is all he needs to complete his Christmas effects."

The girl was straining nervously to build up a conversation before the two men could reach each other's throats. Rainer looked at her quickly, as though she had sounded some chord in him and he found the experience disconcerting.

"Yes," he said after a pause. "Yes, I suppose it is."

He moved to the window, and Roger Wynton studied the hard profile as it was poised against the wintry light. *Like against like*, he thought. *Ice against ice.*

Jeremy Rainer had resigned most of his many directorships and was popularly believed to be financing his retirement out of the fortune he had made. He had earned the reputation of being ruthless in business, and some of the reason for that reputation was revealed now in the hawklike curve of the nose, accentuated in profile, and in the taut line of the mouth that was shut tight above the rigid jaw.

A hard man, unswayed by sentiment. So they said of him. And unswayed he seemed to be—except where Denys was concerned. Roger Wynton had to grant him that. Such humanity as there was in him had crystallized around his ward. There was no doubt of his fondness for her. No doubt that she was at the center of his toughly fibered life.

It was the reason, Wynton's thoughts whispered, for the man's attitude. He could not share Denys. She was the jewel he wished to shut away in his heart, and he could not bear the prospect of loss.

A gray man. That was Jeremy Rainer. Gray hair; gray eyebrows, shaggily massive over the hard eyes that held a grayness as well; gray mustache, close-cropped and stiff; and a gray, forbidding soul.

Damn him! Why should he usurp the right to control the life of another human being? Why should he presume to dictate to Denys?

Momentarily, a surge of anger that surprised him as it came swept through Wynton's mind. He wanted to feel his hands upon the wide, intolerant shoulders, wanted to swing the gray form around and thrust his challenge into the wintry face. Wanted to shout that Denys was his and that he would marry her and that Jeremy Rainer could go to hell.

And then the man had stepped back, and both the gray illusion and the sudden storm of emotion were gone.

"I thought I heard a car not long ago," Rainer said casually. "Anyone turned up yet, Denys?"

"I don't think so," she told him. "It was probably Roger you heard. Is anyone expected today? I thought zero hour was tomorrow."

"I did hear that Professor Lorring might be down," he said, "although most people won't be arriving until tomorrow. Delamere, of course, will probably wait until the day after. He usually leaves his arrival until Christmas Eve. I suppose he imagines he can give us the impression that politicians have to work up to the last minute."

"What about the other new one?" said Denys. "Besides Professor Lorring, I mean. What did Nick say his name was, Roger?"

"Tremaine," said Wynton. "Mordecai Tremaine."

"Who's Mordecai Tremaine?" asked Rainer.

"I'm disappointed," said the girl. "I thought *you* were going to tell *us*."

"Don't know the fellow," returned Rainer. "Someone Benedict's invited down, I suppose, to make up his Christmas party."

Wynton was frowning.

"You know, Denys," he said slowly, "I believe I *have* heard of him. I've been trying to remember where ever since Blaise went out." The frown deepened. And then, suddenly… "That's it," he said. "That's where I've seen his name! In the newspapers! He's some sort of detective!"

There was a sharp, snapping sound. Jeremy Rainer had just taken a cigarette from the silver box that stood on a nearby table. The sound was that of the lid being replaced. "What do you mean?" he said quickly.

"It was that affair down in Sussex last summer," Wynton said. "This chap Tremaine was working with the police. The newspapers were full of it."

"He sounds exciting," said Denys. "What does he detect?"

"The big job," said Wynton. "Murder."

And then he noticed a peculiar thing. Jeremy Rainer was lighting his cigarette, and he was taking rather a long time to do it. Because his hands were shaking.

2

Curiosity won the day. Mordecai Tremaine knew that if he refused the invitation, he would not enjoy his Christmas, because he would be wondering all the time what would have happened if he had gone to Sherbroome and why Benedict Grame had asked him down.

It was not as if he knew Grame well. Their acquaintanceship was so slight, in fact, that the pleasantly worded little note asking him if he would care to spend a few days at Sherbroome House at Christmas had surprised Mordecai Tremaine into allowing his toast to go cold while he had read it at breakfast.

The letter had been written by Nicholas Blaise, whom Mordecai Tremaine knew to be Grame's confidential secretary and companion. There was a postscript that Blaise had added in his neat, artistically flowing hand:

> *Please pay us a visit if you can possibly manage it.*
> *Benedict will be more than ordinarily grateful. As a*

matter of fact, I've a feeling that there's something here
to interest you. Benedict doesn't say much—in fact,
he doesn't know I'm making this comment, so I'd be
glad if you'd keep it confidential. But I can tell there's
something wrong, and frankly, I'm getting scared.

Mordecai Tremaine had already received several invita-
tions from a wide circle of relatives and friends, and he had,
in fact, been making up his mind to spend Christmas in
Dorset, where several nephews and nieces were busily rear-
ing their families, and where he was sure of a welcome from
sundry small boys and girls who were well aware that Uncle
Mordy had a soft spot for them and could be depended upon
to do anything they demanded of him. But that postscript
would not be ignored. It had an air of mystery, and the lure
of mystery was something it was not in Mordecai Tremaine
to resist.

In the end, he sent off regretful excuses to Dorset and a
letter of thanks and acceptance to Sherbroome. He would
arrive, he said, in the afternoon of the day before Christmas
Eve, as suggested.

And having made the decision, he sat down to think over
what he knew of Benedict Grame.

He had met him for the first time the preceding
September at a rather mixed party Anita Lane had given

in her Kensington flat. Anita was a film critic of note, and in appearance was as unlike the successful career woman she actually was as any woman could wish to be. Mordecai Tremaine had known her for several years, and he was very fond of her. In a purely platonic way, he always hastened to tell himself. After all, though she might be in her forties, he himself was past sixty—which was too big a gap to be bridged permanently without a great deal of thought.

The party had been attended chiefly by artists, writers, and theatrical people. Altogether a strange gathering in which to find Benedict Grame who, despite a catholic experience, was inclined to regard such folk with that air of wonder touched with awe with which those who earn their living by the stage and the printed word are often viewed by laymen.

Perhaps because they were all three just outside the magic circles of publisher's contracts and backstage dressing rooms, Grame and his companion, Nicholas Blaise, had gravitated toward Mordecai Tremaine. By the end of a prolonged evening—they had shared a taxi at 4:00 a.m.—they had discovered a great deal about each other. Grame had retired from active business and was now living the pleasant life of a country gentleman untroubled by inadequate capital. Blaise was officially his secretary, but was clearly a good deal more than a mere paid servant, being on terms of intimacy that showed that he possessed Grame's full confidence.

Mordecai Tremaine could not recall much that had passed between them. As he had grown more mellow, he had also grown more hazy—it had not been a noticeably dry party—and at this distance of time, large areas of conversation were completely uncharted.

He had a dim recollection of explaining that he had once been the owner of a flourishing tobacconist's business, and that he was now enjoying the fruits of his past toil. He was aware that he had mentioned his interest in criminology and had spoken of his friendship with a number of police officers.

He did not think, however, that he had gone into details concerning his hobby. He was an amateur, and he had no wish to embarrass his friends—such as Inspector Boyce of Scotland Yard—by proclaiming that he had been allowed to take part in inquiries that should have been the strict prerogative of the police.

The attention he had received from the press at the time of the Dalmering murders was still a somewhat painful memory. He had not sought publicity, but the reporters who had swarmed into the little Sussex village had discovered his connection with the case and had thrust him into the full glare of the limelight. Sometimes he shuddered still at the thought of some of the less-restrained headlines.

He hoped he had not betrayed his passion for sentimental literature. Mordecai Tremaine was a steadfast reader of that innocent but undoubtedly treacle-laden magazine *Romantic Stories*. He followed its serials thirstily, suffering and triumphing with their virtuous heroines. But although he read it so avidly, he was still a little shamefaced whenever he was caught doing so, and would make furtive attempts to smuggle it out of sight. He did not think Benedict Grame was the kind of man who would be likely to understand his weakness, and 4:00 a.m. confidences had a habit of appearing regrettably threadbare by daylight.

The problem of *Romantic Stories* was still hovering anxiously at the back of his mind several weeks later as he climbed into the modest, mass-produced saloon car that was one of his few extravagances and drove carefully through London's traffic maze on a sunny but sharply frosty morning. It was significant, however, that the latest issue of that magazine nestled between the folds of his dress suit in the suitcase occupying the rear seat. Mordecai Tremaine might suffer agony of mind, but he did not retreat.

He was light of heart. He was humming a gay tune the morning radio had provided as an accompaniment for his shave, and he did not leave off even when he was suddenly called upon to perform a miracle of steering to avoid being pancaked between a stationary lorry and a confidently thrusting omnibus. His cheerful mood was not entirely due to the fact that the sun was shining and that through the glass it possessed springlike warmth. Nor was it entirely due to the fact that it was Christmas and that his soul was riding on the wave of seasonal sentiment produced by snowy decorations and fairy lights in the shop windows.

He was running into adventure. Somewhere ahead of him, a problem was waiting for him, and there was an anticipatory tingling within him. Not since those long summer days when terror had lain upon the loveliness of Dalmering had he tasted the thrill of a real-life crime investigation. His appetite for detection had been compelled to feed upon literature, and he had forgotten the sordid background of hate, fear, and jealousy. He had forgotten that the end of the pursuit was sick disillusionment and the destruction of a human creature. He was conscious only of the excitement of the chase and the keenness of testing his brain against the cunning of a murderer.

Quite suddenly, he realized the way his thoughts were running and sobered. What talk was this of murder? Toward what fantastic destination was his imagination leading him? He was on his way to spend a Christmas holiday among newfound friends. It was the season of goodwill and happiness. Why should his mind be traveling along such a forbidding road?

He succeeded in breaking the spell that was on him, but something of his zest had gone. As he drove on, the eyes behind the pince-nez that seemed to be always on the point of sliding off his nose but somehow never did were shadowed and perplexed.

By midday, the clouds were a leaden panoply, and there was only a barren countryside in which bare-armed trees leaned under an icy wind. He was driving deeper into a world of gray light and chill air in which dreadful things could be done.

He knew the truth, of course. He knew that snow had fallen in the West Country and that he must be getting near the edge of it. The only significance in the failing light and the cheerless sigh of the wind was that they were signs that he was near the area of the snowfall. To imbue the wintry landscape with an atmosphere of mournfulness and terror was merely to pander to an imagination straining under the loneliness of deserted December fields.

Fortunately, although it was not long before the snow was all around him, the roads were firm and he was able to maintain a good speed. There was still more than an hour of daylight left as he drove down the long hill leading into the town of Calnford, and he knew that Sherbroome was no more than four miles or so beyond.

It was the knowledge that he would be able to reach his destination before dusk that made him decide to obtain a cup of tea in the town. The turn signal on the saloon had developed the habit of sticking, which meant that he had to keep the window down in order to give his signals by hand, and he was feeling the numbing effect of the icy wind.

Just off the main street was a quiet square that was used as a car park. He pulled toward the curb and, glad of the opportunity to stretch his legs, walked briskly back toward the crowded shopping center.

Calnford was an attractive little town. Wooded hills rising steeply on almost every side had prevented it from breaking out into the usual rash of suburban villas, and it still retained the grace it had possessed when it had been a fashionable spa and eighteenth-century dandies had danced the minuet with Gainsborough's ladies under the candles in its public rooms. In its tall, loftily proportioned houses, the Regency still lived.

But besides the quiet dignity of its residential squares and the peace of the gardens alongside the river across which the stone bridges sat with such an air of unhurried security, the town also enjoyed a throbbing heart that pumped a stream of prosperity along the shop-lined artery running close to the ancient walls of its abbey. Mordecai Tremaine's sentimental soul responded to the warm life pulsing by him as he walked along the crowded pavements, at which gleaming cars, laden with parcels and appearing to radiate the Christmas spirit from their shining chromium fittings, waited for their passengers to come back from the gaily decorated stores.

Even the sad and discolored slush that was all a procession of churning tires had left of the snow possessed an air of magic for him. His gloom had vanished. The strange depression that had overwhelmed him earlier in the day had slunk away in defeat.

He was a child again, snatching at a belief in fairies and in a Santa Claus who came down chimneys and filled a million stockings in one amazing night. The pince-nez slipped even further, but he did not notice them. Sentiment was in control, and for Mordecai Tremaine, this was a moment that would help to sustain him when the time came for him to feel again the knowledge that bitterness and terror and dark despair had their being in the hearts of men.

But he could not afford to delay much longer if he wished to complete his journey in daylight. Most of the big restaurants were already crowded. After a glance at the packed tables of two of them, he turned down a side street and under an arch hard by the abbey where there was an old-fashioned backwater into which the tide of thirsty and hungry humanity did not swirl.

There was a tiny tea shop sandwiched between a bookseller and a basket-maker's premises, and he went through the narrow door, instinctively lowering his head to avoid hitting the oak beam that formed the lintel. At first, he thought the shop was empty, and then he saw the two people sitting at a table set back in the gloom of the paneled wall at the rear and partially concealed by a stand for hats and coats.

They looked up as he came in—quickly, and as though they were startled. When they saw him eyeing them curiously, they looked away again in an equally hurried manner, as if guilty at having been observed.

Tremaine chose a table and sat down. He had his back to the two, but facing him, over the shop counter, there was a mirror in which he could see them as they talked, heads together, whispering in a fashion that had something conspiratorial about it.

An intense interest in people and a highly developed faculty for watching others without being suspected meant that Mordecai Tremaine seldom ignored an opportunity of studying his fellows. And since he had nothing to do apart from drinking his tea, it was inevitable that his eyes should have strayed to the mirror. It was a mechanical process, a natural practicing of his acquired talents. He had no suspicion that the incident was fated to be of such significance.

One of the two was a man and the other, a woman. A colorless, indeterminate creature she seemed, dressed in a coat that was good but dull, and wearing a hat that was clearly not in the current fashion. Her hair was inclined to be straggly and was without luster, although he admitted that he could not see her too clearly as the high collar of her coat was turned up to meet her hat. Her features were delicate, and her face, small and round, was white and peaked as though she spent little time in the open air.

The waitress switched on one of the electric lights, and Tremaine's view was momentarily improved. He saw that although the woman was not young, she was not as old as he had at first imagined. Her style of dress had given him a deceptive impression of her age.

She did not appreciate the sudden light. She half turned, so that her shoulder filled the mirror, and he could no longer see her expression. The movement was so obvious that it betrayed her.

Her companion was not, apparently, so sensitive. He was sitting full face toward the mirror and he did not shift his position, although he blinked under the glare of the light and looked searchingly across the room as if he suspected the action of the waitress to have been deliberately directed against him.

A phrase from *Julius Caesar* came into Mordecai Tremaine's mind:

"Yon Cassius hath a lean and hungry look."

In the mirror there was only the indistinct reflection of a gaunt man wearing a shabby raincoat. A man who could have walked unnoticed through the crowds in the streets outside. But some trick of the electric light upon the glass brought the upper part of his features into prominence so that Tremaine had the uncomfortable experience of looking straight into his eyes. They were dark eyes, set wide beneath a high forehead and with a somber vitality smoldering in their depths. They were disturbing eyes that looked as if they would burn with a visionary fire.

Tremaine drank his tea slowly, trying to appear as though he was unaware of the existence of the mirror. He did not think that the two had any interest in him or that they suspected his interest in them. After that first quick survey, they had taken up their conversation again.

They were still engrossed when Tremaine paid his bill. They did not look up as he left the tea shop. As he walked back to his car, he found himself wondering about them. He always wondered about people. He liked to weave theories about who they were and where they were going and what the pattern of their lives might be. Usually he found it easy to place them and to give them occupations and characters.

But with these two, his imagination would not respond. They were removed from the general pattern.

He recalled the woman's face, saw the over-large mouth with its pale lips. They were tremulous, like the lips of a woman unsure of herself. She was a fragile creature for whom life was not an easy matter. Doll-like, brittle, bewildered by the world—the kind who might break beneath any sudden cruel blow of fate.

What was her connection with her companion? Were they married? He had been unable to see her hands, so he did not know whether she had been wearing a wedding ring.

Still, although they had provided him with material for a brief mental exercise, they had passed out of his life. He would never find out whether his conjectures were near the truth or whether he had invested two perfectly ordinary people with a background of mystery to which their mundane lives could lay no claim.

Ordinary? Somehow he did not think the term was adequate. They had been altogether too watchful, too anxious to remain unnoticed in the gloom.

Within a few minutes, he was too busy trying to get clear of the congested streets of Calnford to continue his speculations. When he had left the town behind and had branched off along the road to Sherbroome, driving became even more difficult. The snow was heavier; there had not been a constant stream of traffic to squelch it into ineffectual sludge, and he was forced to reduce his speed almost to a crawl.

The light was going fast as he drove through Sherbroome village. In some of the houses, the oil lamps were already in use, and the place had an air of fairyland with its smattering of lighted windows showing up against the huddled, gray old houses, the snow thick upon their uneven roofs. It was like a scene from pantomime or some children's fantasy. *The Village of the Elves: Snow Time.* Mordecai Tremaine imagined the whole thing as it would look if it could be picked up by some friendly giant and placed down between the wings of a theater with a row of footlights underlining it.

Sherbroome was a showpiece. It recurred year after year in travel magazines, with photographs of its centuries-old inn and its Norman church illustrating articles on the beauties of England.

Unsuspected by the bulk of the traffic scorching past the modest signpost on the main road, and served by a meandering and strictly limited bus route, it had no railway station nearer than that at Calnford. It had, therefore, remained undiscovered by the larger world of tourist souvenirs and tea gardens, and was unspoiled in the sense that it was still much in the state in which it had been when the eighth Henry had plundered Calnford Abbey. To the villagers, struggling against inadequate sanitation and compelled to rely upon oil lamps in the long winter evenings, it was not entirely a matter for congratulation, but they had at least the satisfaction of knowing that they had not been sacrificed to the false gods of exploitation.

Tremaine was not quite certain of the location of

Sherbroome House, but there was only one road he could take, and he accordingly took it. He was beginning to feel a little uneasy. It would not be long before it was quite dark, and in this lonely countryside, he might easily drive past his destination unaware.

He had traveled about a mile along a narrowing road that was becoming increasingly icebound when he saw a dark figure standing in the shelter of the raggedly bare hedge a hundred yards ahead. He braked gently so that he stopped as he drew level.

"Excuse me," he said, "could you tell me the whereabouts of Sherbroome House?"

The other gave him a prolonged stare. He was a big man, and huddled into a heavy overcoat with the collar turned up around his face, he seemed exaggeratedly so. Tremaine felt uneasy, although the other had made no unfriendly move. He had a menacing aspect, standing there in the wintry gloom without moving, like some monstrous shadow. But at last, he said brusquely, "It's there. Facing you."

Tremaine was too relieved to pay much attention to his hostile manner. He noticed that a few yards on, and set back a short distance from the road, were two stone pillars flanking a driveway.

"Thanks," he returned. "I didn't notice the gates in this light."

He eased in his clutch and brought the saloon cautiously around on the treacherous surface of the road so that he could enter the drive. As he passed close to the big man, he lifted his hand in a gesture of acknowledgment.

The other made no response. Tremaine saw his face and experienced a feeling of shock, for there was but one description of the expression it bore. Malevolent. It was the face of a man with hatred in his soul.

And then he had driven by and was making his way up the drive. Within a few yards of the gate there was a sharp bend, and then, for the first time, he saw the house.

It was perhaps a quarter of a mile away. It was big and black, reaching up tall, gabled roofs toward the snow-filled gloom of the sky. It looked old and mysterious and somber. The few lights that were burning served only to emphasize its grimness.

Mordecai Tremaine tried to banish the wisp of fear that curled across his mind. He tried to forget the chill that was constricting his heart. Because it was almost dark and he was cold and his nerves were strained after his journey, it did not mean that he must allow his imagination to deliver itself of a nightmare.

But he did not succeed in convincing himself. As he drew nearer to the louring old house with its high mullioned windows, he was conscious of the vague but insistent and disturbing feeling that fate was at his side, and that in the great building just ahead, darkness and terror were waiting.

3

The warmth of the welcome Nicholas Blaise gave him and the sight of roaringly healthy log fires drove the sense of oppression and foreboding from his mind. As physical heat seeped comfortingly into his bones, mental well-being returned. This was reality. This was human companionship and the mellow glow of Christmas.

Mordecai Tremaine was fortunate in possessing a child's elasticity of outlook. He could swing with ease from depression to high optimism, from gloomy expectation of disaster to a naive delight with the best of worlds.

"We were just beginning to get worried about you," said Blaise. "Did you have much trouble driving down?"

"None at all," returned Tremaine. "I spent half an hour or so in Calnford, and I'm afraid I cut my schedule rather fine. I hope I haven't put you out."

"Of course you haven't," said Blaise cheerfully. "We keep open house at Christmas. There's still Professor Lorring to come. He was to have been here yesterday but couldn't get away. He's probably traveling by rail, and I daresay the trains are finding it a job to cope with the holiday traffic and the snow at the same time."

"Professor Lorring? Is that the Professor Ernest Lorring who's been doing research work for the government?"

Blaise nodded as he led the way toward the door.

"Yes. He's one of Benedict's latest finds. I believe he thought Lorring had been overdoing things and that a few days at Sherbroome would act as a tonic. By the way," he added with a smile, "I hope you like Christmas!"

Tremaine raised his eyebrows.

"I hope I don't look all that much like Scrooge!"

"Nothing personal," said Blaise. "But I thought it was as well to warn you. Benedict's a Christmas fan. He likes to have all the orthodox trimmings. Christmas carols, holly and mistletoe, Christmas tree, *and* Santa Claus."

Mordecai Tremaine looked dutifully interested.

"Santa Claus?"

"Benedict," explained his companion. "He puts on a red cloak and white beard he keeps especially for the occasion and comes down when the rest of us are in bed and loads up the Christmas tree. There's a present for everyone in the house. I believe he looks forward to it all the year. But let me show you your room, and then you can start to meet everybody."

Mordecai Tremaine did not make any reference to the

postscript that had accompanied his invitation. No doubt Blaise would explain when he judged the moment to be opportune.

By the time dinner was served, all the introductions had been made, and Mordecai Tremaine, still bewildered by a procession of faces bearing names he had not heard before, found himself escorting Rosalind Marsh into the long dining room glittering with silver and cut glass.

She was a very self-possessed young lady, which was invaluable in breaking the ice, for Tremaine had never been able to overcome the disadvantages of being an elderly bachelor who entertained youthful illusions concerning the opposite sex. She was quite ready to talk. To a diffident question he put to her, she replied with a frank directness.

"I'm a working woman," she told him. "I paint. And I run a curio and art shop in town. I'm very expensive, and I make my living off people who have no taste but lots of money."

Mordecai Tremaine hoped that he was not betraying that he was both in awe of her and dismayed by her cynicism. Rosalind Marsh's beauty was of the type for which *statuesque* was the obvious choice. Her fair hair was piled up in an elaborate coiffure that revealed the full grace of her neck, so that she derived the maximum effect from the confident poise of her head. Her features were clear and regular, and her skin was without flaw. Her eyes were wide and brilliant, possessing intelligence and vitality.

But there was something wrong. Tremaine groped in his mind while he listened to her in an effort to discover what that something was. It was, he decided, the suggestion of firmness about her mouth and nose, a suggestion that was too near to harshness. She was too cold, too much the marble goddess. She lacked the warmth of womanhood to soften the too-perfect profile and bring a tinge of color to her cheeks. She was an efficient woman who looked efficient—and was, therefore, a little forbidding.

He realized that she had spoken to him.

"I'm afraid I'm rather a social parasite now," he told her with a smile. "I don't do anything to justify my existence. I used to be a tobacconist."

She was obviously at a loss for a moment or two. And then she said, "I believe this is your first visit here, isn't it? Where did you and Benedict happen to meet?"

It was plain what she really had in her mind. She meant: "You're a queer find in this company. Where on earth did Benedict Grame pick *you* up?"

Mordecai Tremaine's eyes twinkled behind the pince-nez. He said:

"A friend of mine gave a party. We both happened to be there," he replied. The cloud that passed over her face was very faint, but it did not escape him. Nor did it escape him that the look she gave him was speculative, and that with her speculation was mixed a guarded watchfulness and something that was very like a flash of sympathy.

He knew that she wanted to ask more questions. But he made no move to help her, and she did not know how to probe further without appearing ill-mannered. She pretended to concentrate upon her sole Colbert course, and Tremaine took advantage of his release to glance around the table.

By now, the conversation was lighthearted and general. No one seemed greatly interested in the mild-looking elderly man who was peering through his pince-nez at the rest of the company.

So Mordecai Tremaine thought until he looked up to the end of the table and saw Nicholas Blaise. There was no doubt that Blaise had been watching him, and the other made no attempt to hide it. When he realized that he had been caught, he smiled as if he was sharing some secret understanding.

It was only for an instant or two that their glances met, for Blaise turned away almost at once to address a remark to his companion, but it was enough to bring back to Tremaine's mind all the dark suspicions with which he had been beset on his journey to Sherbroome. Why had that invitation been sent? Why was Nicholas Blaise so obviously interested in his reactions to the other guests?

The incident had sharpened the edge of his curiosity. His eyes were keener as he continued his unobtrusive survey.

Underneath the surface gaiety of this happy Christmas party, mystery was lurking. Which meant that there might be subtle hints of it to be noted by the shrewd observer.

Almost opposite him, the bald head of Ernest Lorring shone under the lights. The scientist was bending over his plate, taking no part in the conversation. His beak-like nose, large and inclined to be hooked, the fierce eyebrows and high cheekbones gave him a forbidding air his expression did nothing to relieve.

A great deal of Lorring's work was of a highly confidential nature, and it seemed that constant practice in discouraging the curious had effectively negated what little talent he might once have possessed for taking part in social gatherings. His table companions had made several attempts to draw him and, having failed, had turned their attention to their other neighbors, leaving Lorring in aloof splendor, a rugged, silent island in the midst of a sea of conversation.

Tremaine recalled what Nicholas Blaise had told him of the Christmas atmosphere Benedict Grame delighted to create at Sherbroome, and he wondered whether Lorring would thaw beneath its friendly warmth or whether he would remain chillingly rimmed with frost, a disapproving and icy spectator. At the moment, the odds seemed to be heavily on the frost continuing.

When he looked beyond Lorring there was a glow within

him. He had told himself, when he had been introduced to Denys Arden, that if he could roll thirty years from the calendar, she was the kind of girl for whom he would be searching. Now, as she faced him in an evening gown that emphasized her youthful beauty by its own decorative femininity, she sent admiration happily along his veins. She was so gloriously alive, so eager in her gestures and in her laughter. Beside her uninhibited natural charm, Rosalind Marsh was a marble image whose loveliness was not sustained by any vital flame.

He realized that his companion had raised her head and was watching him. He asked, "Are they engaged?"

"Are who engaged?" she said, although he sensed that she knew quite well of whom he was speaking.

"Miss Arden and Mr. Wynton."

"No," she told him. "At least, not officially."

"A pity," he remarked. "They look as if they should be."

He had formed a good opinion of Roger Wynton at their first brief meeting an hour or so before, and the unashamed adoration with which he was looking at the girl, and the fact that her radiance was an obvious reaction to it, confirmed that first judgment. Wynton seemed to be a sound, level-headed young fellow who knew what he wanted without being insufferably hectoring over it. And he was in love with Denys Arden and she, with him.

If it is open to question whether all the world does indeed

love a lover, it is incontestable that Mordecai Tremaine could never resist the appeal lovers make. *Romantic Stories* provided him with the chief means of satisfying his emotions, but when he came in contact with real-life romance, his sentimental soul went racing away, joyously out of control. He sat regarding them mistily through his pince-nez, his head to one side. They made a charming pair. He sighed.

"There's a spanner in the works," said Rosalind Marsh drily.

Tremaine came back to the dinner table from his sentimental dreams with a start.

"A…a spanner?" he said, just a little disconcerted by her swift perception.

"His name's Rainer," said his companion. She spoke in a low voice so that she would not be overheard, although there was small chance of it in view of the general hum of conversation. "Jeremy Rainer. He doesn't like Roger. Which makes it awkward for Denys because he happens to be her guardian."

"Oh!" said Mordecai Tremaine. "That's Rainer, isn't it, next to Mrs. Tristam?"

Lucia Tristam had arrived shortly before dinner with a middle-aged couple called Napier who apparently lived in the neighborhood. Introductions had been hasty, but no one who had met Lucia Tristam was likely to forget her. She was no longer young, but maturity so far had merely ripened her attractions. With her richly luxuriant auburn hair, tawny eyes with flecks of green mirrored in them, and a superb figure of which she was fully conscious, she was a vivid, exciting creature.

"Lucia the Magnificent," said Rosalind Marsh.

Mordecai Tremaine savored the phrase. Lucia the Magnificent! Certainly it fitted her colorful personality.

Reluctantly, he took his eyes from her to study Jeremy Rainer. It was like turning from brilliant sunshine into gray twilight. Rainer was smiling, but the smile was an artificial one that did not succeed in breaking the grim lines in which his face was set. He reminded Tremaine of Lorring. Like the scientist, he did not appear to be sharing the gaiety of the dinner party.

"He doesn't seem to be enjoying himself much, does he?"

Tremaine became aware that Rosalind Marsh was paying a great deal of attention to what he was doing, and he looked at her curiously. Anticipating him, she said, "You're very interested in all of us."

"I like to study people," he told her. "Besides, I'm anxious to sort everybody out. It's a little bewildering encountering so many new faces all at once."

"If I can help you," she said, "don't hesitate to ask me." There was a hardly noticeable pause, and then she added, "For anything."

He knew that the words were intended to convey a message to him that went deeper than their surface meaning, but this time it was his turn to encounter the blank wall, because she did not offer him any further encouragement. He groped in vain for a clue and was baffled by her apparent indifference.

He looked away from her and glanced along the table once more, and as he did, he realized that his companions were not all complete strangers. Besides Benedict Grame and Nicholas Blaise, there was someone else he had met before.

It was a woman. She was flushed and excited now, and she looked altogether more assured, but there was no mistaking her. It was the woman he had seen in the tea shop in Calnford.

Her companion was not present, but he was not surprised at that. From the secretive atmosphere that had surrounded them in the tea shop, he did not imagine that they would be likely to share the same dinner table. Otherwise, why the clandestine meeting?

If it *had* been a clandestine meeting. Mordecai Tremaine pulled sharply on the rein of his thoughts. He was racing away into the regions of imagination again, creating mystery where he had no sound reason for supposing that mystery existed.

"Charlotte Grame," said Rosalind Marsh, in response to his question. "She's Benedict's sister."

"She lives here?"

"Yes," she told him, "she lives here."

At intervals, Mordecai Tremaine found his eyes straying

toward Charlotte Grame. There was something about her that intrigued him. Something he could not define. She gave him the impression that she was playing a part, trying to conceal her true feelings. Once or twice, indeed, she seemed to him pathetically anxious to appear bright and gay.

He could not tell whether or not she had recognized him as he had recognized her. She was never looking in his direction when he glanced at her, and although he tried, he could not meet her eyes. He waited impatiently for the end of the meal. Although Nicholas Blaise had not overlooked anyone else, he had not introduced Charlotte Grame. Tremaine wondered whether it had been merely accidental or whether he had deliberately refrained from doing so for reasons he would reveal later.

More fancyings, he told himself, and tried to will Benedict Grame into initiating a move from the dinner table.

But Grame apparently was much too content with the situation to suggest a withdrawal. He was seated at the end of the table, beaming upon his guests like some benevolent giant, blue eyes twinkling under the bushy eyebrows, his laugh booming occasionally even above the hum of conversation.

At any other time, Tremaine's sentimental soul would have warmed toward him. He was so openly enjoying himself, so obviously the small boy at a special party at which he was the most important figure. But now, with anxiety to meet

Charlotte Grame bubbling up inside him with an increasing degree of effervescence, his tolerance was in a state any stock-market expert would have described as reactionary.

However, even Benedict Grame's endurance had its limits, and as soon as he was able, Tremaine approached Nicholas Blaise.

One theory was promptly removed from his list. Blaise had not deliberately avoided introducing him to Charlotte Grame. She had been out of the house at the time of his arrival and had returned only in time to dress very hurriedly for dinner.

Certainly, said Blaise, he would remedy the matter. Charlotte Grame was standing at the far end of the room talking to Lucia Tristam. Tremaine was sure that she saw them coming toward her, although she tried to give the impression that she was unaware of them. He saw her figure stiffen. A taut expression drew some of the color from her cheeks. He knew that he was facing a woman tensing herself to endure an ordeal she had been dreading, and doing her utmost to keep her self-control.

As Blaise introduced them, she made no sign that she had ever seen him before, and at first Tremaine made no comment beyond the routine phrases required by courtesy. But when Blaise excused himself on the grounds that Benedict Grame wanted him, leaving them together, he said, "Didn't I see you this afternoon in Calnford, Miss Grame?"

He spoke in the manner of one who uttered a casual remark with the intention of making conversation and with no special interest in the substance of what he was saying. But there was no doubt of its effect upon her. He heard the sighing gasp of her breath and saw her expression change. And then she said, "I-I don't think so. We haven't met before."

"Oh, we didn't exactly meet," he told her. "I stopped in Calnford for a cup of tea, and I thought I saw you in the tea shop. Tiny place just around by the Abbey."

"You must have been mistaken," she said breathlessly. "I haven't been to Calnford today."

She was frightened now. Her eyes flickered away from him, as if searching for someone to whom she could appeal. Then he saw the relief on her face, and he realized that Lucia Tristam was standing at his side.

"Strange," he said. "You must have a double, Miss Grame. I could have sworn that it was you. But the light was poor, and it's easy to make a mistake over faces."

"Yes," she said, clutching at the straw he had deliberately held out to her. "It's easy to be mistaken." Her hand went out to Lucia Tristam's arm. "Lucia…Mr. Tremaine thinks he saw me in a tea shop in Calnford this afternoon. I've just been telling him that he couldn't have. We were together all the time, weren't we? He couldn't have seen me."

"Of course he couldn't, Charlotte," said Lucia Tristam's

cool voice. "Probably he saw someone who looked very much like you. Didn't you, Mr. Tremaine?"

Mordecai Tremaine turned to find himself within the disturbing range of those brilliantly wide eyes, held and yet baffled by the spell contained in the flecks of green that came and went. Lucia Tristam betrayed no trace of embarrassment or nervousness. He felt that she was surveying him with amusement, supremely conscious of her mastery of the situation.

She added, after a deliberate pause, "Charlotte and I spent the afternoon together. We had a lot to talk over."

She meant quite clearly that the incident was closed. Mordecai Tremaine had made a mistake. He had not seen Charlotte Grame in Calnford. It was to be hoped that he would not refer to the matter again.

Tremaine dutifully gave the impression that he understood and would forget all about what he had thought he had seen. But he had no intention of forgetting. Because he had made no mistake. It *had* been Charlotte Grame whom he had seen in that tea shop, behaving like a very guilty conspirator. Her attitude now would have confirmed it, even if he had possessed any lingering doubts, because her dismay had brought back the nervous, uncertain air she had managed to hide at dinner under that forced excitement.

For some reason, Charlotte Grame was lying. And Lucia Tristam was also lying.

Why? What were they trying to conceal? Why were they at such pains to lie to a complete stranger over such an apparently innocent matter as a visit to an ordinary tea shop?

Mordecai Tremaine experienced another of those anticipatory stirrings within him. It was, he felt, going to be an interesting Christmas.

4

More snow fell during the night, and when Mordecai Tremaine looked out of his frosted window, the countryside was smooth, and he could not trace the road along which he had come because the fresh snowfall had repaired the damage caused by car tires and left a uniform whiteness everywhere. He pushed the window open and leaned out. The cold air numbed his face and took his breath away. He shivered and, drawing back into his bedroom, began his exercises.

Normally, he arose at 6:30 a.m. He had decided that to adhere to his custom at Sherbroome would merely mean wandering disconsolately about the house, an object of suspicion to the servants, and he had allowed himself the luxury of an extra hour in bed. By way of a peace offering to conscience, he spent an additional ten minutes on his exercises and dressed with a healthy glow.

Christmas Eve. He wondered what developments the day would bring. He had already seen enough to be aware that his fellow guests and the regular inhabitants formed an intriguingly diverse collection of human beings by whom anything might be concealed and among whom anything might happen. It was equally possible, of course, that despite their apparent peculiarities, they were quite ordinary and unexciting people, but Mordecai Tremaine preferred to give his imagination the benefit of the doubt.

Nicholas Blaise had still made no leading comment, but there had, after all, been little opportunity for confidences. The conversation had been too general. But today…Mordecai Tremaine hummed a little tune as he went down to breakfast. Today might bring results.

As it happened, Blaise was already busily engaged with Benedict Grame, apparently arranging details of the Christmas festivities. But there were compensations. Perhaps because she was also an early riser and they were for a few moments the sole occupants of the breakfast room, perhaps because her eager youth made an appeal he could not resist, he gravitated toward Denys Arden. And perhaps because she sensed in him a sympathetic spirit, she smiled at him and was ready to act as his guide.

"This is your first visit, isn't it?" she said as they finished their meal. "Let me show you around."

"There's nothing I'd like better," he said truthfully. "Provided that young man of yours doesn't object."

"Roger won't be over this morning," she said. "As a matter of fact…" She broke off. The color came into her cheeks.

"Things aren't too…easy. Isn't that so?" Mordecai Tremaine asked.

She looked at him doubtfully, and he added quickly, before she could reply, "I know I sound like an inquisitive old busybody, so I won't be offended if you give me a well-deserved snub."

His rueful tone made her smile, as he had intended it should. She said: "Everyone knows about it, so there's no point in pretending to be annoyed. Jeremy—my guardian—doesn't like Roger. That's why he isn't coming over this morning. I asked him not to. Roger is quick-tempered, and so is Jeremy. I didn't want them to have another row with the house full of people here for Christmas."

"Another?" Mordecai Tremaine looked grave. "It's as bad as that, is it? I'm sorry." He knew that he was approaching uncertain ground, and he gave her a speculative glance over the top of his pince-nez. He said, "Has Mr. Rainer given you any reasons for his objections?"

To his relief, she was not angry with him. Her face puckered into a frown. He thought it gave her a piquant air that increased rather than detracted from her charm.

"That's the baffling part of it," she told him. "He doesn't seem to have any objections. At least, not definite ones. It's just that he doesn't like Roger and he won't make any attempt to improve things. If I knew what he had against him, I might be able to do something to clear up whatever misunderstanding there might be. But this is so…so maddeningly negative. It makes me feel frustrated."

She was unaware of it, but in that moment she betrayed herself. If Mordecai Tremaine had not observed the signs on the previous evening, he would have known then how much she was in love with Roger Wynton.

She seemed to sense what he was thinking. She blushed. And then she took his arm and said quickly, "You don't want to have your holiday ruined by listening to all my troubles. Come along, let me show you the sights."

Mordecai Tremaine enjoyed his morning. The rambling old house would have fascinated him even had his guide been the most senile of antiquarians. Denys Arden was genuinely in love with Sherbroome, and she had the happy talent of being able to communicate its romantic spell to others.

She showed him the tower in which Sir Gervase Melvin had been murdered by his cousin after a quarrel over cards during the wildness of the Restoration. She took him into the spacious chamber in which Queen Elizabeth had slept. They pushed open the eerily creaking door of the cobweb-infested room under the roof in which the lovely Lady Isabel had been kept prisoner for two years—and from which she had flung herself to her death on the terrace below when news had been brought to her of the murder of her lover by her father.

They walked down the gloomy corridor along which her frail ghost was reputed to glide. Relegated to these lumber regions, generations of Melvins stared at them from their painted canvases.

"I often wonder," the girl observed, stopping beneath the gilt frame from which Sir Rupert Melvin, hand on sword, with wide, cavalier brow and dark beard, looked proudly down, "what the family felt at having to give up this house and all it stands for. There aren't any actual Melvins left now. Uncle Benedict bought the property through the lawyers representing a distant cousin who was the nearest surviving descendant. But after all those centuries of ownership, there must still be a tremendous feeling of tradition. Apparently this man who eventually sold it—Latimer, I believe, is his name—was too poor to live in the house, but he used to come here every summer and camp on the grounds. He wouldn't sell until circumstances forced him to."

"It must have been a bitter blow," agreed Tremaine. "It's rather sad to think of a proud family coming slowly to oblivion. I certainly wouldn't like to think I was the last of a great line, compelled to sell what was left of my inheritance."

They examined the inevitable priest's hide, and the girl showed him how to operate the secret panel that formed the entrance.

"There's nothing secret about it now, of course," she told

him. "But there's a legend that in the sixteenth century, a priest was hidden there for a year and never discovered, despite the fact that the house was searched without warning on several occasions."

"It's a horrible thought," said Tremaine, peering into the darkness of the hide. "Just imagine having to live like a hunted beast for all that time, going to earth whenever there was danger."

The hide was situated under the big room on the ground floor adjoining the library and could apparently be reached either from this room or from the library itself. It was one of the first places they'd examined and they did not spend a great deal of time over it, which was why Mordecai Tremaine suggested making a further exploration of it when they came to the end of their tour of the house.

However, when they came back to the oak-paneled room with its wide french doors, they discovered that a transformation scene was in preparation. Benedict Grame and Nicholas Blaise, aided by Fleming, the butler, who contrived to bring dignity even to the task of acting as a draping board for Christmas trimmings, were busily putting up an array of decorations.

Blaise saw them as they came in and waved a hammer in cheerful greeting. "Hullo, you two! Come to lend a hand?"

Tremaine looked around him. Holly and mistletoe had been hung about the room, and gay silver streamers ran from wall to wall. In one corner stood a large Christmas tree. It was firmly entrenched in a big wooden tub, and a tall man standing on tiptoe would only have touched the topmost branch with his outstretched hand with difficulty.

"What do you think of it?" asked a voice, and he saw Benedict Grame beaming at him through the branches from a stepladder on the other side of the tree.

"This is Uncle Benedict's special effects department," said Denys Arden. "Wait until you see the Christmas tree in all its glory. He always does the decorations himself."

"Nothing like it," boomed Grame's hearty tones. "Christmas only comes around once a year. It's up to us to make the best of it!"

Perched on the steps, blue eyes bright in his seamed face, he reminded Mordecai Tremaine of an older edition of Mr. Pickwick. A Mr. Pickwick who had lost his comforting contours and developed something of a grizzled appearance, but who had nevertheless retained his schoolboy enthusiasm. It was, he thought, fortunate that there was no lake on the grounds. Otherwise, Benedict Grame would be rounding up his house party and suggesting an afternoon's skating. And Mordecai Tremaine knew sadly that with his pince-nez flying one way and his legs another, he would not present the most dignified of pictures.

Grame peered dangerously over one of the upper branches

of the tree, a piece of trimming trailing from his mouth. "Sorry I haven't been able to see much of you so far," he said indistinctly. "You know how it is. Can't leave everything to the servants. Must lend a hand oneself. Hope you haven't been bored."

"I've been enjoying myself tremendously," said Mordecai Tremaine with obvious sincerity. "Miss Arden's been showing me around the house. I love these old buildings."

"It's certainly full of history," returned Grame. "And you couldn't have had a better guide than Denys. She knows more about it than any of us. But you'd better take care," he added mischievously. "Don't go spending too long in any of the haunted rooms, otherwise you'll have young Wynton after you!" He glanced inquiringly down at the girl. "By the way, my dear, where is that young man of yours this morning?"

"I told him not to come over," she said. "I-I thought it would be better if he waited until this afternoon."

"This afternoon! When I was younger..." Grame was beginning, and then he pulled himself up. "Sorry, my dear. I suppose it's Jeremy. That stony-hearted old curmudgeon's been making things awkward again, has he? He's been telling Roger to keep..."

Denys Arden was making desperate signs to him in an effort to stop him going on with his tirade. There was a look of appeal in her eyes. Benedict Grame saw it at last, and his voice trailed away. He coughed violently and became very busy behind the tree.

The tension in the atmosphere was unmistakable. Mordecai Tremaine turned his head slowly and cautiously. Jeremy Rainer had come into the room. He was standing in the doorway five yards away.

In the cold morning light, his grayness and his grimness seemed intensified. His shoulders were hunched. His features possessed a gauntness more pronounced than it had been upon the previous evening. He presented a soured, forbidding appearance as he stood facing them.

Mordecai Tremaine felt uncomfortable. It looked as though he was going to be the unwilling spectator to a family scene. He hated domestic squabbles. They jarred upon his sentimental soul.

But Jeremy Rainer did not make the comment he might have been expected to make. He gave no sign that he had overheard Benedict Grame's remarks. His whole attention was fixed upon the tree. He was staring at it as though it held some deep significance for him.

As the only person, apart from Fleming, who was outside the emotional drama, Mordecai Tremaine decided that it was up to him to do something. He said, addressing Grame, "Miss Arden and I did intend to have a thorough exploration of the priest's hide, but we don't want to hinder your activities so I think we'll leave it till later." He turned to the girl. "What do you say to a brisk walk before lunch? Just to work up our appetites!"

She snatched at the suggestion with relief. "I'd love it," she told him, and her eyes gave him his reward. "I'll just run up for a scarf."

"I'll join you," he said. "I'm getting too old to take risks!"

Jeremy Rainer stepped aside to allow them to pass. His manner was quite natural. He smiled at Denys. To Tremaine, he said, "Don't let her take advantage of you! She'll walk you off your feet if you let her!"

"My marathon days are over!" said Tremaine.

Rainer smiled back, but Tremaine knew that there was no real affinity between them. There was a chill bleakness in the gray depths of the other's eyes. He went by him with a feeling of relief that the situation had not developed as he had feared and with the conviction that Jeremy Rainer would be a bad man to have for an enemy.

5

Just as Mordecai Tremaine was going down the main steps with the girl, a car came up the drive. It stopped in front of them. A man climbed out of the driving-seat—a burly, red-faced man. Denys Arden said: "Hullo, Uncle Gerald. Been catching up on your Christmas shopping?"

Tremaine thought that Gerald Beechley had seen them approaching, but judging by the other's sudden start as the girl spoke to him, he had been unaware of their nearness. He had been in the act of taking a brown paper parcel from the car. He thrust it hastily back on the seat and turned to face them. "Oh, it's you, Denys. Yes, I've been making some last-minute purchases."

She tried to peer into the interior of the car, but he shifted his position adroitly so that he blocked the doorway. "Can we see what you've brought?" she asked. "Or is it a secret?"

Beechley seemed awkward and disconcerted. His eyes flickered uneasily away from the girl's laughing face. "As a matter of fact," he said at last, "it's…it's something for Benedict."

Tremaine was standing by the offside front wheel of the car. Through the windscreen he could see the brown paper parcel propped up on the driver's seat. It was loosely wrapped, and where the paper had been pulled aside, he could see a piece of bright-red cloth.

Gerald Beechley became suddenly aware of Tremaine's gaze. He turned quickly and, stretching an arm through the lowered window, tugged the paper back into position over the cloth.

Denys Arden gave him a curious look, but she did not comment on his action. Instead, she said gaily, "Well, we're supposed to be going for a stroll before lunch. See you later."

"Enjoy yourselves!" Beechley called after them, with a return of his usual jovial manner.

They reached the end of the drive, and for the first time, Tremaine noticed the lodge situated to one side of the main gates and partly screened by trees. It did not appear to be tenanted. The windows were bare of curtains, and the whole place had an air of neglect.

They turned right along the road. "I wonder what Uncle Gerald's been up to?" the girl said.

Mordecai Tremaine, who had been pondering that very thing but had hesitated to ask questions, accepted the invitation eagerly. "He seemed very anxious to prevent us from seeing what he'd bought," he remarked.

"I tried to get a good look at that parcel," said the girl, "but he was standing in the way."

"It was cloth of some sort. I caught a glimpse of it where the paper was torn away."

"It's probably something to do with one of Uncle Gerald's practical jokes. There's no knowing what he and Uncle Benedict will get up to at Christmas. Last year, Uncle Gerald spent Christmas Eve pretending to be the ghost of Lady Isabel and frightened poor Aunt Charlotte to death. She wouldn't speak to him for nearly a week afterward."

"Why do you call him 'Uncle' Gerald?" asked Mordecai Tremaine curiously. "He isn't really related to you, is he?"

"Oh no," she told him. "Nor is Uncle Benedict. But I've always thought of them as my uncles. Jeremy and Uncle Benedict have been friends for as long as I can remember, and when Daddy died and Jeremy became my guardian, we were in Uncle Benedict's company so often that I automatically regarded him as my real uncle."

"Are Mr. Beechley and Mr. Grame related?"

She shook her head.

"No—they're just very old friends. But Uncle Gerald counts as one of the family now, although Aunt Charlotte is Uncle Benedict's only actual blood relation."

"Aunt Charlotte?" murmured Mordecai Tremaine

reflectively. "That's the middle-aged lady, isn't it? She struck me as being a rather difficult person to sum up."

"In what way?" asked the girl, and he shrugged.

"I don't quite know," he admitted. "She puzzles me. I thought I saw her in a tea shop in Calnford yesterday afternoon, but apparently I was mistaken. It seems that she was with Mrs. Tristam at the time so she couldn't possibly have been there."

He was searching as he spoke for some reaction on Denys Arden's part that might give him a clue as to why Charlotte Grame had lied so obviously. But she was not looking at him, and he could detect nothing unusual in her manner.

"I feel rather sorry for Aunt Charlotte," she said slowly. "She seems like someone who hasn't been able to get the best out of life and feels vaguely frustrated and unhappy. She must have been quite pretty when she was young. I can't understand why she never married. Poor dear, she's rather helpless at times! It's a good job she has Uncle Benedict to look after her. As far as that goes," she added, "it's a good job for both of them that Uncle Benedict is as generous as he is."

"Both of them?"

"Aunt Charlotte and Uncle Gerald. Uncle Benedict looks after them both."

"You mean," said Mordecai Tremaine hesitantly, "that Mr. Beechley hasn't any money of his own?"

"Not as far as I've been able to find out," she said frankly. "Uncle Benedict always seems to pay his bills for him, and of course, it doesn't cost him anything to live here."

They walked in silence for a few moments, and then Tremaine said, "It's a great pity about your guardian."

It was significant that despite the sudden change of subject, she knew what he meant. Mordecai Tremaine found it equally significant—and oddly gratifying—that she replied frankly and without hesitation. "I don't know quite what to think about Jeremy. It isn't like him to act so unreasonably. And it all started so suddenly. I can't understand what made him change."

"You mean that your guardian hasn't always disliked Mr. Wynton?"

"Oh no. At first Jeremy and Roger were on very good terms. It wasn't until about six months ago that Jeremy began to find fault with him. It seemed to happen overnight. That's what makes the whole thing so baffling."

"Did they have a sudden violent quarrel?"

"No. Unless Roger doesn't want to tell me about it for some reason. And I can't believe that's the case. He's always acted as though he's just as puzzled as I am. I'm sure it's Jeremy who's at fault," she said with spirit. "He's been behaving strangely for a long time—and not just over Roger. I'm sure there's something on his mind."

"In what way has his behavior been strange?" asked Mordecai Tremaine.

There may have been a trace of overeagerness in his manner. Whatever the cause, she seemed to withdraw a little. "Perhaps I'm making it sound too serious. He hasn't been wearing straws in his hair or anything like that!" she said lightly. "It's just that he's been…difficult. He's apt to decide things in a hurry. You can never be sure just what he will do. For instance, until a little while ago he didn't intend to spend Christmas here at all. He was going to America on business. His passage was booked and he'd made all arrangements, and then, without warning, he canceled everything."

"Did he give any reason?"

"He wouldn't say a word except that he'd changed his plans. And that was strange, too, because he doesn't usually have any secrets from me."

"You don't suppose he'd had bad news connected with his business and didn't want to worry you over it?"

"I'm quite sure he hadn't. Jeremy isn't the kind of man to be upset by any business troubles. He's had too many ups and downs."

"What did Mr. Grame think about the American trip? I understand that these Christmas house parties are his special delight. Did he like the idea of Mr. Rainer being away this year?"

"I believe he did feel rather upset," admitted the girl. "Uncle Benedict likes to feel that we're all here. But he didn't say a great deal. His attitude was that he'd be disappointed if Jeremy was missing, but that it was up to him to make his own plans."

Mordecai Tremaine gave her a shrewd glance. He stopped in the roadway, and she, too, came to a standstill, turning to look into the bright-gray eyes behind the pince-nez.

"Don't tell me you're out of breath already!" she teased him.

"No," he said. "But I'm curious. I'm wondering just why you've been talking to me as you have."

"What do you mean?" she said quickly, but the telltale color was in her cheeks.

Mordecai Tremaine thought that it made her look very lovely. He said, "I don't think our conversation has been altogether casual. After all, I'm a stranger, and yet you've been ready to tell me all sorts of things I hardly imagine you usually tell to strangers. And I can't help wondering why."

For an instant or two she faced him, the flush in her cheeks. "All right," she finally said. "You win. What do you want me to tell you?"

"Only why you're troubled. And only if you want to tell me."

"I do want to tell you," she returned slowly. "And yet I

don't know what there is to tell. I know that sounds stupid," she added hastily, seeing his look of surprise, "but there isn't any other way to express it."

"You feel," said Mordecai Tremaine, "that something is going to happen, but you can't give that something a name or do anything to stop it, and you feel restless and frustrated."

"That's it," she said eagerly. "That's just the way I feel. Why is it? What is it that frightens me?"

"I'm a stranger," he told her. "All *I* can see is a rather jolly house party getting ready to enjoy Christmas in a really old-fashioned way."

"Perhaps it *is* like that. Perhaps I'm just suffering from nerves. Uncle Benedict fussing over everyone and enjoying himself by dressing up and playing at Santa Claus; all of us laughing and joking and behaving as if we were one big, happy family; a Christmas tree loaded with presents; a fall of snow at just the right time—it's all so pleasant and secure."

"Only it isn't," observed Mordecai Tremaine gravely. "You're walking about with a feeling of unreality and the sensation that sooner or later you're going to find yourself in the middle of a nightmare."

He was watching her closely. But his carefully planned attack did not achieve its object. She did not reveal her thoughts to him, and after a moment or two he said, "You haven't told me yet why you've been so frank with me."

"I'm afraid I like gossiping," she said. "Sorry. I've probably been acting like an awful bore." She glanced down at her wristwatch, and before he could return to the offensive, she added, "Heavens, we shall have to fly if we don't want to be late for lunch!"

Their walk back to the house was brisk—so brisk, in fact, that there was no scope for conversation. Tremaine decided regretfully that if he wanted to probe deeper into Denys Arden's private thoughts, he would have to wait for another opportunity to talk to her alone. And with Roger Wynton in the neighborhood, that opportunity was likely to be considerably delayed.

It was. After lunch, the girl was nowhere to be seen. Tremaine was wandering disconsolately along the drive toward the empty lodge, having finally given up hope of finding her or of detaching her from Wynton even if he did, when a voice hailed him.

Turning, he saw Nicholas Blaise. He brightened. Maybe the afternoon would not be such a loss after all. "Hullo," he said. "All the decorating finished?"

"All I'm concerned with," returned Blaise smilingly. "Benedict's still fussing over his beloved tree, but I know that he'd rather not have any help with that particular task."

"The tree appears to be something of an institution."

"It certainly is. Wait until tomorrow, and you'll see it in all its glory!"

"A present for everyone… Isn't that the feature?"

Blaise nodded. "That's Benedict's job at the moment…placing the cards on the tree. He sets out all the names on little brackets during the day, and tonight when the rest of us are supposed to be in bed, he'll come down and tie on the presents."

"In the role of Father Christmas."

"In the role of Father Christmas," agreed Blaise. "I'm glad I've found you," he went on, adjusting his pace to his companion's as they walked slowly down the drive. "I've been waiting for a chance to have a talk with you."

"As a matter of fact," said Mordecai Tremaine, "I've been expecting it."

"Of course, you're wondering about that note of mine and just why I wanted Benedict to ask you down here. I'm afraid I've a confession to make. I wanted you here for a sort of busman's holiday."

"The plot," said Tremaine happily, "is beginning to thicken."

But Blaise seemed to have become suddenly uncomfortable. "I hope you won't think too badly of me," he said hesitantly. "I mean, asking you here as a guest and then trying to pour out my troubles upon you. But I've been worried. Damnably worried. And then, quite suddenly, I thought of you, and I knew that you were the person to help me. You see, I couldn't go to the police. I had nothing I could tell them. They would only have told me to go to a doctor and get something for my nerves…and I wouldn't have been able to blame them."

"So there *is* something in it," said Tremaine softly.

"What do you mean?" said Blaise sharply. "What do you know?"

"Nothing," said Tremaine. "Nothing at all. You were saying that you couldn't go to the police. What made you think of them?"

"It's Benedict. What do you think of him? Does he seem…different…since you saw him last?"

"I haven't noticed anything. He seems in very good spirits. He certainly appears to be determined to enjoy his Christmas."

"He isn't the same. There's something on his mind. I think he's afraid."

"Of what?"

"I don't know," Blaise said helplessly. "I don't know. That's why I asked you to come down."

"But what can *I* do? Mr. Grame is hardly likely to take me into his confidence. Not if he hasn't even confided in you, and I imagine from what you've just said that he hasn't done so."

"You're used to this sort of thing. You've had experience in…well, in making inquiries and finding out about things."

"And you want me to try to find out why Mr. Grame is afraid?"

"If you put it like that," said Blaise. "You see, it isn't easy to say what I mean, but the fact is that I've been with Benedict a long time and I've grown fond of him. I think I know him. I know his generosity, the way he'll try to help a lame dog… as I was when I first came to him. I know how simple and enthusiastic he can be—over such things as this Christmas tree, for instance. I hate to see him growing secretive and furtive. I hate to see him losing his enjoyment of life. And that's just what he *is* doing."

"Why don't you ask him the reason?"

Nicholas Blaise made a wry grimace. "Because I haven't the nerve," he admitted. "You know our relationship. I handle all Benedict's business for him. He treats me as a social equal. But after all I'm still only a paid employee. Once or twice when he's been in a sympathetic mood, I've put out a hint and tried to get him to give me his confidence. But all it did was to make him draw back into his shell."

"And you haven't any theories at all as to what is troubling him?"

Blaise hesitated. "No… Well, not exactly," he said. "Only…"

"Only?" prompted Tremaine.

"I've a feeling—it's only that, mind you—that it's something to do with Rainer."

"Oh." Mordecai Tremaine's monosyllable was significant. He said, "I wonder if you and Miss Arden are worrying about the same thing?"

"Denys?" There was surprise in the other's voice. "Why, has she been telling you anything about Benedict?"

"Not about Mr. Grame. About her guardian. She seems to have the same feeling about him that you have about Mr. Grame."

Nicholas Blaise was obviously thinking over the implications of his companion's statement. He said at last, "You mean she thinks Rainer's in trouble of some kind?"

"She does," said Tremaine. "Which strikes me as being interesting. Benedict Grame and Jeremy Rainer, as I understand it, are very old friends. If they're both displaying the same symptoms, it's possible that it's due to the same cause. What about our old friend the shadow from the past?"

He saw Nicholas Blaise's puzzled look and chuckled. "One of the routine theories," he explained. "Old business associates who were accomplices in certain rather dubious affairs in their early days are suddenly reminded of their guilt by the unexpected arrival of one of their former acquaintances. This personage is down on his luck. So he tries to improve his bank balance in the obvious way. By blackmail."

"But that's wildly improbable," objected Blaise. "I'm sure that can't be the reason. They don't act like fellow conspirators."

His protestations were so earnest that Mordecai Tremaine smiled. "I'm not suggesting it's true," he said. "I'm only putting it forward as a possible explanation. Have there been any strangers in the neighborhood lately? That's another standby in cases like this."

"You're not laughing at me, are you?" asked Blaise suspiciously.

Despite a quick denial, he still showed signs of being ruffled, and Tremaine hastened to smooth him down. "I'm perfectly serious, Nick," he said. "I daresay you know everybody in the village by now. Have there been any strange faces around lately?"

Although unwillingly, Blaise nevertheless gave his attention to the question. "I think there have been a couple," he replied. "Not that there's anything unusual in that. Sherbroome's well known, despite its size. People often spend a few days here."

"But not," said Tremaine, "in the middle of winter with an uncomfortable amount of snow around. And not without a reason a little stronger than the mere desire to have a look at a picturesque piece of ancient England. But to get back to these strangers of yours. Do you know anything about them?"

A sudden thought inserted itself into his mind. He had hardly realized it was there when he was saying quickly to Blaise, before the other could reply, "Is one of them a tall, rather gaunt-looking fellow with dark, staring eyes and the appearance of wanting to pick a quarrel with someone?"

He startled his companion to a greater degree than he had

expected. Blaise swung around upon him with an exclamation. "Yes," he said. "That's right. But when did you see him? You haven't been out, have you, since you arrived?"

"No, I haven't been out—apart from a stroll with Miss Arden this morning. I saw him yesterday afternoon. I was looking for the house, and I saw this chap standing in the roadway and pulled up to ask him where it was. He was just by the entrance to the drive. I thought he seemed very interested in the place. Hence my question just now about the presence of any mysterious strangers."

"Probably just taking a look out of curiosity," said Blaise. "It's a fine old house. I believe I've seen the chap about myself. He's probably harmless enough, despite his looks. The truth is, Mordecai, I can't bring myself to pay much attention to your mysterious stranger theory. Benedict and Rainer aren't in partnership over this thing. I feel certain about that, however little I may know about the rest. In fact, I'm not at all sure that Rainer isn't at the root of the trouble."

"I thought," interrupted Tremaine, "that they were the best of friends."

"Officially," said Blaise, "they are. But sometimes I wonder."

"Any particular reason?"

"Well, only one *particular* reason. You know about Mrs. Tristam, I suppose?"

"I met her last night, of course. A very striking woman."

"Very," said Nicholas Blaise drily. "That's just the point. Benedict undoubtedly agrees. And so does Rainer. You… follow?"

"Perfectly. Widows are wonderful. And the two gentlemen have been showing signs of wanting to settle the problem with pistols for two at dawn. Is that it?"

"That's the general idea. Although I don't know about the pistols."

"What does the lady think about it?"

"No one," observed Blaise, "knows what Lucia Tristam thinks." He was silent for a moment or two, as though allowing his companion to assimilate the thought of the magnificent Lucia, and then he said, "Well, how do you feel about things? Will you take on the job?"

"Let me make certain that I understand the position," Tremaine said. "You think that Benedict Grame is laboring under some secret fear. He won't talk about it, but you believe Rainer is the cause of it—"

"No," interposed Blaise quickly, "I'm not going as far as that. It was just…just an instinct, if you like. It hasn't any real foundation, and it may be wildly wrong."

"All right, you don't suspect anybody. In fact, you don't really know *what* to suspect. You just have a vague feeling that Grame's in trouble. Trouble that he won't discuss, even with you, but that is preying on his mind. You want me to investigate this highly nebulous matter, but you don't know where I'm to begin or what I'm expected to find!"

Blaise looked glum. "It does sound pretty feeble," he admitted. "I can understand your not wanting to handle anything so unsatisfactory. But don't let it spoil your Christmas. We'll agree to forget all I've said."

"Wait a moment," said Tremaine. "Who said anything about not wanting to handle it?"

"You mean you *will* take it up?"

"I certainly will. It's much too intriguing to be ignored."

"Thanks, Mordecai," said Blaise. "You've taken a load off my mind. If there's anything you want to know, anything I can tell you or do for you, let me hear about it, and I'll do whatever I can." He added, "There's just one thing…"

"I know," said Tremaine. "Don't tell Grame."

"I don't want to give you the impression that I'm deliberately going behind Benedict's back, but to be perfectly honest, I'm not sure how he'll take it. I don't want him to think I've been spying on him. I owe him too much for that."

"Of course. I appreciate your position."

If the undoubtedly unsubstantiated and half-formed theories Nicholas Blaise had just tried to put before him had arrived out of nothingness, Mordecai Tremaine would probably have been inclined to laugh them aside and accuse the other of having sampled too many mince pies in advance of the Christmas feast, but what Blaise had said had possessed the significance of a sound-track synchronizing with a series of pictures that had already been running through his mind.

There was a picture of the man and the woman he had seen talking so intimately in the tea shop in Calnford. There was a picture of the gaunt man to whom he had spoken at the entrance to the drive on his arrival, dark-faced and seeming to exude such an atmosphere of menace. There was a picture of Charlotte Grame, nervous and pale, denying that she had been in Calnford. There was a picture of Lucia Tristam, amusement in her tawny eyes, coolly supporting Charlotte Grame's alibi, with the look of a woman who knew that she was lying and was reveling in it.

There was a picture of Jeremy Rainer, gray and dour, staring fixedly at the Christmas tree upon which Benedict Grame was busily engaged, as if it drew him with some baleful force he could not resist. And there was a picture of Denys Arden, her scarf flying gaily and her face rosy with the wind, and the shadows in her eyes as she told him of her fears.

Each in itself was without real significance. Each in itself could be easily explained away. But together they created an impression of smoldering drama. And there was, thought Mordecai Tremaine, no smoke without fire.

6

The event of the afternoon was the arrival of Austin Delamere. He was preceded by a lengthy telegram saying that he had been prevented from arriving by the morning train as he had intended, and that he would be traveling later in the day by road. A large chauffeur-driven car brought him to the steps of the house at four o'clock. His plump figure, swathed in a heavy overcoat with a high astrakhan collar, rolled into the hall with cultivated dignity. He raised one hand in greeting to Benedict Grame, who came forward to meet him—the other held a bulging briefcase. His attitude was that of the exhausted statesman, worn by the cares of office.

"So sorry I wasn't able to get here before, my dear fellow," he said to Grame. "Official business, you know. They won't allow us to rest even at a time like this. I'm afraid I've had to bring a few little matters away with me. I hope you won't mind my shutting myself up occasionally while I'm here?"

"Of course not," said Benedict Grame heartily. "I'm only

too delighted that you found it possible to come down. Christmas without you wouldn't have been the same."

If there was a hint of amusement in his eyes, it was not reflected in his voice. Mordecai Tremaine had chanced to be passing through the hall and he was a witness to Delamere's entrance. It was clear that Grame knew his man.

"I suppose there'll be the usual people?" said Delamere, as he allowed the butler to take his coat. "And all the usual trimmings? Including the Christmas tree?"

"Including the Christmas tree," agreed Grame. "Would you like to have a look at it?"

"Oh, there's plenty of time," said Delamere, with a smile. "I'll have a roam around when I've tidied up. Still the same old Benedict!" he added. "I'd have been disappointed if there'd been no tree for us this year! It's good to get away from politics and come into the atmosphere of the real old Christmas. Makes me feel like a boy again. Heaven knows the opportunity is rare enough these days!"

Mordecai Tremaine suspected that the last sentence had been added for his benefit. He knew that Delamere had caught sight of him. Grame noticed his glance and turned his head.

"Hullo, Mordecai," he said. "I don't believe you know Austin Delamere, do you?"

"No," returned Tremaine. "I haven't that honor."

Grame performed the introductions, and he was able to study the politician more closely without betraying that fact.

Austin Delamere's podgy features and high, egg-shaped head, accentuated in its dome-like aspect by sadly thinning hair, were not unknown to him. Although he had never met the other in the flesh before, he had encountered them in newspaper photographs and in newsreels when the politician's unctuous voice had been enlarging upon some item of government policy. He had always thought him a rather pompous little man with far too large a sense of his own importance.

So far, Delamere's career had not been outstanding. It had been plodding rather than meteoric. But in some quarters, he was reputed to be a coming man, one whom it might be well to cultivate if one had an eye on long-term prospects.

There was certainly no disputing his ambition. Delamere made no secret of the fact that his goal was the top. It was whispered that he was not particular about the methods he used to get there, but such scandal as there had been had not passed beyond the stage of the whisper. There was no proof to connect him with anything unsavory, and without proof, it was an error in tactics to slander such a man as Austin Delamere.

At one time, however, there had been a hint that something more concrete might result and that he might find himself in a very awkward situation—a situation in connection with which the name of the director of public prosecutions had been mentioned. Mordecai Tremaine searched his memory during the brief moments he was facing the object of his thoughts. Something to do with contracts and bribery...

But whatever it was, it had become too deeply embedded in the rusty details of the past to be uncovered now. He realized that Delamere was making polite conversation. He released the other's soft hand that had rested in his without making any attempt to grip. "It's my first visit," he said. "I'm looking forward to the festivities."

"Benedict is determined to go down in history as the man who kept the spirit of Christmas alive in an age of cynical materialism," Delamere said.

He sounded like a man who was quite willing to go on talking, but Mordecai Tremaine was sensitive to atmosphere and he knew that the other's mind was not on him, and that he was merely employing the politician's trick of speaking diplomatic phrases while his attention was engaged elsewhere.

And in a few moments, Delamere was on his way up to his room and he was left to ponder the subject of the latest addition to his fellow guests and the question of whether the politician had any part to play in the drama that seemed to be underlying the seasonal trimmings and decorations. Although there was nothing to suggest that he did, there was equally nothing to suggest that he did not. But

Delamere was one of the regular members of the Christmas party. Which meant that the odds were therefore slightly in favor of his having some connection with whatever intrigue was in existence.

Mordecai Tremaine told himself that his thoughts were leading him onto unmarked paths again and drifted toward the library. He was well inside the room before he realized that it was occupied, and by then it was too late to withdraw with dignity.

Gerald Beechley was there. He was seated at the telephone. He was saying: "I've told you it's all right. I'll see you get the money." His voice rose urgently. "No…don't do that! You'll be paid. He's good for that much…"

He broke off. Mordecai Tremaine had coughed. Gerald Beechley's furious eyes glared at him for an instant, and then the other turned back to the telephone. "I'm going to ring off," he said quickly. "I'll explain later. But don't do anything hasty. You'll get what you want."

He replaced the receiver viciously. He said: "What do *you* want?"

Mordecai Tremaine said mildly, "I didn't realize there was anyone here."

Beechley seemed to realize suddenly that he was betraying himself. And Mordecai Tremaine, standing there with his pince-nez on the verge of slipping off and a look of complete ineffectiveness on his face, was so obviously harmless that it was impossible to remain angry with him.

"Sorry," Beechley muttered. "You rather startled me."

"That's all right," said Tremaine. "It was my fault for coming in so quietly."

His attitude was a mixture of diffidence and benevolence. He might have been a sheltered spinster who had inadvertently strayed into the wrong bedroom and who didn't know quite what to do.

Beechley was clearly uncomfortable. "I'm afraid you caught me in rather a bad moment," he said hesitantly. "A…a friend of mine rang me up. As a matter of fact, he wanted to borrow some money. I don't like refusing him, although it isn't the first time. I told him I'd help him out, but at the same time I felt that I ought to speak my mind to him."

He gave Mordecai Tremaine a sideways glance, as if trying to estimate how convincing he was being, but that gentleman's blank expression told him nothing. Which, of course, was Mordecai Tremaine's intention.

"I quite understand," he murmured. "These things are sometimes a little…er…delicate, aren't they?"

He gave no hint that he did not believe Beechley's story or that he had added one more peculiar episode to his growing collection. According to Denys Arden, Gerald Beechley was entirely dependent upon Benedict Grame. It did not seem likely, therefore, that he was in the habit of lending money to his friends, but on the other hand, it did seem distinctly probable that he was capable of a good deal of borrowing. One of his creditors had been on the telephone making inconvenient demands. That was the reason for his sudden flare-up of temper. He had not relished his financial difficulties being made known to a stranger.

"I'll see you get the money… He's good for that much…"

That Benedict Grame was the *he* in question was a logical enough assumption. Evidently it would not be the first time he had been asked to come to Beechley's aid.

The weather had not encouraged many people to go outdoors, and despite the size of the house, it was inevitable that anyone as addicted to wandering as Mordecai Tremaine should encounter most of the other guests in turn. It must be admitted that his journeyings from room to room were not without purpose. His love of a mystery had been fully aroused by now. Had his friend Inspector Boyce (of Scotland Yard) been on the spot, he would have recognized the symptoms the moment he set eyes on the mild-looking figure, pince-nez askew, drifting from place to place as though unable to settle permanently in any one of them. Mordecai Tremaine was engaged in the task of collecting impressions of the intriguing party of human beings among whom his Christmas was to be spent, and he was thoroughly enjoying the proceeding.

The rustle of a newspaper attracted him as he passed a door that stood just ajar. He glanced inquiringly into the room and saw a bony hand holding the wide pages of the *Financial Times*. The hairless dome of Professor Ernest Lorring, shining in the firelight, was visible over the back of an easy chair.

Mordecai Tremaine seated himself facing the professor. He knew that the other had seen him, although he had made no sign of recognition.

"Stock markets don't seem to be too healthy just lately," he observed in the overbright manner of one trying to start a conversation and choosing an obvious opening.

"No."

It was more a grunt than a word. It signified that as far as its author was concerned, the conversation had both opened and closed. But Mordecai Tremaine's apparent diffidence concealed a tenacity many a bulldog would have been proud to own.

"I suppose it's the holiday influence," he went on. "The markets always seem to sag at holiday times. I daresay it's a general lack of interest."

"I daresay it is," Lorring said.

"I expect they'll begin to recover again next week. Don't you think?"

A sound that was laden with unconcealed exasperation

came from behind the *Financial Times*. With ostentatious cracklings and rustlings, the newspaper was folded. Mordecai Tremaine allowed himself a quiet smile of victory. "It's my first Christmas here," he said. "Are you one of the regular members of the party?"

"If you mean have I spent Christmas here before," said Lorring, "the answer is that I have not."

"Then we've a pleasure in common to look forward to," Mordecai Tremaine replied, impervious to the gaunt, frowning face staring aggressively into his own now that the newspaper barrier had been removed. "I understand that Mr. Grame's Christmases are very happy affairs."

"Christmas!" said Lorring.

This time the grunt was a definite snort.

"I saw them decorating the tree this morning," persevered Tremaine. "It's going to be quite a splendid piece of work. Have you seen it yet?"

It was as though he had pressed the switch that closed a circuit. The scientist sat up suddenly in his chair as if an electric impulse had vitalized him.

"No," he barked, "I haven't. I've no time for this childish humbug. The whole thing is just an excuse for self-indulgence on the part of people who are old enough to know better."

And then, just as Gerald Beechley had done, he seemed to become aware of the unwarranted violence of his manner.

He said, "Forgive me if I sounded rude. I've been working under pressure lately. I was looking forward to a few days of quiet, and the thought that there might be a crowd of rowdy young people to contend with—or, worse, a crowd of elderly people trying to play at being young—is inclined to put me on edge."

Mordecai Tremaine did his best to look sympathetic. Lorring's change of front was no more genuine than Beechley's had been, but there was no point in revealing what he felt.

"Of course," he said. "You've been engaged in a good deal of special research work."

Lorring's face became suddenly wary. He stiffened visibly, as though to resist attack. There was nothing, thought Mordecai Tremaine, to be learned from him now. The scientist was on his guard, and a man who was both a curmudgeon and watchfully suspicious was unlikely to give anything away.

He made an excuse that was received with undisguised relief and left the room. As he closed the door, he heard the rustle of the *Financial Times* as Lorring continued his reading. He wondered why Benedict Grame had invited the gaunt-looking scientist to spend Christmas with him. Certainly he seemed completely out of place as a member of a house party reputed to keep the season in a wholehearted and traditional manner. There was nothing jolly about Ernest

Lorring. If Benedict Grame was drawn after Mr. Pickwick, then Lorring was drawn after Ebenezer Scrooge.

Perhaps Grame would try to thaw his guest's icy manner. He might even persuade him to don the traditional robes of Father Christmas and distribute the gifts from the Christmas tree. The image that came to mind of Lorring's face decorated with a white beard and peering miserably through the foliage was so incongruous that he broke into a chuckle.

"You seem pleased with your thoughts, Mr. Tremaine!"

He looked up, startled. It was Rosalind Marsh. She had just come into the hall with Gerald Beechley. She had evidently been out, and the color in her cheeks made her look decidedly lovelier. It had softened that hard whiteness of the goddess. He could think of her now as a flesh-and-blood woman, one who would experience a woman's fierce emotions.

He smiled at her, but he did not explain his chuckle. She was obviously disappointed, but in her turn, she made no further reference to it.

"You haven't been out this afternoon?" she said inquiringly, and he shook his head.

"No, I've been wandering about…talking to people."

There was speculation in the look she gave him. "Have the results been…interesting?"

"Oh yes," he told her. "Very interesting."

From her expression, he thought she was about to put

another question to him, but she changed her mind, after all. She glanced toward Gerald Beechley. "Give me a cigarette, Gerald. Do you mind? I've left my case upstairs."

"Of course."

The big man attended to her needs and then offered the case to Tremaine. That gentleman shook his head. "No, thanks. I smoke very little. A cigarette after meals. Perhaps a pipe occasionally."

"You sound like a medicinal smoker!" said Beechley. He was his bluff and jovial self. His red face whipped by the keen wind, his high-necked pullover, his rough tweeds, and his massive hands, one of which was grasping a stout oak stick, made him look the typical countryman. He was the simple farming man, hearty of appetite and manner. He seemed to have forgotten the embarrassment of that scene in the library.

Rosalind Marsh drew at her cigarette. Mordecai Tremaine suspected that she had only asked for it in order to gain time. Time for what? "I see Austin Delamere's arrived," she said. "That completes the party."

"There'll be quite a lot of us for dinner, won't there?" said Tremaine.

She nodded.

"Pretty much the same as last night. The Napiers will be over again with Lucia Tristam. They'll spend the night here… probably a couple of nights. They usually do at Christmas. I wonder what Benedict's planning? Any idea what's on the agenda, Gerald?"

Tremaine's mind went back to that little scene outside the house when the big man had been so obviously unwilling to reveal what it was he had brought back in his car. He said, "I rather imagine Mr. Beechley could tell us something if he wished. Eh, Mr. Beechley?"

His tone was deliberately arch. He was the garrulous old busybody trying to draw confidences by hinting that he already knew what was going on. Gerald Beechley gave him a scowl of dislike. He would clearly have liked to change the subject, but Rosalind Marsh had been quick to take up the point.

"Don't tell me you're going to give another of your famous performances, Gerald!"

Mordecai Tremaine pushed his pince-nez into a more secure position. He blinked at the big man. He looked rather like a friendly dog, pleading to be granted some attention.

"Another?" he said. "Why, does Mr. Beechley usually entertain at these times?"

Rosalind Marsh threw back her head and laughed.

"I think *entertain* is the right word," she said, "although it doesn't mean quite what you imagine it does. Gerald is a notorious character in Sherbroome. People are never quite sure what he'll do next. Most of the villagers are convinced that he's quite mad. What was the last episode, Gerald? Was it when you set up a stall in the market and started selling homemade toffee apples in exchange for jam jars?"

Tremaine could see the veins standing thickly in Gerald Beechley's neck where it bulged redly over the yellow pullover. The big man was staring at Rosalind Marsh's white throat as though he would have delighted to take it between his powerful fingers and crush the life from it.

Or was it just some queer trick of the light that made that murderous expression appear to be in his face, and was he really smiling broadly? Not for the first time that day, Mordecai Tremaine experienced a feeling of unreality. He stared at the other, trying to be sure, and found that he could not.

And then that brief, disturbing impression was gone and he was facing the bluff countryman who really was smiling at the joke and whose booming voice was saying, "Doesn't do to have long faces all the time, you know!"

"No, indeed," Tremaine said as though he had never suspected anything was wrong. "It does us all good to laugh now and again."

"Let's go crazy while we can. Life's too short to spend it all being serious."

The big man seemed to be speaking genuinely enough now.

Tremaine remarked, "You and Mr. Grame must have a great deal in common."

"We understand each other," said Beechley. "Benedict's a great fellow…one of the best. Don't know what we'd do without him. He's certainly put up with me longer than most people would have done. Which reminds me… I promised to see him as soon as I came in. I daresay he wants to give me my briefing!"

Rosalind Marsh made no comment until the other had left the hall. She was standing apparently casually, her cigarette drooping between her fingers, a slightly bored expression on her face. But her eyes were anything but bored. She said to Mordecai Tremaine, "I wish I understood what you were after."

Tremaine regarded her doubtfully. "What I'm after?" he echoed in an attempt to collect his thoughts.

She came closer to him. "If you were to be frank with me," she said in a low voice, "perhaps I could help you. It might be to our mutual advantage."

There was a sound from the shadows at the end of the hall. It startled her, and she drew away from him. "I'll have to run up to my room," she said in a voice that was obviously designed to be overheard. "I'm in urgent need of running repairs!"

As she went up the stairs, Tremaine turned slowly to gaze

at the newcomer. It was Fleming—a middle-aged, dignified figure, whose trained poker face revealed nothing. He walked through the hall, evidently on some errand connected with his duties, with a subtle unobtrusiveness that implied that he neither saw nor was seen.

It would, thought Tremaine, be enlightening to get behind the mask of the upper servant and contact the real man. He recalled the incident of the morning when the butler had been helping Benedict Grame to decorate the Christmas tree and Jeremy Rainer had made his appearance. Fleming had given no sign that he was aware of the tension in the air, and yet he must have known what was going on.

There was a leather-seated chair in the hall, partly concealed in the gloom of a recess under the stairs. Tremaine sat down to meditate and was still there some twenty minutes later when Gerald Beechley came back.

The big man looked as though he had received a shock and had not recovered his self-control. He was muttering angrily to himself. He was only a yard or two from Tremaine when he realized that the hall was not empty. A sullen antagonism came into his face. He pushed past without speaking, but the glare he gave was eloquent enough.

"Not in the best of tempers," Tremaine murmured to himself.

He waited until the ostentatious slam of a door told him that Beechley had gone, and then he went quickly toward the room from which the other had come.

He had expected to find Benedict Grame. His host turned sharply at his entrance. The blue eyes surveyed him keenly. The bushy eyebrows had the air of having been brushed the wrong way. Grame looked like a man who had taken part in a somewhat undignified scene.

Mordecai Tremaine was not surprised. The telephone conversation he had overheard earlier and Gerald Beechley's attitude in the hall had acted as unmistakable signposts. Beechley was pressed for money. He had approached Benedict Grame. And he had been rebuffed.

Benedict Grame was awkward in the presence of his guest. "Have you seen Gerald?" he asked.

His manner was so clumsy that it was painfully obvious he was trying to hide something.

"I saw him in the hall a few moments ago," said Tremaine. "As a matter of fact," he added, apparently guilelessly, "I thought he was with you. Did you want him?"

"It doesn't matter," said Grame hastily. He was obviously casting about in his mind for some means of changing the subject. He said, after a pause, "I hope you haven't been too bored. I'm afraid I haven't had as much opportunity of talking to you as I would have liked."

"I'm enjoying my stay immensely," said Tremaine. "So far I've found it most interesting."

The bushy eyebrows went up in an arc. "Interesting?"

"Does it seem a strange word to use?" Tremaine smiled. "I'm a student of human nature. Don't forget my hobby!"

Grame's slightly puzzled features relaxed. "There isn't a very fruitful field for an amateur criminologist here. We're all painfully law-abiding! Unless you'd like to make a special study of Delamere. I accept no responsibility for politicians."

But despite his attempt to appear lighthearted, there was a suggestion of weariness in his manner. He gave the impression of being an aging and inwardly worried man. Tremaine thought of Nicholas Blaise and the subject of their conversation that morning. There seemed to be confirmation here of what Blaise had said—at least as far as his belief that Benedict Grame had something on his mind was concerned. But Nicholas Blaise had said nothing about Gerald Beechley being the cause, and it was Beechley who appeared to be the reason for Grame's present dejection.

For an instant or two, Tremaine suffered from the temptation to take advantage of his companion's existing mood to put a leading question to him. Perhaps Grame might unburden himself if he approached the matter boldly now that the ground had been prepared. But the thought of his promise to

Blaise held him back. If Grame took offense at his probing, it might put Blaise in a difficult position.

Regretfully he decided against a frontal attack. Instead, he remarked, "I haven't seen your sister about this afternoon. Has she gone into Calnford?"

"Charlotte? Heavens, no! She's in her room…resting. I can't recall the last occasion when Charlotte went as far as Calnford. She very rarely goes out. She spends a great deal of time in her room. Too much, I'm afraid. I often wish I could get her to mix with people more."

"She seems very reserved."

"She always has been. She's always had a horror of leading anything that might be called a social existence, and the idea of marriage just seems impossible to her."

The sentimental part of Mordecai Tremaine's soul that was the driving force behind his love of *Romantic Stories* and similar literature stirred protestingly.

"A pity," he said. "Really, a great pity. I should imagine that she was quite a beauty as a girl. She's still a good-looking woman."

"Charlotte could have had her choice," said Grame. "But she's always acted as though love and marriage were something repugnant. I've done what little I could, of course, but I haven't been able to influence her. She's gradually become more and more shut in upon herself—almost a recluse. That's why

I was so glad when she and Lucia—Mrs. Tristam—became so attached to each other. They've been together a good deal lately, and the difference in Charlotte has been striking."

"Mrs. Tristam's an unusual woman," said Mordecai Tremaine. "She has a vivid personality. I can understand your sister being attracted by her."

Benedict Grame did not say anything, but it was almost possible to see pride inflating him. There was no doubt about the extent of Lucia Tristam's conquest.

Tremaine looked at him understandingly. "If you'll forgive my making such a comment," he said, "and put it down to the remark of a candid friend, you haven't been having too easy a time."

"You mean my flock have been difficult to handle?" said Grame wryly. "Perhaps they have at times, but after all, I've enjoyed the feeling that I've been holding things together. And there have been compensations. They know that they can trust me and confide in me. But this is Christmas, and you're here to enjoy yourself! This is no time to be dragging make-believe skeletons out of dusty cupboards!"

It was on that note of banter that their conversation finished. Mr. Pickwick was himself again, radiating youthful enthusiasm and eager that the right atmosphere of Christmas cheer should be abroad among his guests.

But when he was alone once more, Mordecai Tremaine

found himself probing beneath the surface of Benedict Grame's cheerfulness, and what he found did not support outward appearances. Despite the other's attempt to seem undismayed, it was clear that he was finding it difficult to preserve the illusion of harmony in his household and to maintain the pose of the benevolent ruler of a happy if slightly unorthodox family.

Tremaine experienced a surge of sympathy for his host that was all the more real because of his own sentimental soul. He, too, was a romantic. He, too, liked to feel that all was well in the best of worlds. That was why he had warmed toward Benedict Grame, why he had taken so mellow a view of the other's eagerness to create the atmosphere of the Dickensian Christmas, and had appreciated the warmhearted simplicity that lay behind the gesture of the decorated Christmas tree.

Benedict Grame wanted to be the benevolent despot. He wanted to be the friendly, solacing figure to whom his protégés would come when they were in trouble and who was always ready to give them his advice and help. And he had discovered that while the theory was rosily attractive, the reality was prickly with thorns.

His mind was still dwelling on Charlotte Grame and the difficulties she presented for her brother when he realized that she was crossing the hall toward the stairs. Before he had recovered from the mild shock of the coincidence, she was halfway toward the second floor. He took a step forward.

"Miss Grame!"

She did not turn, and he thought she could not have heard him. He called again, and this time he knew that she was deliberately pretending deafness because she quickened her pace. She reached the head of the stairs and vanished from his sight.

"Curiouser and curiouser," said Mordecai Tremaine. *Alice in Wonderland* occupied a favorite corner in his heart, and the expression was dear to him.

The frail and nervous Charlotte's reaction had not altogether surprised him, for although he had not expected her anxiety to reveal itself quite so plainly, he knew that she was in dread of finding herself alone with him. The afternoon was, however, fated to produce yet another intriguing incident and one that was to give him an entirely new field of speculation.

It occurred when the gray winter light was giving way before the darkness and the shadows were creeping ever more greedily through the house. Tremaine had been sitting at one of the windows, gazing out over the snow and allowing his thoughts to drift. He came out of his musings to discover that he was both cold and stiff, and that the gloom had stolen upon him.

The notion came to him as he rose to his feet to take another look at Benedict Grame's Christmas tree. He had no precise reason for the impulse; it sprang from some instinctive source within him.

He was growing familiar now with the layout of the house, and he found the big room in which the tree had been placed without difficulty. The door opened soundlessly under his touch. The french doors had not been curtained, and in the half-light he could see the gaily decorated tree standing against the wall, its spreading branches carrying tiny silver lanterns and festoons of tinsel.

It made a brave show, even in that gloomy setting. Under the glow of the electric light and with a merry party atmosphere to breathe a warm vitality into its gift-laden arms, it would possess the magic of fairyland. Benedict Grame had undoubtedly succeeded in creating his cherished illusion where the tree was concerned.

There were no gifts upon it as yet. They would come later when Grame put on his robes of office and made his nocturnal visit in the role of Santa Claus. But Tremaine could dimly make out the brackets, each with its square, white name card, showing where the gift for each guest was to be hung.

Usually one associated a Christmas tree with a children's party, but even mature adults who had believed themselves long past such things could derive pleasure from Grame's handiwork. It was so spontaneous a gesture, so intimately bound up with the sentiments of peace and goodwill.

Mordecai Tremaine smiled a little wistfully. He was not a bachelor by choice. It would have been good to have had children so that one could have watched their eager faces as their eyes fell upon such a tree as this.

And then he realized that he was not alone in the room.

There was a man sitting in a deep chair in the shadow of the wall between the two sets of french doors, directly facing the tree. A man who sat with such rigid stillness that he did not seem to be there.

It was Professor Lorring. Tremaine saw the high-domed forehead, the hooked nose, and the prominent cheekbones as he peered through the gloom, and accustomed now to the grayness, his eyes made out the other's shape. He did not think that Lorring had seen him. His entrance had been so quiet, and the other's attention had seemed to be fixed with such a strange intensity upon the tree in front of him.

Mordecai Tremaine watched for a moment or two, and a shiver went through him. He was glad Lorring did not know he was there. For upon the other's gaunt features was an expression of sheer malignant ferocity that it was not good to witness upon the face of a human being.

1

Dinner had indubitably been a success. It was as if each of those present had decided to make a personal contribution to the gaiety in an attempt to give Benedict Grame the kind of Christmas Eve they knew he wanted.

Mordecai Tremaine looked around the crowded table and smiled benignly. Crackers had been exploded and gay paper hats distributed. A carnival air reigned over the relics of the feast.

Austin Delamere was behaving as though he had been released from the restrictions of officialdom and was determined to forget that he was a man with a future. He seemed to be enjoying the fact that a Napoleon hat was tilted rakishly over his left eye: his plump hands were waving animatedly as he explained some obviously humorous point to Charlotte Grame, who had regained the strained air of excitement she had revealed on the previous evening. Her eyes were bright, and the high color was back in her cheeks in two vivid patches.

At the head of the table, Benedict Grame sat beaming. He showed quite frankly that he was reveling in the sight of his guests giving way to the Christmas tradition. His was the unashamed delight of the small boy who sees his party going with a swing.

Even Jeremy Rainer had lost his frozen grayness and was talking with a lightheartedness that vitalized his dour features and gave him the carefree appearance of a man whose mind was unclouded. It might, thought Tremaine, not be entirely unconnected to the fact that he was seated next to Lucia Tristam. One would need to be icy indeed to remain unthawed by the warmth of the magnificent Lucia's colorful personality. With her green evening gown contrasting under the light with her luxuriant and superbly coiffed auburn hair, her beauty tonight was dazzling.

The only exception to the rule of exhilaration was Professor Lorring. As had been the case on the previous evening, the scientist had eaten in an ostentatious silence, his head lowered, oblivious to the conversation around him.

Several times, Grame had attempted to draw him out, but he was seated too far from the other to make a sustained effort, and Lorring was apparently determined to remain uncommunicative. Tremaine saw Nicholas Blaise regarding the scientist thoughtfully, and it was not difficult to guess what was in his mind. In Lorring's attitude, he was finding what might be a significant factor as far as Benedict Grame's uneasiness was concerned.

After dinner, chairs were pushed back and rugs and carpets rolled into corners. Dance music was provided by records, but the atmosphere was informal enough by now to make that disadvantage a very minor one. Mordecai Tremaine found himself dancing with Denys Arden and liking it more than a little.

"I didn't see you about this afternoon," he remarked, as he steered expertly past a chair jutting into their path.

"No, Roger and I went out for a long walk," she told him. "We didn't get back until late." She added, "You dance marvelously."

"You sound surprised. Do I look so very old and feeble?" he said with mock dismay.

"Oh, I didn't mean it that way. But you're not a bit like I expected."

He peered over the top of his pince-nez in the manner that always made him look most harmless and that in reality was a warning that he was most to be feared. "What did you expect?" he said, and he added softly, "And why?"

At first she did not appreciate the significance of the second question. "I don't quite know," she said. "Someone much more official looking. Someone hawklike…almost frightening. I suppose it's because Sherlock Holmes always comes into my mind when I think of a—"

She broke off quickly, as though she had only just realized where her frankness was leading her. She colored and pretended to be suddenly interested in the music to which they were dancing. But Mordecai Tremaine was not to be so easily shaken off.

"When you think of a what?" he prompted gently, and when she did not reply, he said, "It wouldn't be a detective, would it?"

"Yes," she said unwillingly. As though she felt called upon to explain, she said, "You *are* one, aren't you?"

"Well, in a way," said Tremaine. "I'm interested in criminology, but I haven't any official position. But who told you about my little hobby?"

She hesitated. He had the impression that she was seeking in her mind for an assurance that in telling him she would not be incriminating anyone. "It was Roger," she said at last. "He mentioned it several days ago…when we heard you were coming. He saw your name in the newspapers in connection with a murder case."

"Publicity," said Mordecai Tremaine, "seems inseparable from murder. It's very regrettable. I hope the knowledge hasn't caused any embarrassment."

She looked at him suspiciously, but the mild eyes only half concealed by the pince-nez betrayed nothing of what he was thinking. "What do you mean?"

"I wouldn't like to feel that my presence here was causing anything in the nature of…well, constraint. Who else besides Mr. Wynton knows my dark secret?"

"Only Jeremy, as far as I know. But that's because I haven't talked to anyone about it. I imagine that Nick and Uncle Benedict know."

"How did your guardian react to the news?" he asked her casually.

He could tell from the instinctive look of defense that came into her eyes that he had touched upon a sensitive spot. But at that moment the music stopped, and before he could follow up his advantage, Roger Wynton had come up to them and the opportunity had gone.

He decided to turn his attention to Charlotte Grame and looked around for her so that he could ask her for the next dance. Whether she saw him and guessed his intention, he could not tell, but an interchange of glances took place between her and Gerald Beechley, and the big man reached her first.

Mordecai Tremaine smiled. Charlotte Grame was becoming an exciting fish to play. She was making it more obvious than ever that she had something to hide.

However, he was not to have the chance to question her when the waltz she was dancing with Beechley came to an end, as he had planned. Benedict Grame had been absent for a few moments, but now he came back, and it was obvious from the look of eagerness on his face that he had an announcement to make. He stood at the end of the room and held up his hand.

"Listen, everybody, the village carolers have arrived. They're under the command of the rector. He thought we might like to hear them, since it's Christmas Eve, and brought them up here. It seemed to me to be an excellent idea, and I've asked them inside. They're waiting for us now."

He led the way, and in a few moments, they were all in the big room that housed the Christmas tree, making themselves comfortable in a wide semicircle around the assembled carolers, who were trying desperately to conceal their embarrassment at finding themselves the center of attraction in what had for centuries been the "big house" of the village. Although the old ruling family had long since passed from among them, something of the awe associated with it still lingered in the lofty rooms in which its members had held sway. There were coughs and shufflings. It was as though the ghost of the feudal system had suddenly and disconcertingly made them aware that they were under the roof of the lords of the manor.

Only the rector seemed unimpressed by the atmosphere. White-haired, benign, and perfectly in character, he stood in front of his flock, waiting for the guests to settle themselves.

The tips of his fingers were pressed together in the expectant attitude he adopted every Sunday in the pulpit of the ancient village church when the congregation came to the last verse of the hymn before the sermon and he prepared to begin his delivery.

Tremaine deduced that the carolers sprang mainly from the ranks of the village choir. He studied them idly and found himself counting them as they stood in front of the gaily decorated tree and being sorted now into treble, alto, and bass. Seven, eight… He was confused by the maneuvering for position and had to begin again. There was a middle-aged lady of noble proportions at the piano. With the rector, she made thirteen—no, fourteen…

His attention became fixed, no longer desultory. At the back, partially hidden by the branches of the Christmas tree, was a face he knew. The face of the man whom he had seen outside the house on his arrival. The face that had seemed to him then to hold a strange malevolence.

Like Lorring. The thought came into his mind hard on the heels of his recognition. It startled him with its concise impact, and he realized that it was strange that it had not occurred to him before.

Professor Lorring had looked in the afternoon like a man in whose heart hate was deep-rooted and his expression had been akin to that which this stranger had borne when he had encountered him outside the gates. Why? What possible link could there be between the distinguished scientist and this village caroler?

Someone had turned off all the lights except one that burned above the piano. The rector turned and raised his hand, and the pianist struck a warning chord.

It was an old carol they chose as their first. A beautiful medieval hymn that somehow seemed in full keeping with the setting of the noble old house. It found a response in Mordecai Tremaine's soul. It held a message of peace. Of peace and glad tidings and goodwill.

And yet he was not at peace. Like a cloudy barrier across his vision, there was an image of those two malignant faces. He stared at the stranger. He could gaze at him without fear of being observed now, for he was in the shadows. He would appear as no more than a white blur, not to be distinguished from a number of similar blurs all turned in the same direction.

But his scrutiny told him nothing beyond the fact that there was no sign of that earlier disturbing expression on the other's face now. He seemed to be concerned with nothing but the carol in which he was joining with every appearance of earnestness.

Not for the first time, Mordecai Tremaine wondered whether a vivid imagination was causing him to see things that had no real existence. The other's face had a natural darkness that gave him a saturnine appearance that might have no connection with his thoughts. All the carolers had taken off their outer garments when they had come into the house, and without the overcoat that had muffled him at that first meeting, and removed from the fantasy-laden setting of a gloomy winter afternoon and a snow-covered landscape lying under a fading light, the man did not give such an impression of bulk. No doubt he had been well protected against the weather and had seemed much bigger than he really was.

The only thing about him now that spoke of more than ordinary size was his head. This was not so large that it was abnormal, but it was certainly noticeable. It was, Tremaine thought, a rather noble head. It had dignity and a certain proud poise. It was, in fact, an unusual head to find on the shoulders of a man who was apparently no more than a simple villager.

It was difficult to see the other's features clearly, because he was at the rear of the singing group and partially hidden by the branches of the tree. Black, thick hair surmounted broad features with wide nostrils and an expressive mouth. As he sang, with head held back, some trick of the light in association with the darkness of his jaw gave him the appearance of possessing a short, pointed beard.

All through the first two carols, Mordecai Tremaine kept his eyes on the dark man. Was he becoming surer of himself? Was he relaxing what had at first been a guarded attitude and beginning to look about him as if he wanted to impress every detail of the room upon his memory? Or was he reacting like the average villager who, after being awestruck by his introduction to new surroundings, gradually finds himself becoming accustomed to them and begins to display natural curiosity?

Having failed to arrive at a satisfactory conclusion, Tremaine transferred his attention to his fellow guests. Benedict Grame was enjoying the whole thing, sitting back in his chair blissfully content. Denys Arden was listening eagerly—the carolers sang well together, and their voices blended perfectly in the lofty room—and Roger Wynton was deriving his pleasure from her happiness. Reaction among the others varied from the polite boredom of Rosalind Marsh, whom he caught stifling a yawn behind a graceful white hand upon which a single stone flashed, to the unconcealed antagonism of Professor Lorring, whose expression was that of a man forced to endure the unendurable.

Tremaine glanced slowly along the ragged line of faces. Austin Delamere was plumply peaceful. His hands were folded over his stomach, and he was lying back in his chair with his eyes half closed. He might, of course, have been taking advantage of the lull to think out some weighty matter of state, but the signs were certainly against it.

On the other side of Delamere, Harold and Evelyn Napier were seated. They were a colorless couple, pleasantly nondescript. Tremaine judged them both to be in their early forties. The husband was a plumpish, inoffensive-looking individual, rather like a somewhat harassed edition of Delamere but without the politician's elaborate air of importance. The wife was a soft-voiced shadow of a creature who had once been pretty and who still retained a timid, faun-like appeal and had a disconcerting trick of looking to her husband before making a reply to a question, as if seeking his support.

Tremaine had not exchanged more than a few words with them, and his inquiring mind had not yet been able to classify them with any satisfaction. They were apparently well-established inhabitants of the district, and yet they gave him the impression of being oddly out of place in it, as though they were town folk doing their best to live up to a country estate and finding the process both difficult and uncomfortable.

Evelyn Napier had seemed reluctant to talk about their connections with the neighborhood. Although there again, Tremaine admitted, he might have been allowing his over-sensitive imagination to lead him astray. Watching her now as she sat listening to the carolers, a little faded, streaks of gray infringing upon what had once been the soft brown of her hair, she reminded him of Charlotte Grame. There was the same suggestion of inhibition, the same nervous defensiveness.

When they had been introduced, he had made a commonplace enough opening gambit with a remark about the charm of Sherbroome village. She had agreed readily...even enthusiastically. And he had gone on, thinking she came from local stock. "I imagine your family roots go deep into its history?"

That was when her smile had become a mechanical thing that owed nothing to her emotions. That was when she had ceased to be natural and had revealed herself to be on her guard. At least—perhaps.

"Oh no," she had told him. "We haven't been living down here very long."

Delicately probing, he had said, "You couldn't have chosen a more perfect spot in which to settle down. I suppose that like most of us, you were anxious for peaceful country life, away from the noise and bustle."

"That's it," she had said eagerly—too eagerly. "Both of us had begun to find town life unbearable."

And then Gerald Beechley had come up, and he had been left with the frustrating feeling that he had been on the verge of a discovery and had had an opportunity snatched from him.

Evelyn Napier made a sudden movement. He thought

at first that she had felt his eyes upon her, but she did not look in his direction. He saw that her left hand was feeling stealthily for her husband's. Harold Napier felt her gentle touch. Tremaine saw him give his wife a smile and saw their hands come together.

It quickened his sympathy. His sentimental soul warmed toward them. He was romantic enough to believe firmly in the sanctity of marriage.

He shifted his attention from the Napiers and allowed his thoughts to dwell on Lucia Tristam. It was a pleasant occupation. Mordecai Tremaine was an admirer of beauty wherever it was to be found.

She seemed to be listening eagerly to the carols. Lucia Tristam was a person who brought intensity to everything she did. It was easy to imagine her sweeping royally through life, undisturbed by thoughts of convention or what the rest of the world might say about her actions.

Perhaps she was the most intriguing personality in the room. Warm, vital, and disturbing, the sort of woman who could set men on fire merely by looking at them on a crowded street.

Thinking that he had been studying her too long and too ardently, he looked away and found himself staring into the questioning eyes of Nicholas Blaise. The other smiled. There was approval in the smile. Evidently Blaise was satisfied that his request was bearing fruit.

The carols came to an end. After his official speech of thanks, Benedict Grame escorted the rector and his little band from the room, evidently to see that they were suitably refreshed before they went on their way. The dark man was the last to leave. Tremaine saw him hesitate in the doorway, saw him give a last, searching glance about him.

As soon as he could, he took Nicholas Blaise aside. The other gave him an expectant glance. "Things," he said, "are beginning to move. Am I right?"

"Not exactly," Tremaine said. "But I thought you might be able to give me some information. Is Mr. Grame in the habit of keeping fairly large sums of money in the house?"

"He has a safe in his room in which he keeps various odd amounts, but it's rare for him to have much loose cash. Nothing worth stealing, if that's what you mean."

"I didn't say that was what I meant," returned Mordecai Tremaine evasively. "But since you've mentioned the point, is there anything worth a burglar's visit?"

"As a matter of fact, there is. A diamond necklace."

"A family heirloom?"

The quickening of interest in Tremaine's voice brought a smile to Nicholas Blaise's face. "I'm afraid not. But it does possess certain sentimental associations," he added. "It's intended to be a present. For Denys."

"For any particular occasion?"

"Her wedding day."

"Does Miss Arden—Denys—know about this necklace?"

"Yes. She's tried several times to persuade Benedict against it. She's told him it's far too expensive a gift for him to give. But he's made up his mind about it, and when Benedict makes up his mind over a thing, you can't change him."

"He's very fond of Miss Arden, isn't he?"

"He treats her as his own daughter—you've probably seen it already. He's been working on the necklace for years, collecting the stones and trying to get a perfect match."

"So it's no secret?"

"It's a very open one. All of us in the house know about it. Gerald, Charlotte, myself…"

"And Mr. Rainer?"

"And Jeremy," agreed Blaise. His eyebrows went up. "You don't mean… You're not suggesting that *Jeremy* might want to steal it?"

"Is the suggestion so unthinkable?" Mordecai Tremaine said gently.

For an instant or two, Blaise did not know what to say. "Not what you might call unthinkable," he said at last. "But I must confess that it isn't one that would have occurred to me. After all, what reason could he have? He isn't short of money, and he's as fond of Denys as Benedict himself. I'm certain of that. Why should he want to rob her?"

"Perhaps he wants to rob her husband. You said that it was intended to be a wedding gift. And he doesn't make any secret of his dislike for Roger Wynton."

"True enough," Blaise admitted. "But I can't accept that as a sufficient reason. After all, they aren't married yet. Suppose Denys marries someone else?"

"In that case, it wouldn't be necessary to steal the necklace. Unless the next prospective husband happened to be equally disliked!"

Nicholas Blaise looked at him suspiciously. "I wish I could tell when you were pulling my leg. You aren't seriously putting forward the theory that Jeremy might steal the necklace merely to damage Wynton's interests? I don't suppose Wynton's a wealthy man, but he certainly isn't a poor one. I don't know what the necklace is worth. I daresay its value runs into thousands, but if it ran into millions, it wouldn't affect his wanting to marry Denys."

"You sound like the young man's champion," said Mordecai Tremaine, and his eyes were twinkling. "Don't go trying to read any significance into all this," he added. "The fact is that Mr. Grame keeps a valuable necklace in the house which he intends to give to Miss Arden as a wedding present when the time comes, and everybody knows of its existence. Does 'everybody' include the servants, by the way?"

"I wouldn't like to say," returned Blaise. "I imagine

that most of them have heard about it. There aren't many secrets as far as they're concerned. You know how such news spreads."

"Yes," said Mordecai Tremaine, "I know."

Despite the antagonism of Lorring and the boredom of Rosalind Marsh, the carol recital had undoubtedly brought an atmosphere of peace and goodwill in its train. The carefree spirit that had prevailed at dinner remained throughout the evening. Benedict Grame, his paper cap riding perkily on his bushy hair, circulated tirelessly among his guests, and as the gaiety grew, so did his smile broaden and his schoolboy's laugh sound more frequently.

It was not a protracted party. Perhaps that was why the merriment did not flag. It was a tradition, apparently, that there was an early retirement on Christmas Eve, as though to make up for the feasting that was to come on the succeeding days.

Mordecai Tremaine knew that he should be reacting to the general festivity, that he should be expanding mentally under its generous glow. But somehow he could never quite bring himself to the point of abandonment. He could never quite enter so thoroughly into the spirit of the gathering that he was able to forget everything but the satisfying sensation that he was enjoying himself in the way that one should at such a season. It was as though there was a barrier between his companions and himself. It was as though he stood watching them but could not join in their revels because he could not accept them as real.

He knew, of course, that the barrier was a mental one. He knew that it existed only in his own mind, and that he could break it down if he made the effort.

When he was in his room and it was no longer necessary to display an interest or to make conversation, he tried to analyze his emotions. Why had he been unable to surrender himself to the gaiety of Benedict Grame's Christmas party, a gaiety to which he had looked forward with such pleasant anticipation? What had been troubling his mind, stifling spontaneity?

The answer was an instinctive one. It had been because he was waiting for something. Because he knew that something was going to happen, and because he was tensed to meet it.

He brushed the argument aside, and when it still pursued him, he tried to thrust it deep into the background of his mind. What could happen? This was Christmas Eve, the night when peace and tranquility lay quietly over the earth in spirit, just as the snow was lying outside, blanketing the scars made by man and blending the whole landscape into a soft, white pattern.

It was a night when joyous magic was abroad, the kind of magic for which mankind had so great a need and in which there was no fear. Why should he be so heavy with foreboding, so laden down with a dread he could not name?

He switched on the reading lamp at the side of his bed and settled back against the pillows with *Romantic Stories* in his hand. Here was the anodyne. Here he would find balm for his soul. As literature, it might be the subject of scorn by the critics, but at least it was mellow and kindly. It offered love and romance and the humor and humanity that formed the mainspring of the world.

But he read without seeing and without understanding. Tonight, at least, *Romantic Stories* could not help him. He laid the magazine down, and moved by a sudden impulse, he slipped from the bed and went toward the window, pulling his dressing gown around him.

He drew back the curtains, but the light behind him made it difficult to see out, so he turned back and switched off the reading lamp. The clouds were lying heavy across the sky, but as he looked, the moon cleared and he saw the snow spreading fairylike across the grounds of the house and the neatly hedged fields beyond. It sparkled with frost, and he could imagine how it would crunch beneath his feet, were he to walk on it.

He opened the window and leaned out, and as he did so, he gave a sudden low gasp of surprise. Almost immediately below him, moving along the terrace, was a figure. That in itself was possessed of no great significance, but the clothes in which the person was dressed caused him to stare wide-eyed, for it was the figure of Father Christmas! He could see the long, red cloak and the red cap with little patches of snow upon it that showed plainly in the clear light.

For a few unreal moments he wondered whether his brain was betraying him. Undoubtedly it was Christmas Eve, when Santa Claus rode abroad to delight the hearts of children. But this was fantasy!

And then his thoughts were able to focus on the screen of his mind, and the explanation was clear. The red-robed figure was no hallucination. It was, of course, Benedict Grame. Now that his guests had gone to their rooms, he had dressed himself in the traditional manner and was setting out to decorate the Christmas tree.

Tremaine leaned out of the window. From where he knew the village to lie, the sound of a bell was coming. The moon was still free of the drifting clouds, and the Christmas card effect of his surroundings was emphasized by its cold radiance. The bare arms of the trees formed a boundary to the big house; the snow lay unbroken between the main steps and the road they bordered.

The red figure was in perfect keeping with its setting. Now it was no longer moving. It was as though Tremaine was not looking out upon a real scene but gazing at a Christmas picture in a shop window, a picture that possessed a stereoscopic quality that gave it the illusion of life, but which must remain eternally unchanged.

But it was only for a moment that the illusion lasted. A faint wind sighed eerily up from behind the hills. A great mass of dark and ominous cloud passed its grim finger over the clear face of the moon and stole its brightness from it.

And with the darkness came menace.

The blackness of the earth seemed to be giving shelter to the forces of evil. Malignity and terror were abroad. The whole world lay under a deep, inky shadow in which the figure of Father Christmas had been swallowed up. Above the house, the clouds had gathered. They were pressing down upon it, threatening and implacable, as though it had been singled out for some essential act of evil and that now the hour was come.

Wrapped in his dressing gown, Mordecai Tremaine did not feel the chill wintry air. But he shivered.

8

The scream awakened him.

Mordecai Tremaine sat up in bed with the sound of it ringing in his ears, and at first he could not tell whether it was real. Imagination and reality, fantasy and fact had become so entwined within him that, aroused suddenly from a troubled sleep, he was left groping after truth.

And then the scream came again, and this time its shrill desperation impacted upon his mind with an effect that shocked him into full consciousness.

He groped for the bedside lamp, found it, and blinked at his pocket watch. It was ten minutes past two. He could not have been sleeping for long; the heavy, drugging legacy of first sleep still lay upon him.

As he huddled into his dressing gown, the screams went on. They formed a hysterical background to the slow working of his thoughts. He was listening to them and trying at the same time to assimilate their meaning. There was something he had to learn. There was some message for him. It was not merely that the screams were underwritten by terror; there was another, less obvious meaning.

But although he was conscious of it, he could not define it. His awakening had been too sudden. He had had no time to sort out his impressions clearly. This was it, his mind was saying. This was the *something* he had been expecting.

As he opened the door of his bedroom and stepped into the corridor, he could hear movements from other parts of the house. A voice called out in inquiry. There was a note of irascibility in it, and he thought it was Lorring's. He heard the sound of running feet.

The screams were less frequent now. They had a sobbing note, as though exhaustion was reducing whoever was responsible to semi-impotence.

It was a woman who had screamed. The mists had cleared from Mordecai Tremaine's mind now, and that much at least had resolved itself. He wondered as he padded along the corridor what he would find. He had located the source of the screams as the ground floor, and as he made his way toward the stairs, Gerald Beechley came out of a room just ahead of him.

The other heard him and turned. His normally red face had lost its high color and was drawn and tense. "What is it?" he said. "What's happened? I was asleep…wondered what was going on. Is it Benedict?"

Mordecai Tremaine regarded him curiously. "I don't know," he said. "What makes you think it might be Mr. Grame?"

Fear flickered in Gerald Beechley's eyes. His glance wavered. He gave a convincing impression of a man who had made a mistake and was trying to avoid being caught in a trap. He said haltingly, "It seemed the…the most obvious thing. I-I thought it must be Benedict. All the others are in bed."

They were going down the stairs now. Mordecai Tremaine did not look at his companion. It was a method that encouraged people to talk more freely, either defensively in an attempt to throw up excuses against what they construed as cold suspicion, or confidently in the belief that they had nothing to fear.

"You mean you thought it was Mr. Grame because you knew that he would be downstairs attending to the Christmas tree after everybody else had gone to their rooms?"

"That's right," Beechley said eagerly. "You know Benedict's habit, of course. He always stays up on Christmas Eve to get the tree ready for the morning. He likes to have the presents all waiting for us when we come down."

"I see," said Mordecai Tremaine. "The only thing is," he added gently, "it was a *woman* who screamed."

This time, he glanced sideways at his companion. Beechley's newfound assurance had collapsed as rapidly as it had been inflated. The hesitant, fearful look was back in his face, and one hand had gone to his collar to caress his neck nervously.

As if, thought Tremaine suddenly, *he was anxious on account of it…*

Downstairs, lights were blazing through an open doorway. They heard the sound of voices and, crossing the hall, went into the room in which the activity appeared to be centered.

The first thing Mordecai Tremaine saw was the Christmas tree. He saw it as though it was a symbol, as though it was the dominant factor in a dark tragedy. And as though, in some strange way and as though it possessed a thinking brain, it *knew*.

It was, of course, only a fleeting and fantastic impression born of its momentarily seizing his attention as he went into the room. In the next instant, the full scene of which it was a part was photographed upon his mind.

It was Charlotte Grame who had screamed. She was seated in one of the easy chairs from which the house party had listened to the village carolers. Grief and horror had distorted her face, and her expression held the indefinable misery of someone who felt herself to be lying under the hand of doom.

She was dressed in a dark tweed costume that exaggerated her paleness into a pallor that shocked and that accentuated the dark rings marking her tortured eyes. Her emotion had stormed itself out, but it had left her weak and pitiable, huddled into the chair.

Austin Delamere was with her. The plump man had lost his official pose. He was no longer the potential elder statesman carrying the cares of office and relaxing with conscious dignity in between signing documents of historic importance. He was only an over-fat, harassed little man, whose thin hairs were straggling wildly down into his eyes and who was faced with a situation with which he was unable to cope.

He was patting one of Charlotte Grame's hands, making an ineffectual attempt to revive her. For all the interest she was showing in him, he might not have been there. She was staring past him. She was staring at something that lay beyond him on the floor.

It was a heap of red cloth. It lay almost under the Christmas tree. It lay motionless, and it was the fact that it was so still that made it so terrible.

Mordecai Tremaine's hand gripped Gerald Beechley's arm. He said sharply, "Don't go any closer! Don't touch anything!"

It was an unnecessary warning. Beechley had stopped almost as soon as he entered the room. He stood there trying to say something, but with only inarticulate sounds coming from him.

Tremaine walked forward and looked down. His eyes

moved over the crumpled red cloak, the plain red cap with edges trimmed with white, the long white beard that had slipped out of position and rested grotesquely against the dead man's cheek.

It *was* a dead man. There was a darker red on the cloak. It was a red that had stained. It was a red that had seeped through when a bullet had drained the lifeblood from the heart. He stooped. He could see the hole—discolored around the edges, slightly irregular but quite small—through which the bullet had passed. It was in a vertical line with the heart, but well below it.

This was Father Christmas, Tremaine's brain was saying crazily over and over again. It was Christmas Eve, and Father Christmas had arrived. Only he was lying dead under the Christmas tree. Father Christmas had been murdered.

Murdered? That was something it remained to prove. He peered about him. There was no sign of a weapon.

On the floor by the dead man's hand, something glittered. Cautiously he picked up one of the bright particles lying there and examined it. It looked as though it might have come from one of the decorations on the tree. He turned and saw that one of the little bells hanging from the branches had been broken. The remnants were hanging precariously from the lower part of the tree, a pathetic morsel of wreckage.

Despite the fact that the carol singers had left ample

evidence of their presence, the floor immediately around the tree was reasonably clear. Tremaine was able to pick out the four marks that disfigured the woodwork between its base and the body. They looked as though they had been made by something that had been dragged an inch or two under pressure, and they formed an almost perfect square. Between the dead man and the french doors was an uneven trail of moisture.

The other occupants of the room had watched him without speaking. He had felt their eyes upon him, questioning, frightened, but they had said nothing, as though there was nothing they could find to say.

Austin Delamere was the first to break the silence. He cleared his throat. "Should we… Do you think we ought to send for a doctor?"

"A doctor," said Mordecai Tremaine, "cannot bring a dead man back to life."

"He…he *is* dead?"

"Yes," said Tremaine, "he is dead."

There were voices in the hall. People eddied into the room. The bald head of Professor Lorring showed in the lead. He thrust his way forward, gaunt features soured with the anger of a man robbed of sleep.

"What the devil's going on down here?" he demanded. "People screaming their heads off in the middle of the night! I'll—"

Mordecai Tremaine cut him off. He stood up quickly. "Stay where you are!" he ordered sharply. "All of you!"

The note of command in his voice, so much at variance with his mild appearance, would in any case have surprised them into obeying. But they had seen the crumpled form under the tree, and they were suddenly at a loss.

Lorring's face went white. His eyes swept to the tree, fiercely searching, stayed for an instant, and then swung back to the body.

"It isn't—*murder*?"

All his antagonism had gone. He was a frightened man. He was looking at Mordecai Tremaine as though he wanted to be given comfort.

"That," said Tremaine, "is a matter the police will have to decide."

"The police!"

It was a woman's voice. The voice of Rosalind Marsh. It came in a taut, involuntary sigh.

"Of course," said Tremaine. "The police. They will have to be told. Don't you…like the thought?"

She recoiled at that. The desperate expression of a hunted wild thing came into her eyes. But it was only for a moment or two. She came back at him with a kind of challenging fury. "Why shouldn't I like it? Are you trying to accuse me of something?"

"Oh no," said Mordecai Tremaine apologetically. "I'm

sorry if I expressed myself clumsily." He looked so inoffensive as he stood there in front of the tree, pince-nez askew, his slight form seeming to flinch beneath her attack, that she was partly reassured. She regarded him suspiciously but without the same open hostility.

Tremaine's eyes were passing over each member of the little group at the doorway. They thought that he was bewildered by what had happened and not quite certain what to do next, despite the surprising manner in which he had at first assumed command of the situation. They could not tell that his brain was working coolly and steadily, taking them one by one and trying to memorize their manner and their appearance, trying to analyze what they were thinking—and trying to extract the significance from those things.

For this was the vital time. This was the period when the murderer—if he or she were present—might make the mistake that would be a betrayal of guilt.

Gerald Beechley had not moved from the time he had entered the room. He was displaying no interest in any of the others. His attention was fixed alternately upon the Christmas tree and upon the sprawled figure beneath it. His gaze swung from one to the other in an unending rhythm. His face was still but a bloodless shadow of its usual high-colored self, and the expression it bore was a curious mixture of fear and bewilderment.

Professor Lorring was just behind him. In contrast to Beechley's complete disregard for anyone else, the scientist was now displaying an intense interest in his companions. His head was thrust forward in that challenging manner with which he had rebuffed all attempts at drawing him into conversation. It was as though he was striving by his aggressiveness to eradicate those first moments of betrayal. His eyes were peering this way and that; he had the look of a predatory, if uncertain, eagle searching for its quarry.

It was Austin Delamere with whom he was most concerned. His fierce glance returned continually to the politician, who was still leaning over Charlotte Grame, one plump hand yet holding her wrist as though he had forgotten it was there.

Delamere became suddenly conscious of the scrutiny. He looked up to meet Lorring's stare, and his face flushed. At first Tremaine thought that he was going to make an angry comment. He did make an abrupt movement, and his lips opened. But no words came. Whatever he had been about to say, he'd changed his mind, and his only response was a deepening scowl.

Rosalind Marsh had recovered her self-possession. She was once more the cold beauty who knew how to wrest a living from an unfriendly world. She gave no indication of being unnerved by the presence of murder. She was the unemotional woman of experience, whom life had schooled to remain indifferent to tragedy.

The one person who might have been expected to show a calm acceptance of the situation betrayed the most reaction. Lucia Tristam came in behind the Napiers. She was panting, as though she had been running hard from her bedroom. When she saw the crumpled Father Christmas on the floor, she stopped abruptly. She gave a gasp, and her hand went to her throat.

She swayed. Tremaine thought she was going to fall, but she managed to retain her hold on her senses with visible effort. She stood by the door unsteadily, her hand grasping the jamb for support, her face very white.

The Napiers were as they might have been expected to be. Dressing-gowned, the husband's straggly hair tousled, the wife's enclosed in a net that drew it tight around her head, they were any nondescript, middle-aged couple pitchforked into the midst of strange events that left them at a loss and pathetically ready to accept guidance from anyone with a stronger mind than theirs.

And yet, Mordecai Tremaine was not altogether sure that his first quick judgment was correct. There was something about Harold Napier and his wife that he could not place. They *looked* ordinary. They *looked* just what one would imagine them to be. But he was not satisfied. There was about them a queer, elusive quality that hinted at the existence of something more complex behind their facade of ordinariness.

His survey was too hurried to give him any opportunity of indulging in a detailed analysis. It was over in a matter of seconds, for it had to be accomplished in the brief space of time in which shock and alarm might reasonably be expected to keep the hurriedly aroused house party inactive around the doorway, waiting for a lead to be given them.

It was a photographic series of impressions that he received, images that were thrown upon his mind in quick succession, and that he was given no time to develop and study at leisure.

As it was, there were already stirrings. Lorring said, "Well, what's going to happen now? If Grame's been murdered, hadn't we better notify the police at once?"

There was a truculent, almost defiant note in his voice. But before Tremaine could reply, there was a movement by the doorway as Nicholas Blaise appeared. He was in his dressing gown, dark hair brushed back, alarm on his face. He saw Mordecai Tremaine and came straight toward him.

"What is it?" he asked. "I heard screams…"

Tremaine had been standing in front of the body. He drew back. Blaise looked down suddenly. He saw the red cloak and the beard.

"No…"

He took a pace backward, horror rising in his eyes. He swung slowly around upon his heel so that he faced the others. He surveyed them accusingly, searchingly, and with cold purpose. And then he turned back to Tremaine. "It's happened, Mordecai," he said shakily. "It's happened. I wanted to prevent it, and I was too late…"

Bitterness and grief choked his voice. For a moment, he could not go on. But they saw him struggling to hold himself in check, and when he spoke again, his tones were firm. "It's up to you, Mordecai. Now that you're here, you've got to handle this—"

"The police…" began Tremaine, but Blaise took him up.

"I know they'll have to be brought here," he said. "But they'll listen to you. And you can tell them the kind of things they'll want to know. You can help them to find out who did it."

"Perhaps," Tremaine observed, "they will resent my interference."

"Why should they?" Blaise said. "Your name needn't be mentioned outside. If they're allowed to take the credit, surely the police aren't likely to object." He caught Tremaine by the shoulders. His grip was strong, and his fingers probed deep. "You know why I asked you here. It was because I was afraid for Benedict. It's too late to save him now, but at least we can make sure his murderer hangs!"

Blaise was momentarily oblivious of the others. His eyes were on Tremaine, passionate and pleading.

"Will you do it, Mordecai? Benedict's lying there because of some foul creature who thinks he'll go scot-free—"

"It isn't Mr. Grame," said Tremaine gently.

Nicholas Blaise did not understand him for an instant, so much was he in the grip of his emotion. Then his eyes widened. He stared incredulously. "Not…Benedict?" he said.

He went on his knees by the side of the dead man. He leaned over, the better to see his face. His hand went out. Gently he moved the beard.

They saw him start back and heard his gasp.

"God in heaven!" he breathed. "It's *Rainer!*"

9

Nicholas Blaise came slowly to his feet.

"I don't understand," he said. "I don't understand. I thought it was Benedict…"

He gestured toward the red robe the dead man was wearing. Mordecai Tremaine nodded.

"When you saw Father Christmas lying there," he said, "you thought it was Mr. Grame because Mr. Grame likes to play the part of Father Christmas on Christmas Eve. But it looks as though for some reason Mr. Rainer decided to play it instead." He studied Blaise inquiringly. "Has he ever taken Mr. Grame's place before?"

The other shook his head. "It's the last thing I would have expected him to do. He thought the whole business was a little…well, childish. He wasn't the kind of man to enjoy dressing up."

Blaise was speaking mechanically, like a man who was doing his best to answer intelligently but who was unable to concentrate. He was trying desperately to preserve an attitude of calm, but it was clear that the murder had been a terrible shock to him.

"I believe," said Mordecai Tremaine, "that there is a telephone in the library next door. Is there a police station in the village?"

"There's a village policeman," said Blaise. "I'll ring him now."

"He can pass the news on to his superiors," said Tremaine. "I imagine that he takes his orders from the police at Calnford."

"What about a doctor?" Blaise was recovering now. He obviously felt that it was incumbent upon him to give a lead in dealing with the situation. "Should we send for the local man?"

"I don't think so," said Tremaine. "I'm afraid that there isn't any doubt that Mr. Rainer is dead, and the police will bring their own surgeon."

"You don't think..." said Blaise, in the manner of a man who knew what the answer would be, but who felt that he must put his question. "You don't think it could have been an accident? Or...or suicide?"

"That," said Tremaine, "we must allow the police to decide."

"Of course," said Blaise. "Of course. I'll telephone the village." He turned away and took a step toward the door, then hesitated and glanced back at Tremaine. "Is there anything else we should do?"

"No one must leave the house. We must be careful not to disturb anything. I think it would be wise to awaken the servants. Beyond that, we can only wait until the police get here."

Blaise nodded. He was making his way through the silent group around the door when Denys Arden appeared. She came face-to-face with him.

"What is it, Nick? What's happened?"

He did not answer, but his expression told her of the gravity of what had taken place. She stepped past him, her eyes wide with inquiry. She saw Charlotte Grame and Delamere, and from those two, her gaze went to Mordecai Tremaine. And then she saw the sprawled thing on the floor.

"Jeremy!" She ran forward, and Mordecai Tremaine stepped quickly to meet her.

"Don't come any closer, Miss Arden!" he said urgently.

"But it's Jeremy," she said. "He's been hurt…"

"I'm sorry," he told her. "Dreadfully sorry. But it would be better if you didn't touch him. You see, the police—"

She did not allow him time to finish. "The *police*?" Her wide eyes were suddenly horrified. "What have the police to do with it?"

"Everything," said Tremaine quietly. "Mr. Rainer is dead."

"Dead…" she whispered. "Oh no…"

"He's been shot," said Tremaine. "Mr. Blaise has just gone to telephone the police."

The sight of the agony in her face was torment to him.

But she had to be told. And if it had to be done, then it was well that it should be done quickly.

She stood swaying, one hand to her mouth. Rosalind Marsh and Lucia Tristam moved together to support her with gentle hands. It was strange, thought Tremaine, that such an instinctive sympathy should come spontaneously from them—from the cold beauty who seemed so aloof and unmoved, and from the vivid creature who seemed too full of primitive vitality to have within her the springs of pity.

The others watched. Lorring's gaunt face might have been carved from stone. Gerald Beechley, his face now puffy and patchily red and white, had backed to the wall, prey to his own somber thoughts. The Napiers were standing hand in hand, a pathetic, frightened pair, afraid of some unnamed thing. Austin Delamere was still hovering over Charlotte Grame, in whom the mainspring of life had broken.

"Come and sit down, my dear," Lucia Tristam said gently.

She slipped an arm about Denys Arden's waist, and Mordecai Tremaine saw that the difference between them went deeper than surface appearances had suggested. Denys Arden was the hurt, bewildered child, seeking pathetically for consolation; Lucia Tristam was the mature woman who had known life and death and who possessed the richness of wisdom.

On Rosalind Marsh's face was a look that softened it and

gave it the virtue of compassion. He wished she would always look like that.

"Denys!"

The cry startled them. It was a man's voice, sharp with anxiety, and it came from the terrace outside. The french doors were pushed suddenly open. A figure shouldered its way into the room.

"Denys! Are you all right?"

It was Roger Wynton. He had no eyes for anyone but Denys Arden. He went straight toward her, and his arms went about her protectively.

Mordecai Tremaine's gray eyes blinked over his pince-nez, shadowed with speculation. How had Roger Wynton been able to make such a timely entrance? He was supposed to be several miles away, sleeping beneath his own roof. Quite apart from the fact that he could not have heard Charlotte Grame's screams at such a distance, there had not been time for him to make the difficult journey along winding, treacherous roads. Still less had there been time for him to arrive fully dressed.

The inference was that he had been somewhere near at hand. It was an inference that brought suspicion with it.

Mordecai Tremaine knew that he was not the only person to whom the suspicion had occurred. Lucia Tristam was looking at Wynton in a manner that left no doubt as to what was in her mind. She did not speak, but after a moment or two, her eyes went back to the dead man.

Roger Wynton wanted to marry Denys Arden. It was not in dispute that Jeremy Rainer had done his utmost to prevent the match. And now Jeremy Rainer was dead.

Wynton himself seemed oblivious to the suspicions he had aroused. He had taken the girl into his arms and was trying to comfort her.

For the moment, at least, she found nothing strange in his presence. She yielded to him willingly, finding relief in the fact that he was there. "Oh, Roger," she said brokenly. "It's Jeremy. He…he's dead…"

He looked beyond her to where the dead man lay. His gaze went inquiringly to Mordecai Tremaine. He said, "You mustn't think about it, my darling."

He came further into the room, still supporting her. As he came nearer the light, Tremaine saw his face clearly for the first time. There was an ugly mark down his cheek, and there were traces of blood on his skin. The heavy overcoat he was wearing had been pulled back from his shoulders. One of the buttons had been torn away.

Tremaine said, "Did you stop him?"

Wynton's head came up suddenly, as though something that had been driven from his mind had suddenly recurred to him. He said: "No. He let drive at me with a stick or a club of some kind. I was dazed for a moment or two, and by the time I'd gotten to my feet again, he'd had too much of a start. But he can't have gotten far. We must get in touch with the police at once!"

"Mr. Blaise has gone to telephone them. Did you recognize the man who struck you?"

Wynton shook his head. "The moon had gone behind the clouds. Besides, he was too well muffled up. I managed to get one blow at him though. I may have marked him."

A strange sound came to Mordecai Tremaine's ears. A frightened, sighing sound. He looked slowly around. Charlotte Grame was sitting upright in her chair, displaying more interest in what was going on around her than she had so far evidenced. Her lips were half open. She was gripping the arms of the chair so tightly that her whole frame was rigid. She was looking at Roger Wynton, and there was terror in her eyes.

Tremaine did not think that anyone else had noticed it. Attention was fixed upon Wynton. Gerald Beechley took a step forward. There was a curious, almost feverish expression on his face. "It's strange you didn't manage to see him clearly when you were close enough to hit each other," he said.

The accusation in his voice brought a flush to Wynton's face. He swung toward Beechley. "What is so strange about it?"

"I would have thought you could have told us a little more, that's all. You haven't said yet what you were doing here."

Gerald Beechley was no longer the jovial, bluff countryman. His manner was that of a snarling, vindictive creature, trying to incriminate someone else beyond the hope of redemption. As though, Mordecai Tremaine thought, he was driven by fear and prepared to use any method to save his own skin.

Wynton reacted with a heightening of his angry color. But it was significant that he did not offer any instinctive explanation as an innocent man might have done.

Mordecai Tremaine foresaw the violent scene that was dangerously near, and interrupted quickly. "I don't doubt that Mr. Wynton has a satisfactory explanation for all his actions. We must leave it to the police to ask any questions that may be necessary."

Fortunately, the antagonism that had flared between the two men had no chance to develop. Voices sounded in the hall, and a moment or two later, Nicholas Blaise came back.

"I've just seen Fleming," he said. "He's gone to call the rest of the servants. The police will be here very shortly."

He had recovered command of himself now. He spoke with the incisive tones of a man who was, in addition, beginning to master the situation. He caught sight of Roger Wynton, and his eyebrows went up inquiringly.

"Mr. Wynton arrived a moment or two ago," said Tremaine. "He was involved in a struggle with someone who was outside on the grounds, but unfortunately he wasn't able to stop him from getting away."

Nicholas Blaise stared hard at Wynton, doubt and suspicion clouding his face. He said slowly, "You mean…you actually laid hands on the murderer?"

"I don't know whether it was the murderer," said Wynton. "I certainly laid hands on someone."

"Did you see him leaving the house?"

"I saw him in the drive. I'd heard the screams, and I was on my way to find out what was happening. When I called out, he started to run so I went after him. He gave me this." Wynton fingered his bruised jaw. "By the time I'd collected my wits, there was no point in going after him in the dark so I came up here."

"That's queer," said Blaise. "Damned queer." He stood in thought for a moment or two. Wynton's story had evidently opened up an unexpected possibility to his mind. He turned suddenly to Charlotte Grame. "It was you who screamed, wasn't it, Charlotte? Did *you* see anyone?"

It was the question for which she had obviously been waiting. She said: "No…no, I didn't see anyone." Her voice was a tremulous whisper. She stared back at him, piteously anxious to be believed.

"What *did* you see?" said Blaise urgently. "What made you come downstairs?"

"I-I couldn't sleep," she told him. "I had a headache. I thought I-I heard noises. I came down with a flashlight. At first, I didn't see what it was. And then I stumbled over something, and when I looked down…" Her voice faltered. "It was horrible…horrible…"

"But there was no one else here?"

"I-I don't know. It was dark. And I was so terrified…"

Blaise leaned over. He took her by the shoulders.

"You must think, Charlotte. You must try to remember. The police will be here soon, and they will want to know. You're sure you saw no one? You're *quite* sure?"

"The room was empty," she said. "Except for…except for—"

"Except for the body?"

"Except for…for the body. There was no one else."

Austin Delamere spoke for the first time. He addressed himself to Blaise. He said: "If Rainer wasn't taking Grame's place, why hasn't Grame decorated the tree as he usually does? Why hasn't he been here? It's almost half past two."

"He *has* been here," said Nicholas Blaise. "Look at the tree."

He turned as he spoke and indicated the Christmas tree. The topmost bracket carried a small package neatly tied with colored ribbon. Tremaine moved nearer so that he could read the name on the little card fixed to the bracket. It said: *Jeremy*.

"Where," said Delamere shakily, "are the rest of the presents?"

"Perhaps…" said Gerald Beechley. "Perhaps Benedict still has them."

It seemed as though it was not what he believed but what he wanted to believe.

Mordecai Tremaine had been a thoughtful and highly intrigued spectator. But he judged that the time had come for him to say what was in his mind. "Where *is* Mr. Grame?" he interposed gently.

Nicholas Blaise spun around on his heel. Alarm and confusion had once more stripped him momentarily of his self-possession. "Of course," he said. "Benedict—"

"He's the only one," said Tremaine, "who hasn't come down."

It was a moment or two before Blaise replied. "You don't think… You don't suppose anything has happened to Benedict, too?" he asked.

"The only thing we can do," said Tremaine, "is to find out."

It was Blaise who led the way to Benedict Grame's room.

They did not have far to go, because it was in the main part of the house on the floor above them. The door was locked. Blaise hammered on it furiously.

"Benedict! Are you there? Benedict!"

They heard stirrings from inside the room. In a moment

or two, the lock was turned and the door opened. Benedict Grame's tousled head appeared. He blinked in the light, stupidly, like a man just dragged from a heavy sleep and not yet fully awake.

"What is it, Nick?" he demanded querulously. "What's all the din about?"

And then he saw the others crowding behind Blaise's dressing-gowned form, and the expression on his face changed.

"What's the trouble?" he said. "Has anyone been hurt?"

"It's Rainer," said Blaise. "He's dead."

"Dead?" Grame stared at the younger man, and then he repeated the word, as though its significance had only just impacted upon his mind. "*Dead? Jeremy?* You mean there's been an accident?"

"I don't know," said Blaise, "about an accident. He's been shot. It looks like murder."

"Murder!" The word came in a startled gasp. Benedict Grame stepped out into the corridor. There was no trace of sleep about him now. "Where is he?"

"Downstairs," said Blaise. "In front of the Christmas tree. Dressed in *your* Father Christmas outfit."

His tone was exaggeratedly noncommittal. But Grame was shaken. He could not speak for an instant or two. And then he passed his tongue over his lips.

"It…it's absurd," he said. "He can't be. My things are *here*."

There was a silence. It was a tense, oppressive silence, in which accusation slowly mounted. Benedict Grame looked around him. And then, abruptly, he went back into his room.

Nicholas Blaise made a movement as though to follow him, then changed his mind and stopped. It was seconds only before Grame reappeared. He was carrying a long, red cloak over his right arm, and in his hand was a white beard. His attitude was a mixture of challenge and appeal.

"There," he said. "There. I told you they couldn't be mine."

The top button of his pajama top was undone, and the lapel protruded untidily over his dressing gown. He made an odd figure as he stood there with his wiry hair all ruffled, holding the cloak and the beard in front of him. But no one found him an object of humor. Tragedy was too painfully near.

Mordecai Tremaine edged his way toward the front of the group about the door. "Did you ask Mr. Rainer to take your place in putting the presents on the tree tonight, Mr. Grame?"

"No," said Grame. "No. Of course not." His voice rose slightly. "Why are you asking? Are you suggesting *I* know anything about it?"

"Dear me, no," said Tremaine placatingly. "I was just wondering what caused Mr. Rainer to put on those clothes and go down to the tree."

"Well, *I* can't tell you," said Benedict Grame shortly. There was a trace of resentment in his manner. His voice carried a hint of sulkiness, even, as though he was piqued because some special plan of his had gone awry. And then, after a moment or two, it seemed that he realized the impression he was creating and realized, too, that the situation had thrust responsibilities upon him as the head of the house. He turned to Nicholas Blaise. "Hadn't we better inform the police, Nick?"

"I've told them," said Blaise. "They'll be here shortly."

It seemed that he was going to add to what he had said and then decided against it. The glance he gave Grame was both puzzled and wary. Mordecai Tremaine had the impression that he was anxious not to say too much until he knew more of what the older man was thinking, in case what he said proved to be the wrong thing.

The news that the police had already been informed seemed momentarily disconcerting to Benedict Grame. But he recovered himself quickly. "You'd better show me where… where Jeremy is, Nick," he said brusquely.

He allowed Blaise to take the lead and followed him down the stairs. The others, who had formed a ragged ring of spectators in motley, moved instinctively after them like a collection of puppets suddenly stirred into action under the impulses of their guiding strings.

Benedict Grame saw the huddled figure on the floor, but he hardly glanced at it. It was to the Christmas tree that his eyes were drawn. He uttered an exclamation. "What the devil!" He swung upon Nicholas Blaise. "Who's been playing the fool, Nick? Who's been meddling with the tree?"

"Do you mean," interposed Mordecai Tremaine, quietly but insistently, and before Blaise could reply, "that you placed all the presents in position?"

"Of course that's what I mean!" snapped Grame, without looking to see from whom the question had come. "I had everything ready before I went to bed! Who took them off? Was it Jeremy? Did *he* take them?"

"If he did," said Tremaine, "where are they?"

There was certainly no sign of the missing presents in the neighborhood of the body. There was no sack or bag in which Jeremy Rainer could have carried them. It was, of course, a possibility that he had taken them out of the room and had been killed when, for some reason, he had returned later.

"They aren't all gone," said Nicholas Blaise. "There's one left. It's Rainer's own. Perhaps he didn't have time to take it down."

"You mean," remarked Mordecai Tremaine gently, "that there *was* one present left. It isn't there now."

"But you know it's there," said Blaise. "Up at the top of the tree. We saw it when…" His voice trailed off. His eyes widened in stupefaction. The hand he had been raising to indicate what he meant to Grame dropped back to his side.

The tree was now completely bare of presents. The bracket that bore Jeremy Rainer's name was empty.

10

Mordecai Tremaine looked as though he was sleeping. He was huddled in his chair, and his head drooped limply upon his breast. He gave the impression that lack of sleep had exhausted him and that he was waiting in a kind of stupor for the coming of daylight.

The impression was a deliberately false one. Despite his crumpled appearance, his brain was both fresh and active. It was going over the events of the night. It was recollecting, considering, probing. It was searching for the clue that would reveal the murderer.

The police had arrived two hours before. Under the leadership of Superintendent Cannock—burly, scrupulously polite, and yet with a certain something in his manner that discouraged opposition and held a warning that only complete frankness would suffice—they had taken charge of the situation. Fingerprint men and photographers had already been at work. The police surgeon had made his preliminary examination of the body.

The room in which Jeremy Rainer had died had been barred to the members of the house party. The police experts had no intention of allowing their investigation to be complicated by the presence of spectators.

But Mordecai Tremaine had made good use of such time as he had had. The many hours he had spent in memory training had proved their value, and he could have drawn a satisfyingly accurate picture of the room. The Christmas tree, the chair in which Charlotte Grame had sat, the steps against the far wall, the trail of moisture across the floor, the body itself—they were all tabulated in his mind.

In the moments of confusion that had followed the discovery that the last present had vanished from the tree, he had created the opportunity of making a quick and what he believed to be an unobserved examination of the setting of the crime. He had noted that the dead man had been wearing rubber boots. They had not been visible as he lay, but when Tremaine had lifted the long red cloak that had been concealing them, he had seen the dark patch of wet they had left on the floor. He had followed the trail of moisture that led back to the french doors.

The marks of Roger Wynton's entrance had been plain, because he had rushed in too hurriedly to trouble about the snow caking his shoes, and it had melted into a series of pools wherever he had stood. Beyond the windows, one of the moon's fitful appearances was revealing the cold whiteness of the lawn, broken by three trails of footprints.

It was difficult to be certain without a closer examination, but Tremaine had thought that two of them led toward the house and one of them led away from it. All three trails came to an end at the terrace just outside.

He put up a hand to straighten the eternally askew pince-nez and contrived to glance around at his companions. Under the guidance of Fleming—immaculately grave even in pajamas and dressing gown, and with his impassive manner unshaken even by murder—relays of coffee had been brought in, and there had at first been an occasional remark from one or other of them. But now reaction was at work, and even the spasmodic conversation the coffee had stimulated had died away.

At intervals, a uniformed constable would appear, and another member of the weary party would depart to face the ordeal of an interview by the superintendent. They were long interviews, conducted without haste. Cannock was in no hurry, despite the lateness of the hour. His attitude, Tremaine thought, was that if people would go in for murdering one another at inconvenient times, they would have to take the consequences.

To such a keen student of human nature as was Mordecai Tremaine, it was both fascinating and instructive to observe the manner in which each of his companions came and went. In most of them, the struggle to appear unconcerned was evident. They made desperate attempts to show that they had nothing to hide and therefore nothing to fear.

Professor Lorring had just come back. As he had appeared in the doorway, every eye had been turned upon him, and he had walked to his seat, trying to convey that he did not know they were watching him guardedly and that they were looking for some trace of discomfiture in his expression.

It was not that there was any special suspicion directed against Lorring. The same reception had greeted the others. It occurred to Tremaine that it was odd that all the members of the house party who had so far been interviewed had chosen to return to an uncomfortable vigil in an overcrowded room rather than seek their beds. It was unlikely that Superintendent Cannock would send for them a second time. Having heard their stories, he would undoubtedly have told them that he would not require them again until at least the morning.

There was a universal reluctance to part company. It was as though each of them hesitated to be the first to leave in case something happened in their absence, and as though that was a possibility they dared not contemplate.

But why? Mordecai Tremaine's eyes flickered once more about the room. They could not all have been involved in the murder. At least, it was highly unlikely that they had been. What, then, was the link that bound them?

Lorring was facing him. From his dour countenance, it was not possible to tell the results of his interview with Cannock. But Tremaine did not think the superintendent would have discovered anything Lorring did not want him to know.

He had come to the conclusion that Professor Ernest Lorring was a gentleman who would repay study. It was a belief that had germinated when he had found Lorring surveying the Christmas tree with that peculiarly malignant expression on the previous afternoon, and that belief had blossomed with tropical rapidity two hours ago. Because, unless Mordecai Tremaine's intuition was seriously at fault, the hand that had removed the last present from the tree had been Lorring's.

He had recalled to his mind the sequence of events when he had followed Nicholas Blaise up to Benedict Grame's room. He had subjected to a detailed analysis the mental photograph he possessed of the group that had been about Grame's door. And he was certain that Lorring had been the last person to join it. That he had, therefore, been the last to leave the room in which the body lay.

Lorring, of course, had denied it. Had denied it so vehemently that it had been obvious that he had been well aware of what accusation would follow any admission that he had been the last person in the room.

"Nonsense!" he had snapped angrily. "I went up the stairs with the rest of you!"

No one had been able to give him the lie. The movement toward the stairs had been too confused for any of the others to be sure of their neighbors. And Lorring had seized his opportunity. "Miss Grame was behind me," he had gone on. "So was Delamere."

He had glared at them, as if defying them to challenge his statement. Delamere had looked as though he was going to make a protest, and then, realizing that he was on unsure ground, had thought better of it. Charlotte Grame had not seemed to care. She had given no sign either of understanding or of resentment at the inference of what Lorring had said.

Tremaine had not pressed the matter. He had hesitated to undertake anything in the nature of a cross-examination in the face of Lorring's ugly mood, and in any case, the arrival of the police had cut short all other activities.

Benedict Grame had been surprisingly silent. But if it might be considered strange that he had revealed so little emotion over the brutal murder of a man who had been his closest and oldest friend, he had at least done nothing to arouse suspicion. His lack of positive reaction could be explained by the fact that he had not recovered from the initial numbing shock and the fact that his duties as host required him to maintain an impersonal attitude.

The constable appeared in the doorway. Rosalind Marsh heard her name and rose to her feet. Her face was expressionless, but the tip of her cigarette had glowed with sudden brightness at the summons.

Tremaine watched her go out of the room. Here again was no pliant material for Superintendent Cannock. To all his questions, she would present an icy calm that would checkmate him—temporarily, at least.

As he waited for Rosalind Marsh to come back, Tremaine looked around again and realized that only Lucia Tristam and himself remained to be interrogated. It was then that the idea came to him that there was reason behind the manner in which the guests had been required and that he was deliberately being reserved until last. Nebulous at first, the thought gained strength in his mind, and when Rosalind Marsh returned and Lucia Tristam's name was called, he felt no surprise but only a pleasant sense of curiosity.

Analyzing his own emotions, he knew that his sense of well-being had its origin in the fact that he was no more than a spectator. He had nothing to hide from the police and was, therefore, quite ready to be questioned by them. Had there been any guilt upon his conscience, he would have sat like his companions—strained and anxious, going over and over again in his mind the story he proposed to tell, making himself perfect in all its details and testing it for flaws.

He drew back from the assumption that he could read more than a natural tension in the faces around him and fell to wondering what Superintendent Cannock would make of the magnificent Lucia. Although the past two hours had left their dark traces under her eyes and her expression carried an elusive something that seemed a brother to fear, she was still a woman to awaken admiration. Somehow, despite the other's air of official stolidity, he did not think Cannock was the type to remain unstirred by her generous beauty.

When she reappeared in the doorway, she gave him no clue. Perhaps her color had heightened a little, perhaps her eyes were a shade brighter, but Tremaine could not be sure that it was so or of the reason for it. She gave him a glance as she went back to her seat. Quite clearly, she was wondering what might be his thoughts of her. He felt oddly relieved that she could not know how empty of any real conclusions he was.

As he rose to his feet and followed the constable from the room, he knew that every eye was upon him. And not this time with the sharp curiosity and the eagerness to find some sign of betrayal that had marked the manner in which the others had gone, but with a kind of painful intensity.

It gave him the feeling that he was the unknown quantity, that there was something quite different about him, something that momentarily bound them together against him as if against a common enemy.

It was a disconcerting sensation. He was glad when he was in the corridor and no longer conscious of the staring eyes behind him.

Superintendent Cannock had established himself in the library. He was seated at a table facing the doorway, his head bowed over the notes he had evidently been taking. He looked up. "Sit down, Mr. Tremaine," he said quietly.

His voice was reassuring. He showed no sign of weariness or exhaustion. His big frame, overflowing the chair in which he sat, radiated a disarming friendliness. *Only confide in me,* he seemed to say, *and all will be well.*

It was, no doubt, part of his stock-in-trade. It was calculated to induce a feeling of reassurance. And when, passing from relief to overconfidence, the victim made the first careless mistake, the velvet would be abruptly removed from the claws.

Tremaine realized that he was being subjected to careful scrutiny, and he returned the superintendent's gaze to find himself confronting a pair of shrewdly brown eyes set in a face that was round, fresh-colored, and jovial. It did not look like the face of a policeman. It looked as though, wrinkled and weather-wise as it was, it should have belonged to a farmer.

The body, however, betrayed the policeman. It was big, solid, and somehow official. It was easy to imagine it clothed in a blue uniform and proceeding majestically along a beat. Superintendent Cannock had, in fact, climbed the hard way, taking each rung of the ladder in his ascent.

It seemed that he found Mordecai Tremaine's attitude refreshing. A brief smile lifted the wrinkles around his eyes. He said: "I'm afraid you've been kept waiting rather a long time. But I'm sure you appreciate that in such a serious matter, even the most apparently insignificant details have to be carefully examined. That's why I like to talk to people while events are still fresh in their minds. Memory is apt to play queer tricks, especially the morning after."

"I quite understand," said Tremaine. "You have to do your duty, superintendent. In any case it wouldn't have been any use my trying to sleep." He added, "None of the others have gone to their rooms."

Cannock did not appear to have noticed the remark. He was once more consulting the papers in front of him. "I believe this is your first visit here?"

"Yes."

"Do you know Mr. Grame well?"

"Not really well. We've met before, of course."

"But you're sufficiently acquainted for him to have invited you to spend Christmas with him," murmured the superintendent, as though to himself. "What about the other guests? Have you met any of them before?"

Tremaine shook his head. "Only Mr. Blaise…Mr. Grame's secretary. The others are strangers. At least they were when I arrived."

"I see." The superintendent consulted his notes again, and Tremaine became aware that it was a routine action designed both to convey the impression that he already knew so much that it would be unwise to attempt to fool him, and to give him time to frame his next question. "Will you give me your account of what took place when the murder was discovered, Mr. Tremaine? I mean, of course, as far as your own part in it was concerned."

"I heard screams. At first I thought I was dreaming, but when I realized that they were real, I got out of bed and went into the corridor to see what was the matter."

"Did you see any of the other guests?"

"Mr. Beechley came out of his room as I was passing. I'd decided by then that the screams had come from the ground floor, and we went down the stairs together. The light was on in the room where Mr. Grame had placed the Christmas tree, and as I went in, I saw the body lying on the floor."

"Was there anyone else in the room?"

"Yes. Mr. Delamere and Miss Charlotte Grame. It was obvious that it was Miss Grame who had screamed. She was very upset, and Mr. Delamere was trying to comfort her."

With an occasional interjected question from the

superintendent, Tremaine told his story. He omitted nothing save his own brief investigations, and when he had finished, Cannock nodded approvingly.

"Thank you," he said. "You've been very helpful." He waited a moment or two, his eyes seemingly far away. Mordecai Tremaine experienced a prickle of anticipation along his spine. Cannock said idly, "Jonathan Boyce and I are very good friends. We walked the same beat together in our younger days."

"Indeed?" Mordecai Tremaine said, careful not to betray his excitement. "That's interesting. Do you see anything of him now?"

"We haven't met for some time," said Cannock. "Duties won't permit. But we keep in touch. He sends me all the news."

Significance underlined the last sentence. But the superintendent's official expression mirrored no reflection of it. He leaned back in his chair. As though he had dismissed all personal thoughts from his mind, he went on. "You know, Mr. Tremaine, in a case like this, our investigations can't be altogether satisfactory. The very fact that the police are carrying on an inquiry seems to make people reluctant to talk. They behave unnaturally. They don't let themselves go in a normal manner. Consequently, it's difficult to find out what they're really like. Of course, we seldom get the opportunity, but the ideal thing would be to have a sort of unofficial observer. Someone to whom people would talk freely, and who would be able to give us a much more accurate picture of things than we're able to get for ourselves."

Mordecai Tremaine fenced delicately. "I realize your difficulties, superintendent." His mild glance was all innocence. "Of course, it wouldn't do for you to ask anyone outside the police force to help you. It would lead to all sorts of awkward questions."

"Precisely," said Cannock. And added, "If it became known." By now, Mordecai Tremaine knew where he stood, and the knowledge encouraged him to play his hand boldly. He said inquiringly, "I take it there are no more questions you want to ask me at the moment, Superintendent?"

"No," said Cannock unwillingly. "That's all."

Was there a trace of disappointment in his manner? Mordecai Tremaine found it pleasantly flattering to think that there was. He rose as if to go. And then, with the air of a man to whom the idea had only just occurred, he said, "There is one matter I should perhaps mention."

Cannock looked at him. "Yes?"

It is said with truth that what a man wishes to find is what he *will* find. Mordecai Tremaine was looking for eagerness on the part of the superintendent. It must be admitted, therefore, that it was easy enough for him to convince himself that it was there, and that the monosyllable was invested with the sharpness of hope about to reach fulfillment.

"It's about Miss Grame," he said.

"Yes?" said Cannock again.

"She said that she had a headache and couldn't sleep. She thought she heard noises and came downstairs with a flashlight to find out what was happening. That was why she was the first person to discover Mr. Rainer's body. Is that the same story she told *you*?"

"Why are you asking?" said Cannock evasively.

"I very much doubt," said Tremaine, "whether it is the truth. From what I've seen of Miss Grame, I do not think she is the kind of person to go downstairs alone in the middle of the night to look for burglars. In any case, if she *did* hear noises and decide to investigate without calling Mr. Grame or any of the servants, it seems reasonable to suppose that she would merely have slipped on a dressing gown."

He stopped. He looked at Cannock. The superintendent said encouragingly, "Well?"

"Well," said Tremaine, "she was fully dressed. She was wearing a tweed costume and even had a thick scarf about her neck. She only needed a top coat and a pair of rubber boots, and she would have been ready to go out. Of course, she *might* have done all that just to go downstairs. But it seemed rather odd to me."

Cannock was glancing through his notes. "I understand that her manner was agitated. Would you say that it was an entirely natural agitation in view of the circumstances? Or would you say that she seemed excessively disturbed?"

"I can only," said Mordecai Tremaine, "give you my own opinion."

"Of course."

"I thought she seemed more than shocked and alarmed. You'd expect her to be distressed after such an experience. But I thought she was—*frightened*."

"What, precisely," said the superintendent, "do you mean?"

Mordecai Tremaine looked over his pince-nez in a manner Inspector Boyce would have recognized. "If," he said gently, "I knew precisely what I meant, I could probably be of much greater assistance to you, superintendent. Miss Grame is the person who discovered the body. The house was in darkness. She was using a flashlight to find her way about. She actually stumbled over Jeremy Rainer's body. It must have been a terrible moment for her when the flashlight showed him lying there.

"You can imagine what a dreadful scene it was. Everything still and hushed and with the whiteness of the snow outside contrasting with the blackness within. Father Christmas sprawled across the floor, with his red cloak and long, white beard. And that decorated tree throwing monstrous and mocking shadows as the light wavered in her hand.

"It would have unnerved a person of strong control, and

Miss Grame certainly isn't that. She went to pieces. She screamed. She aroused the household. When I reached the room, she was sitting in a chair in a state of collapse and Mr. Delamere was trying to help her.

"So far, so good. It was understandable. It was how anyone might have thought she would react. But it seemed to me that there was something more. She looked like a woman who was possessed by a fear she could not hold in check. And that was not so understandable. Because although she might reasonably be horrified and almost hysterical on account of what she had found, there was no reason why she should continue to be so obviously afraid now that the lights were on and help had arrived. Which led me to the conclusion that she was afraid not because of what had happened *but because of what she feared was going to happen*."

Superintendent Cannock was impressed. His forefinger smoothed gently along his chin. "You haven't any…theories?" he asked.

"I haven't any facts," said Tremaine.

He waited a moment or two and then he said, "You know, superintendent, I feel envious. You have organization behind you. It's possible for you to call upon practically every source of information there is in the world. If you set yourself to discover the innermost secrets of a man or a woman's life, it's within your power to do it. Whereas the ordinary citizen, no matter how much he may wish to do so, can't make complete inquiries because he's unable to draw upon official sources for the knowledge he needs."

"Sometimes," observed Cannock, "it's a boring business. We have to get at the needle by taking every individual piece of hay out of the stack."

"But you *do* get it," said Tremaine. He added, as if he was merely expressing his thoughts aloud, "It would be fascinating to find out all there is to learn about the people who are staying here. Two days ago, apart from Mr. Grame and Mr. Blaise, I hadn't met any of them. And now we've all been thrown into an intimate relationship. Murder has made us bedfellows, so to speak. We've become completely entangled with one another because we're the people who were here when Jeremy Rainer died. It makes me wish that I knew more about them so that I wouldn't be at such a disadvantage. I'd like to know all about their backgrounds, how they spend their time and how they make their living, the places they've seen and the people they've met…"

The superintendent's brown eyes were smiling. There were lines of humor crinkling the weather-beaten face. "I think," he said, "we understand each other."

A pagan song of elation was striving to find expression in Mordecai Tremaine's soul as he left the room and went back along the corridor. In sending Superintendent Cannock to investigate the murder of Jeremy Rainer, fate had been more generous than he could have expected. That the superintendent should have recognized his name was not surprising in view of the embarrassing blaze of publicity in which he had basked not so very long ago. A police officer might have been expected to recall an amateur who had achieved such prominence. But that he should also be one of Jonathan Boyce's old friends who still corresponded with the Yard man was luck indeed, for undoubtedly it was the reason for the superintendent's attitude.

Cannock hesitated to make any open moves. Perhaps he feared to make himself a figure of ridicule in the eyes of his subordinates by enlisting the aid of a man who had no official status, or perhaps he had a chief constable who would not take kindly to such a departure from orthodoxy. But it was evident that Jonathan Boyce had told him a great deal, and that as far as he was able, he was prepared to turn a blind eye to any investigations Mordecai Tremaine might choose to make.

Now that his position appeared to be secured, Tremaine realized just how much he had secretly desired to be allowed to play an active part in the pursuit of the murderer. It was not merely that he had been a guest in the house when the murder had been committed and that he was therefore already concerned, even if in a minor role, in the inevitable police inquiries. His interest went deeper than that. It went back to the reason for his visit to Sherbroome. It went back to what he had heard and seen and felt from the moment of his arrival.

The sight of that fantastically clothed body sprawled under the Christmas tree had merely been the climax. The drama had been in progress the whole time. Its influence had been there beneath the surface, underlying the appearance of lightheartedness and goodwill that Benedict Grame had been trying so pathetically hard to sustain.

And Mordecai Tremaine wanted to be more than a mere spectator in the stalls. He wanted to know what was taking place in the wings. He wanted to know how many acts the drama was scheduled to possess—and how many of the cast were aware of the significance of the parts they played. He wanted to know who had killed Jeremy Rainer and why he had died in that incongruous garb.

As he entered the room where he had left his fellow guests, a stillness fell upon them. He sensed it, and he stopped upon the threshold. It must be admitted that his action was deliberate and a little theatrical.

He looked around at them, meeting the intensity of their eyes, held by a strange and rather terrifying exhilaration that had its origins in the time when his remote, forgotten ancestors had known both the thrill and the tight-throated danger of the hunt in the primeval forests. Among those eyes might be the eyes of a murderer.

11

During the night, frost had come and used the windowpanes to sketch its fantasies. Idly, Mordecai Tremaine mused upon the delicacy of the icy tracings revealed against the clear, white light beyond them. He was in that pleasant, all-too-fleeting state that lies between sleeping and waking, when the mind is floating in blissful space and conscious thought has not fettered it with anxiety. All there was of the world lay in that frosted square.

And then the brief spell was broken and the thinking processes had begun.

The first realization was that this was no ordinary day. He groped after the special significance that set it apart from other days, and was vaguely surprised that he should have needed to do so. Of course, this was Christmas Day! The clear light that was filling the room was the light of Christmas morning.

The second realization came tumbling upon the heels of the first. It was that the light was very much stronger than it should have been. It was much brighter than even the magic of the fact that it was Christmas morning could explain away. Six thirty on a December day should be decently shrouded in winter darkness.

He raised himself on his elbow and peered at his watch. The hands pointed to eighteen minutes past ten. But even as his eyes were carrying the astounding message to his brain that he had overslept by almost four hours, memory was rushing upon him with a vehement desire to remind him of what had happened.

Jeremy Rainer was dead. He had died in the darkness, and his body had lain fantastically under the Christmas tree in the red robes of Father Christmas. Charlotte Grame's screams had roused a startled household.

And then the police had come, and Superintendent Cannock—politely reassuring but quite evidently grimly determined to allow no possible scent to grow cold—had settled down to a patient taking of statements. Dawn had been near before anyone had gone back to bed. That was the reason for this ten o'clock awakening. Placid routine had been shattered by murder.

Mordecai Tremaine looked around his room, and it seemed to him that it was no longer as bright as it had appeared. This was Christmas morning. Peace and goodwill to all men. That was the message this day should bring, and down below there was a dead man whose blood cried out to the law for retribution upon the guilty, and through all the rooms in the house were stealing the three frightful shades whose names were fear, suspicion, and terror.

Although he had had so little sleep, he knew that if he closed his eyes again, it would only be to watch memory's images flickering across his mind, and that his thoughts would only go around in an interminable series of questions.

Why had Charlotte Grame been fully dressed? Why had it taken so long to arouse Benedict Grame? Why had Professor Lorring stolen the last present from the Christmas tree? And why had Jeremy Rainer been wearing the robes of Father Christmas?

Tremaine shaved, dressed, and went downstairs in search of breakfast. Murder might strike terribly across the scene, but for those who lived, the essential functions must still continue.

Austin Delamere and Ernest Lorring were seated at either end of the long table in the dining room. Each had apparently decided to ignore the other.

Lorring was eating purposefully, as if he had no interest in what was taking place around him. Delamere, on the other hand, was picking moodily at his meal, plainly with no enjoyment. He looked up as Tremaine came in and then glanced quickly away again with a muttered "Morning" in response to his greeting.

The scientist merely grunted without raising his eyes

from his plate, but despite his air of self-sufficient indifference, Tremaine suspected that Lorring was not as unmoved as he wanted to appear. As he walked across to the buffet and began to remove the various coverings, he would have offered long odds that the other's glance was upon him from under the shadow of the fierce eyebrows. Ernest Lorring was a man who had something to hide, and he was therefore suspicious. And especially suspicious of someone who had already shown a decided tendency to probe and curious to know just what that someone intended to do.

But Mordecai Tremaine betrayed no sign that he suspected he was under observation. He sat down at the table and began his breakfast. It gave him mild satisfaction to know that he had Lorring guessing.

He had almost finished his meal when Charlotte Grame came in. She slipped apologetically through the doorway, and only her half-whispered "Good morning" told him that she had appeared.

She had not, he thought, slept a great deal. Her face was very white, and the dark patches of strain under her eyes had become intensified.

At first she did not look at him, and then, as if she was being driven by a force she could not control, her glance lifted waveringly to his face. He smiled at her, and she returned the smile tremulously.

"I hope," he said, "you're feeling better this morning?"

"Yes," she said. "Yes. I am. Much, much better. Thank you."

He knew that she was lying. Knew also that she was aware that he knew and that the knowledge was no light addition to her burden of discomfort.

He was glad when he had finished breakfast and was able to make his escape from the dining room. Utterly dissimilar though they might be in all other respects, his three companions shared one thing in common—suspicion of him. It expressed itself in different ways, but it was there in each of them—in Charlotte Grame's obvious terror, in Ernest Lorring's aggressive silences, and in Austin Delamere's constant and nervous sideways glances, mixed, in his case, with a kind of petulant resentment.

It was Rosalind Marsh who put the situation into words. He found her in the library, a book open in her hands, but her eyes staring unseeingly through the windows.

"Oh…hullo," she said, turning as he came in. She added, with deliberate cynicism, "Merry Christmas."

"It isn't," he said, "the kind of Christmas morning I was expecting. I'm afraid poor Rainer's death has put a stop to any festivities."

"*Poor* Rainer?" she queried. "What makes you think so?"

He looked at her. She betrayed no signs due to lack of sleep; certainly she showed nothing of the haggard anxiety that marked Charlotte Grame. Her cold beauty was as perfect as ever, and she was in complete possession of her nerves.

"Perhaps I should have chosen my words more carefully," he said. "But it's the sort of expression one does use. After all, he *was* murdered."

"Oh yes," she agreed. "He was murdered."

Mordecai Tremaine felt a little shocked. He could not help the feeling that her calmness verged on the indecent. "You sound," he said slowly, "as though you think he was the kind of man who *deserves* to be murdered."

"Do I?" she said. She seemed amused. "Jeremy Rainer wasn't exactly a saint. During his lifetime, he was mixed up in quite a lot of shady things. He had secrets he wasn't at all anxious for the police to hear about."

"You mean that there were things that were outside the law?"

"Of course," she said. "After all, there must have been."

It was not conjecture. It was a casual statement of fact from a person who was in no doubt. Mordecai Tremaine felt that he was slipping out of his depth. She saw something of it in his face. She said, "Perhaps you don't know as much as I thought you might. Or as much as certain other people think you do."

"I'm not very good at riddles," he told her, and she surprised him by the spontaneity of her laugh. "You're either a very modest detective or a dangerously subtle one. You've succeeded in setting everybody by the ears, anyway. They're all afraid to move in case you start suspecting them."

A sick disappointment clawed unpleasantly at Mordecai Tremaine's stomach. Superintendent Cannock's hopes of gaining an uninhibited insight into what went on inside Sherbroome House seemed to be sliding away. If his fellow guests already suspected him of being linked with the police, they would be no more anxious to talk to him than they would be to talk to the superintendent or his men. And if he could give nothing to Cannock that Cannock did not already know, then he could expect nothing in return.

"What makes everybody think I *am* a detective?" he asked, trying to keep the chagrin from his voice.

"The whisper has gone through the prairie grass," she told him lightly. "And your lengthy interview with the superintendent has been giving it close support."

"Perhaps the superintendent spent rather a long time with me because he wasn't altogether satisfied with my story," he said carefully.

"Perhaps," she said in disbelief. Her handbag was on the chair beside her. She took a cigarette from a monogrammed gold case, lit it, and drew upon it thoughtfully.

Mordecai Tremaine said, "All right. Suppose I admit that I'm interested in crime investigation. As an amateur, of course. Naturally, when a murder takes place in a house in which I'm a guest, I feel I want to know all about it. But that doesn't mean that I have any official standing or any link with the police."

A faint echo of something Jonathan Boyce had once said to him was stirring in his mind as he spoke. The Yard man had told him that he was a murder magnet, that whenever anyone was killed, he either found the body or was somewhere near at hand. And one half of his mind was reflecting now that it was undoubtedly strange that he should have been on the scene yet again when murder had been let loose.

"Is there anything," he said to the woman facing him, "you'd like to tell me?"

"I presume you mean is there any confession I'd like to make?" she said. "I suppose I'd better make the obvious remark. I didn't kill Jeremy Rainer." She eyed him through a smoke cloud. "Now you can try to decide whether I'm innocent but scared and anxious to clear myself, or whether I'm guilty but clever and trying to put you off the scent by pretending to admit that I know I might be suspected."

"*Did* you kill him?" Mordecai Tremaine asked mildly.

"I know who *might* have killed him," she countered.

Over the top of precarious pince-nez, a pair of highly interested eyes regarded her. "Yes?"

"Yes," she returned. "But the name is not for publication.

Because I haven't a scrap of proof, and it's unwise to go around accusing other people of being murderers."

She flicked her cigarette dexterously over an ashtray, and as his eyes followed her movement, Tremaine saw that the tray already contained several stubs bearing traces of lipstick. He looked at her thoughtfully. So her self-assurance was only skin-deep after all. She sensed what he was thinking, and a trace of color came into her cheeks. But she was saved any further embarrassment, because at that moment the door opened and Nicholas Blaise came in.

His dark eyes went questioningly from one to the other of them. "I don't want to interrupt you," he said slowly, "but the superintendent has just been talking to Benedict. He doesn't want anyone to leave the neighborhood of the house for the present. It's just a formality, of course, while the police complete their investigations."

"We understand, Nick," said Rosalind Marsh. "We can't have a murder without undergoing a few inconveniences. Don't worry. We'll be good."

"I suppose," said Mordecai Tremaine, "that they've put some of the rooms temporarily out of bounds to us?"

"*The* room," said Blaise. "They're still measuring and taking photographs. They've roped off part of the lawn as well."

"I haven't seen Benedict this morning," Rosalind Marsh said casually. "How's he taking all this, Nick?"

Blaise hesitated. A wary expression came onto his face. "In what way do you mean?" he asked, playing for time.

"After all, Jeremy Rainer was his greatest friend," she observed. "It must have been a tremendous shock to him."

"Yes, of course. At first he just didn't seem able to grasp it. He isn't a young man, you know, and he and Jeremy were together for years. But he's really bearing up remarkably well."

They reminded Mordecai Tremaine of two fencing opponents, each circling watchfully about the other and searching for an opportunity to deliver a scoring stroke.

Rosalind Marsh smiled. It was a peculiar, significant smile. It was as though she was telling Nicholas Blaise that she appreciated his defense of his employer but was not convinced by it. "I've a feeling that you two would like to talk to each other," she said. "I think I'll go and commiserate with Delamere. He's probably seeing his career in ruins around him after this affair!"

"Don't let me drive you away, Rosalind," Blaise said a little too quickly.

"I'm sensitive to atmosphere, Nick," she told him gently. "Let me be suitably discreet."

After she had gone, Nicholas Blaise turned to his companion. "She was right, Mordecai. I *do* want to talk to you."

"I thought you might," said Tremaine.

Blaise seated himself on the edge of the table. One long

leg swung nervously. Against the light from the window, his lean face was anxious.

"This is a damnable business," he said. "That's trite enough, of course, but it's the plain truth. I asked you down here because I thought that there was something mighty queer going on, but I never dreamed that it would end like this. I never thought that it would come to murder."

"You're worried about Benedict Grame, Nick. Isn't that it?" said Tremaine soberly.

Blaise did not reply at once. The leg stopped swinging. Then he said, "That was why I asked you to come."

"I'm talking about a different worry," said Mordecai Tremaine. "The *new* worry. The worry about whether Benedict Grame killed Jeremy Rainer."

A gasp he could only partly stifle escaped Nicholas Blaise's lips. He had become very still. When at last he spoke, his voice was husky. "Why do you say that?" he asked.

"There may be other answers," said Mordecai Tremaine, "but suppose we take the obvious one first. Lucia Tristam."

Blaise was looking toward the window. His hands were held tightly against the table's edge. "What of Mrs. Tristam?"

"The magnificent Lucia," said Tremaine softly. "I rather like that, Nick. It has the full-blooded ring of the kind of period to which she belongs. The period of the Borgias, for instance, when the world was full of flamboyant color, and loving and hating were on the grand scale. And when murder was the obvious solution to most problems."

"I don't understand you."

"I think you understand me very well, Nick. Two men in love with one woman. Both of them men who in the past have been in the habit of taking what they wanted without paying too much attention to ethics. It's a situation that can quite easily get out of hand. Suppose the woman isn't quite sure herself which of them she favors. Suppose one of the suitors decides to settle the issue by getting rid of his rival. Men will do strange things for the love of a woman. And a man who is well past the age of discretion will often act more rashly than the most callow boy."

Nicholas Blaise made a helpless gesture with one hand. "I can't believe it. It's altogether too improbable. Things like that just don't happen."

"They happen every day," said Tremaine. "Only we're so used to reading about them in the newspapers that we don't pay much attention to them. Until they happen to us, and then we're so blind that we delude ourselves that we've been especially picked out by fate to act as a target for the unusual."

His voice suddenly lost its note of mildness. He said: "Benedict Grame's bedroom is immediately over the room where Jeremy Rainer was killed. When Charlotte Grame discovered the dead man she screamed so hard that she awakened all of us. People were moving about the house. There were loud voices. And yet our host made no attempt to discover the reason for such a disturbance in the middle of the night."

"Benedict's a heavy sleeper," said Blaise. "He may not have heard."

"I agree," said Tremaine, "that there may be an explanation."

It was clear from Nicholas Blaise's face that his thoughts were bewildered and uncertain, and that he hesitated to commit himself until he had had an opportunity to think things out more clearly. He said slowly, "You haven't…you haven't mentioned anything of this to the superintendent?"

"No. I thought it was the kind of thing that was best discussed between the two of us—at least for the time being."

Blaise nodded. "Thanks, Mordecai. Although I don't suppose it will be long before it occurs to Cannock…if it hasn't already done so. He seems capable enough."

"Policemen are," said Mordecai Tremaine. "They may appear to move slowly sometimes, but they don't miss a great deal."

Blaise had moved from his position on the table. He was pacing the room with nervous, uneven strides. He said, "I can't believe it of Benedict. I just can't. Unless—"

"Unless?"

But evidently Blaise thought that he was carrying his

conjectures too far. He did not finish what he had been saying. "I can't go any further into it now, Mordecai," he said haltingly. "This…this business means that all kinds of arrangements have to be made, and Benedict's relying on me to deal with them. After all, I'm working for my living, you know. I have to find the others and let them know what's happening."

"I quite understand, Nick. Naturally you have to carry out your duties."

Blaise did not make any immediate move to go. Apparently, there was still some problem exercising his mind. "Benedict's been very good to me," he said at last. "I owe him a great deal. We've had our differences, of course, but I'm fond of him. I think I understand him. You'll let me know if the superintendent…if he begins to have any…any suspicions?"

"I'll let you know what I can, Nick. But I can't tell you, of course, what may be in his mind. He's hardly likely to take me so far into his confidence."

"I think," said Blaise, "he'll tell you quite a lot. He knows who you are, and he knows that you may be able to help him."

He left Mordecai Tremaine in a very thoughtful frame of mind. He was obviously expected to be on intimate terms with Superintendent Cannock. If the superintendent did not prove so approachable, despite that first impression, his personal stock would suffer an embarrassing decline. And on the other hand, if Cannock *was* prepared to admit him to an unofficial equality and the knowledge of it had the effect of freezing his relationships with his fellow guests, it would be impossible for him to give the superintendent any real aid. Either way, he reflected, he was on the losing side.

He was still staring moodily out the library window, gazing unhappily at the two detectives busily engaged in examining and measuring the footprints on the lawn, preserved, fortunately, by the night's frost, when a sound from the doorway made him turn. Denys Arden had come into the room. "I'm so glad I've found you," she said a little breathlessly. "I've been looking everywhere for you."

The flush on her cheeks and the brightness in her eyes, somewhat feverish in origin though he guessed it to be, gave her a vital quality that accentuated the appeal of her youth. Mordecai Tremaine's sentimental soul described a somersault. But he said placidly, "Old men like me don't often have the pleasure of being pursued by attractive young ladies!"

She acknowledged his pleasantry with a hurried smile. It was a mechanical change of expression in which she obviously had no real interest. "I've got to talk to you," she said. "It's about Roger."

Mordecai Tremaine performed the ritual of gazing at her over his pince-nez. "Ah, yes," he said. "Roger."

She hurried on, as if she expected him to interrupt her and was desperately anxious to tell her story first. "He's under suspicion," she said. "The superintendent thinks that he…that he killed my guardian. It's because he came here last night. It isn't true! Roger didn't…*couldn't* do such a terrible thing!"

"What," said Mordecai Tremaine, "makes you think the superintendent believes he did?"

"Roger rang me up just now. The police have already been over to the manor asking questions. They've told him he isn't to leave the neighborhood."

"That doesn't prove that they suspect him any more than they suspect the rest of us," he told her reassuringly. "We've all had to answer questions. And we've all been asked to stay within the grounds of the house. But just as a point of interest," he added, "*why* did that young man of yours come here at such a critical moment last night?"

She hesitated. She said slowly: "I can…I can speak to you in confidence?"

"I cannot promise," said Mordecai Tremaine gravely, "to keep back from the police any information I feel they should have. So if there is anything you do not want them to hear, it would be better if you did not tell me."

"I understand," she said in a low voice. "You're quite right, of course." She raised her head, and he was glad that her eyes held no veiled secrets. "Roger came because he was worried about me. He had a feeling that there was something strange going on in this house. He had no proof of anything, and I tried to laugh him out of it, told him that he was imagining things.

"Last night he seemed more convinced than ever that something was wrong. He wanted to stay in the house, and although Benedict wouldn't have objected, Roger knew that Jeremy would have made a scene about it. That's why he left when we all went to bed. At least, that was why he *appeared* to leave. I didn't know at the time, of course, but he drove his car a little way down the road and then came back to the house on foot. He stayed outside watching. He said he wanted to be near me in case anything happened. I suppose it sounds rather impossible and foolish now, but you see"—her voice wavered—"you see…Roger's in love with me."

"I believe," said Mordecai Tremaine, "that he is."

His eyes were warmly understanding. There was an image in his mind of a lover who kept watch for his beloved, waiting loyally in the bitter darkness of a winter's night so that he could be near if danger threatened. It was the crazy folly of youth, but it was a brave, dear folly. It was something rare and precious that glowed in a cynical world of gloom.

But it was undoubtedly something that would need a great deal of explaining to a jury of hardheaded citizens who had long since ceased to cherish romantic notions. It was something that would lose its magic when it was dragged out into the critical light of a police inquiry. For the police, being severely practical men, would require a more materialistic explanation of Roger Wynton's presence.

Mordecai Tremaine was troubled. Any suggestion of true love imperiled was enough to arouse his sympathies. The incurable romanticist in him made it inevitable that he should be ranged on the side of the lovers. "I take it," he said, "that this quixotic young man of yours has given the police the explanation you've just given me, and they weren't altogether impressed."

"They weren't," she told him. "The superintendent was quite polite, but Roger said that he made it clear that he didn't believe that it was the whole story. He wanted to know what made Roger feel that something was going to happen." A sense of helplessness had crept into her voice. "The trouble is that there isn't anything either of us can say. There's nothing definite we can give them."

"And what," said Mordecai Tremaine, "do you want *me* to do?"

She turned to him with a look of appeal. "There *was* something wrong," she said. "You know how you can feel things even when there's nothing you can actually describe? You could tell from Jeremy's attitude that there was something on his mind. If you could find out what it was…if you could discover the reason for his strangeness, you might be on the way to finding out who killed him. You might be able to find out exactly what happened here last night."

"In other words," he said, "you want me to find the murderer in order to convince Superintendent Cannock that Roger Wynton isn't guilty, and you've come to me because you think the superintendent has already made up his mind that he is."

His directness disconcerted her for a moment or two. "Yes," she admitted slowly, "that is the reason." And added, "Say you will try to help us...*please*."

Mordecai Tremaine regarded her seriously. "Naturally it's the business of the police to find out who killed your guardian," he told her, "but I confess that I'm interested, and if I can do anything to help you, I'll certainly be pleased to do so. You realize, of course," he went on quickly, anticipating her gratitude, "that if you give me your confidences, I may discover things you might prefer left unknown. It will be too late then to conceal them."

A hint of fear seeped into her eyes. "What do you mean?"

"I mean that as far as the police are concerned, Roger Wynton had both the opportunity and the motive for the murder. He was here last night at a time when he should have been at home and in bed. He's in love with you, and your guardian had quarreled violently with him and made it clear that he would never consent to his marrying you. If Superintendent Cannock *does* think as you say he does, it's just possible that he may be right."

"Oh no," she said, and her hand went to her lips. "No—not *you*. You can't mean that *you* think Roger is guilty."

"I haven't said so," he told her. "But *someone* must be."

Her face had lost some of its color, but her voice was under control. "You're quite wrong," she said steadily. "You're only speaking like that because you don't know Roger."

Compassion and perhaps just a twinge of conscience were at work upon Mordecai Tremaine now. "I don't want you to think," he said, "that I'm prejudiced against Mr. Wynton. After all, you know, each of us is under suspicion to some degree. Now," he went on cheerfully, trying to put her at her ease, "what is there you can tell me that might help? What about the fellow who was in a hurry to get away from the house? Is there anything you know about him that might offer a clue?"

She shook her head. "No—Roger said he can't give a description that wouldn't be guesswork because it all happened so quickly. But he did tell me something over the telephone this morning that he hasn't told the police."

"About last night?"

"Yes. He saw Jeremy. He said it was about half an hour after we were all supposed to have gone to bed. He saw him come out of the house and go down the drive to the lodge. It isn't occupied now. He went inside and was there for about twenty minutes."

"Did Mr. Wynton speak to him?"

"I don't think so. He didn't want anyone to know that he was there."

"What happened?"

"When Jeremy went into the lodge, he was wearing his ordinary clothes, but when he came out, he was wearing the Father Christmas cloak. Roger said that he went straight across the lawn and up to the french doors. That was the last he saw of him until—until he rushed into the house after Charlotte screamed."

"Anything else?"

"Not until the screams. That was when Roger saw some-one hurrying toward him. He tried to stop him, but he was knocked down and stunned for a few moments. There didn't seem any hope then of catching whoever had attacked him, and he thought the best plan was to come up to the house and find out what had happened."

Mordecai Tremaine silently considered the information he had been given. And then: "Why," he said, "didn't Mr. Wynton tell the police that he'd seen your guardian?"

"I've been waiting for you to ask that," she said. "I'd rather explain it to you than to the superintendent because I think you'll understand. It was on my account. Roger didn't want to say anything about—Jeremy until he'd had an opportunity of telling me first."

"Very human," said Mordecai Tremaine, "but very unwise.

I'd like to talk to your young man, my dear. He'll have to tell the superintendent everything, of course, but I think I can guarantee," he added, with a confidence he did not feel, "that in view of the circumstances, the police will overlook his not having told them earlier."

Her look of gratitude warmed his heart and steeled him for the encounter with Superintendent Cannock. "Thank you," she told him. "I knew you would help us."

Her trust in him was so obvious that he felt he must repeat his earlier warning as insurance against what might happen later. "You won't forget," he said, "that nothing must be concealed? No matter what it may mean?"

"I won't forget," she returned, and she left him with the feeling that Roger Wynton was an exceedingly lucky young man.

Mordecai Tremaine hoped that fate would be kind to her. His vision, although sympathetic, was not limited by the illusions of love, and he knew that Roger Wynton was in a highly suspect position. If only in view of his known antagonism toward the dead man, the police could not take the risk of accepting his story at face value. Wynton was likely to be confronted with a series of awkward questions, and it remained to be seen whether he could provide the right answers.

If not... Mordecai Tremaine considered the alternative unhappily. If not, there would be a grim and sudden ending to romance.

12

All the morning, the police were busy in the house and grounds. There was no doubt that Superintendent Cannock was conducting his campaign with efficiency. His men were courteous and as unobtrusive as the situation would allow, but they gave the impression of being part of a remorseless machine that would leave nothing to chance.

Wrapped in her fur coat, Lucia Tristam was standing on the terrace by the main steps. Ostensibly, she had gone outside in search of fresh air, but Mordecai Tremaine, who had been studying her for the past few minutes, knew that she was more concerned with the movements of the detectives who were working near the open french doors of the room in which Jeremy Rainer had died.

His voice insinuated itself softly into her thoughts. "They *are* a little frightening, aren't they?"

He could not see her face, but he knew from the sudden tenseness that came into her attitude that she was trying to hide her emotions from him. She turned slowly. "Why should they be?" she said coolly, and superficially, her manner was as casually self-possessed as it had been when she was lying so brazenly on Charlotte Grame's behalf. Only the glint of ironical humor was missing from her eyes to betray her real state of mind. Lucia Tristam was no longer amused.

"They look so…so inevitable," he said, watching her. "I'd hate to watch them at work if I had anything to hide. I'd feel too scared. I'd be imagining every moment that they were uncovering my secret."

"Imagination," she said, "can sometimes be a curse. Fortunately, you and I haven't anything to hide, have we?"

The green eyes met his own challengingly. They possessed a hard brilliance this morning, as though they were diamonds reacting to the frosty light.

"Haven't we?" he said, echoing her tone.

She did not allow herself to be drawn out, although it was obvious from her expression that she knew what he was trying to do. She looked away from him, out over the lawns. Despite the fur coat pulled around her, he could still admire the grace of her figure and feel that superb quality in her, both vital and voluptuous, that could drug men's senses. For a moment or two, he was almost glad that the blood was no longer running so strongly in his veins.

"Jeremy was a strange man," she said musingly. "I wonder if any of us really knew him."

"He was a jealous man," Mordecai Tremaine observed, and once again he knew that he had touched her, for she could not conceal the fact that she was on her guard.

Was it fear that lay behind her eyes? It was certainly something akin to fear, and yet he did not think that fear provided an entirely satisfactory explanation.

"I'm glad that at least two people don't find it too cold to venture outdoors!"

The voice was unexpected and near enough to startle. Tremaine turned hastily to find Benedict Grame at his side. The other's approach had been silenced by the snow.

He realized that it was the first time he had seen his host at close quarters for more than a moment or two since Grame's dressing-gowned figure had appeared in his bedroom doorway in the early hours of the morning. He had had no opportunity of studying him when he had looked into the dining room and had said good morning to Delamere and himself as they had been finishing breakfast.

His tone was surprisingly cheerful. A certain amount of it was, no doubt, due to the natural anxiety of a host to ease matters for his guests, but he was undoubtedly far removed from the badly startled man he had been when Nicholas Blaise had pounded on his door. He looked confident. More than that, thought Mordecai Tremaine curiously, he looked almost as though he was enjoying the situation.

That was absurd, of course. It must be some trick of the light playing across the lined face that was adding the glint to the blue eyes and the ironic twist to the bushy eyebrows. Benedict Grame could surely find no cause for humor in the present situation, with his best friend murdered and the responsibility for a houseful of uneasy guests sitting heavily upon his shoulders.

"I couldn't stand it inside, Benedict," said Lucia Tristam. "I simply had to come out for a breath of air, despite the cold."

Grame nodded understandingly. "I'm afraid it's a depressing Christmas for you. I've been trying to find everyone to offer my apologies for the way things have turned out."

She laid a hand on his arm. "It's all right, Benedict. No one is likely to lay this at *your* door. We all know how you feel."

Her voice held a caressing note. It was, Mordecai Tremaine thought, a note a man might be flattered to hear when such a woman was speaking to him.

"The trouble is," said Grame, "that I'm at such a disadvantage. Quite apart from the fact that the police have taken charge of the house, I can hardly go ahead with the arrangements I'd made for entertaining you. I hope you won't find things too difficult."

Once again, Mordecai Tremaine had the impression of a false note being sounded. Benedict Grame looked as he might have been expected to look. His words were ones he might have been expected to use. And yet the effect of truth was not there. Benedict Grame was behaving as he *ought* to behave, but it was not the way his heart was inclined.

Tremaine made use of his most benevolently harmless expression. "Have the police discovered any clues?" he asked.

There was genuine surprise in the blue eyes. "I thought," said Grame, "that *you* would have known that before any of us. In fact"—he spoke more slowly, as though anxious to employ the right words—"in fact, I was about to put that very question to you."

"There are opportunities open to you that are denied to the rest of us," said Lucia Tristam. Her voice sounded urgent. "Isn't there anything you can do to help find out who killed Jeremy Rainer? As long as the murderer goes free, innocent people are bound to be under suspicion."

Benedict Grame shook his head gravely from side to side. "It was a dreadful tragedy," he said. "Poor Jeremy! I feel I'll never rest again until his murderer has been found."

"You knew him perhaps more closely than anyone else," said Tremaine. "Can you offer any theories? Can you, for instance, think of anyone who might have had a motive for killing him? Anyone connected with his past?"

Grame did not reply at once. He seemed to be anxious to give the impression of a man who was speaking reluctantly. "Not his past," he said. "But—"

"Yes?"

"It's been so obvious," said Grame, "that I don't suppose I can do young Wynton any harm by speaking. You know how things are between Roger and Denys. For some reason, Jeremy was dead against it. I'm fond of Denys, and I did what I could, but it only seemed to make matters worse. Jeremy could be completely unreasonable at times. When he took a dislike to anyone, it was impossible to argue with him, and he certainly made it plain that he didn't like Wynton."

"So you think," said Mordecai Tremaine, "that Roger Wynton killed him?"

"Oh no," said Grame quickly. "The fact that he was here last night does seem rather odd, of course, but I'm sure he has a satisfactory explanation. My feeling is that it's better to state these things openly rather than have a situation where everybody is talking about them secretly and nobody has the courage to come out with them. I think it's in Wynton's interest that nothing should be held back."

"When a man is innocent," said Mordecai Tremaine, "it undoubtedly is the best policy."

Benedict Grame nodded. He seemed to be deep in thought. At last he said, "Has Gerald said anything to you?"

Mordecai Tremaine showed his surprise. He blinked over his pince-nez and said, "I haven't seen Mr. Beechley this morning. *Should* he have said anything to me?"

"Well, I thought he might have done," said Grame awkwardly. "I don't see what point there could be in concealing it—"

"What Benedict is trying to say," interposed Lucia Tristam, "is that Gerald bought a Father Christmas outfit in Calnford yesterday. An outfit like the one Jeremy was wearing when he was found."

"It doesn't necessarily mean anything, Lucia," said Grame. "After all, you know Gerald. There's no telling what he's likely to do. He's always been fond of his practical jokes. It's just that I thought he might have seen the wisdom of telling the police or...or someone...in view of what's happened."

Mordecai Tremaine was recalling how he had encountered Beechley just outside the house on the previous day and how the other had quite obviously done his utmost to prevent Denys Arden or himself from seeing what he had bought. And he was recalling the glimpse of red cloth he had caught before Beechley had hurriedly pulled the covering paper back into position.

So it had been a Father Christmas outfit he had bought. It had been one like that in which Jeremy Rainer's dead body had been clad. It was, he thought, decidedly interesting.

Benedict Grame shivered suddenly. "This is no place for me," he announced. "Coming inside, Lucia?"

"Yes, I think I'm rapidly turning into an icicle," she told him.

When they had disappeared inside the house, Mordecai

Tremaine moved slowly along the terrace. He was well served by fate, for just as he reached the open french doors a few yards away, Superintendent Cannock came out. He looked wryly at Tremaine's muffled figure. "Merry Christmas," he said.

His tone was an encouragement. It said that he was still approachable and that his earlier mood had not been succeeded by an official coldness.

"It's hardly a happy Christmas morning, I'm afraid, superintendent. I don't suppose your wife appreciates your having to spend it like this. If you *are* married," he added.

"I am," said Cannock. "But fortunately she's used to the trials of a policeman's household." His broad face lost its smile. He said seriously, "Anything interesting?"

Tremaine nodded. "A little. Rainer was seen outside the house last night not long before he was killed. Roger Wynton saw him go into the old lodge by the entrance gates."

He told his companion what Denys Arden had said. Cannock listened thoughtfully, a frown on his face. "Why didn't he tell me all this before and save me a great deal of trouble? I'll have to talk to that young man."

His tone was forbidding. Mordecai Tremaine said hastily, "I've more or less offered myself as security that you won't do anything drastic. I think he'll tell you all you want to know if you send for him."

A faint smile appeared in the depths of the brown eyes.

"Cherchez la femme, eh?" Cannock murmured softly. "The young lady's been at work on you, has she?"

Mordecai Tremaine felt himself coloring and was annoyed. He tried to change the subject. "Have you…have you found anything?" he asked.

"We've been having a look around," said Cannock. "But why don't you come inside?"

It was an invitation for which he had been hoping. Having received it, Mordecai Tremaine accepted it eagerly.

The room was still a more or less true reflection of the image in his mind. The Christmas tree, incongruous in the morning light, still bore its gay decorations. The steps were still standing against the wall. The chair upon which Charlotte Grame had sat was still where she had left it. Only the body was missing. The polished floor in front of the tree no longer carried that ominous heap of red.

Mordecai Tremaine looked curiously about him. "Have you found the gun?" he asked.

"Yes," returned Cannock quietly. "We found it an hour ago in Jeremy Rainer's room."

"In *Rainer's* room?" Mordecai Tremaine's pince-nez seemed to be on the very edge of disaster. "Where was it hidden?"

"We discovered it," said Cannock carefully, "under one of the pillows on his bed."

"Any fingerprints?"

"Several. I've already had them checked. They're all Rainer's."

Mordecai Tremaine assimilated this second surprising item of information. "Jeremy Rainer's gun and Jeremy Rainer's fingerprints," he said. "That makes it look like suicide. Except…"

"Except," agreed the superintendent, "that it's a very unusual suicide where a dead man walks upstairs and slips the gun under his pillow and then walks back down again and lies on the floor ready to be found. The doctor swears that he must have been killed instantaneously. The bullet lodged in his heart. Incidentally, it struck him very low in the body, under the ribs in fact, and traveled almost vertically upward through the thoracic cavity. It would have taken a miracle for him to have walked a yard after he was hit, quite apart from the fact that he would have wanted a pretty intense motive to make him do such an apparently crazy thing."

"Suppose it *was* suicide after all. Suppose somebody found him and deliberately took the gun away to make it look like murder."

"And then spoiled the whole effect by leaving the gun in Rainer's own room with his fingerprints on it?" The superintendent shook his head. "I don't think so."

"Neither do I," admitted Mordecai Tremaine.

He walked across to the tree. The pathetic remnants of the shattered bell still hung from its branch; particles of it still glittered on the floor. He peered into the big wooden tub in which the tree was set. There was an indentation in the soil, and he leaned over to study it more closely.

He looked up. The brackets with the names of the guests upon them were still in position. Something caught his attention. He peered upward, but it was difficult to see clearly, and after a moment or two, he fetched the wooden steps from their place against the wall and climbed up so that he could make his investigation more easily.

There was something tied to the branch bearing the bracket with Jeremy Rainer's name on it. It was a piece of thin but stout twine, dark green in color and hardly distinguishable against the background of the tree. It ran back over a stouter branch a few inches higher, its other end dangling downward. Tremaine reached over and examined it. It looked as though it had been cut.

Superintendent Cannock was watching him with interest. "What have you found?" he asked.

"I'm not sure," said Tremaine slowly. He said, as he descended the steps, "I suppose the gun you found is the one that killed Rainer?"

"The ballistics people will want to play around with it, of course, but there isn't much doubt about it being the right one."

"Do you think I might have a look at it?"

"I daresay," said the superintendent, "that it could be

arranged." He added, and now there was a definite twinkle in his eyes, "I've always wanted to see how an amateur sleuth looked when he was hot on the scent!"

Nevertheless, there was a serious note behind the banter. Tremaine knew that the other was not allowing him so much liberty without reason. He was doing it because he believed that it was a policy that might yield him rich dividends.

Which meant that Jonathan Boyce must have been warm in his praises when he had been writing to his colleague. Mordecai Tremaine buried his head in the tree to hide his embarrassment. He hoped he would be able to live up to the flattering portrait the Yard man had obviously drawn.

"Any clues?" came Cannock's voice.

There was a vague stirring in Mordecai Tremaine's mind. Something the superintendent had told him and something he himself had seen had linked significantly. But his thoughts were too nebulous for him to risk voicing them. It would be best, he decided, to safeguard his reputation by appearing mysterious.

"I'd like," he said, "to see that gun before I start offering any theories." He added musingly, "Rainer was a fairly tall man…taller than average, anyway."

"He was five feet eleven," said Cannock. "Is it important?"

"It might be," returned Tremaine. He replaced the steps against the wall. As he came back toward his companion, he said, "Have you been told about the hide?"

"The priest's hiding place?" The superintendent nodded. "Mr. Blaise told me all about it and showed me the entrance in this room. He's been very helpful," he added appreciatively. "He's given us a great deal of information…the location of everyone's room, the routine of the house, and so on. I understand that Mr. Grame thinks a great deal of him and that he's more or less one of the family."

"Nick runs the household," said Tremaine. "I've only been here a very short while, of course, but I've noticed that although he doesn't say a great deal, he does a tremendous amount of work behind the scenes. I imagine Benedict Grame would be lost without him."

Cannock had moved over to the tree. He was staring reflectively at the decorations. "Mr. Grame's Christmas parties are something of a local tradition," he said. "This must be a terrible blow to him."

Tremaine accepted the obvious invitation. "It's my first visit so I haven't had a great deal of time in which to judge, but I believe he tries to keep Christmas in the Dickens style, with all the festivities we associate with the season."

"I wonder," observed the superintendent, "that he's never held a children's party for all the kiddies in the neighborhood. It seems the kind of thing that such a man would naturally do."

Was there any significance in his tone? Tremaine looked at him curiously, but Cannock's broad face told him nothing.

And after a moment or two the superintendent said, "I suppose you noticed those stray pieces of blue cord on the tree?"

Tremaine had noticed them. Attached to several of the branches in the vicinity of a number of the brackets with the name cards were short pieces of cord. It was not easy to see them because in most cases they were very tiny—just a loop around the branch and a fragment dangling below it.

"They look to me," he said, "like pieces of the cord that Grame used to tie the presents. Have you spoken to him about them?"

"I have, and they are," said Cannock. "The odd thing is that we found a supply of that cord in Rainer's room."

"Anything else?"

"If," said the superintendent, "you mean did we find any of the presents there, the answer is that we didn't. And Grame swears that he tied them on the tree last night. He seemed to be taking their disappearance to heart at first, but apparently he's gotten over it now."

Mordecai Tremaine pushed his pince-nez back over his nose just in time to prevent his companion from leaning involuntarily across and doing it for him. The superintendent was not used to their providence-defying air. He eyed his companion reprovingly.

"It's a strange business," he said. "Benedict Grame puts the presents on the tree in his usual manner, and a little later

Jeremy Rainer is found dead beside it, dressed in a Father Christmas outfit, and with the presents nowhere in evidence. And just to make things a little more complicated, the gun that did the killing is found in Rainer's own room with only his own fingerprints on it."

"Don't forget," said Tremaine, "that Rainer's present was still on the tree when we found his body."

"But it isn't there now," remarked the superintendent. "It looks as though it was overlooked for some reason—probably because it was at the top of the tree—and the murderer came back for it as soon as the opportunity occurred."

"The murderer?" queried Mordecai Tremaine quietly.

"Who else? Who else took all the other presents? Perhaps Rainer disturbed the killer when he was at work and before he'd had time to take them all."

"And handed over his gun so that he could be murdered more conveniently?"

Momentarily, the superintendent looked disconcerted, and then he smiled. "Perhaps not," he said. "But who took those presents and why? Robbery doesn't seem to me to be a satisfactory motive. After all, I don't suppose they were really valuable articles. As I understand it, the tree was more in the nature of a seasonal gesture."

"You've checked up on everyone's whereabouts, of course?"

"The same answer in each case...and the obvious one.

They all claim to have gone straight to bed when the party broke up last night. Except Grame, and he says that he saw and heard nothing unusual while he was attending to the tree and went to bed himself immediately afterward."

"He didn't go outdoors at all?"

"No."

"No one heard the shot or any other suspicious sound?"

"Silencer," returned the superintendent briefly. "It's reasonable that it passed unnoticed. After all, *you* didn't hear it."

"That's true enough," admitted Tremaine. "But I *did* see Father Christmas. I was looking out of my window just before going off to sleep," he added in explanation. "I saw a figure down below on the terrace. At first I thought my imagination was playing tricks, and then I remembered that Grame was supposed to dress up on Christmas Eve and play at being Father Christmas. I thought it *was* Grame, but if he didn't go outside the house, then it couldn't have been him."

"Probably it was Rainer. You said that Wynton saw him at the lodge."

Mordecai Tremaine shook his head.

"No, it wasn't Rainer. It was too early for him to have been coming *back* from the lodge—it wasn't long after we'd all gone to our rooms—and he didn't wear the Father Christmas outfit on his way to the lodge. And this Father Christmas had snow on his cap."

The superintendent stared at him, and Mordecai Tremaine enjoyed the mild sensation he had caused.

"No," he said, "I'm not mad. When I saw Jeremy Rainer's body, I noticed that the cap he was wearing was a plain red one except for white trimming on the lower edge. But the cap on the Father Christmas I saw on the terrace had little pieces of cotton wool set all over it to represent snow."

"Then if it wasn't Grame and it wasn't Rainer, who *was* it?"

"Perhaps," said Mordecai Tremaine, "it was Gerald Beechley."

Cannock reached out a foot and hooked a chair toward him. He sat down. He crossed his legs with deliberate slowness. He said, "I think you'd better give me the whole story."

"I'm afraid it isn't much of a story." Tremaine told the other of his meeting with Beechley and of that gentleman's reluctance to display his purchase and of Benedict Grame's comment of a few moments before. "Why Grame told me, I don't know," he finished. "He *said* he thought it would be in Beechley's best interests to let you know the facts."

The superintendent was frowning thoughtfully. "We started off with one Father Christmas, and that seemed crazy enough, but now we've discovered *three*!"

"I hope," said Tremaine diffidently, "that I've been of some use to you, superintendent." He added, "I take it that in view of Roger Wynton's statement, you'll be going to the lodge?"

The spark of humor came back into the superintendent's

brown eyes. "We've already been," he said. "It was routine in any case." He rose from his chair and crossed to a small suitcase lying on the floor near the doorway. He opened it and took out a cardboard box. Carefully he opened the box. "Do you recognize that?" he asked.

It was a gold signet ring. Tremaine recognized the somewhat flamboyant seal. It was a ring he had observed on Jeremy Rainer's finger. "I know it," he said. "It belonged to Rainer."

"It was found in the lodge," said the superintendent. "So was this."

He replaced the ring and took something else from the case. It was a piece of notepaper, creased and slightly dirty, as though it had been hurriedly thrust into someone's pocket and had fallen unnoticed upon an unswept floor.

It bore no address and was unsigned, but it carried several lines of typescript. Tremaine took it from the superintendent's hand and read slowly.

> *Go to the old lodge at twelve-thirty. Wait for half*
> *an hour, then return to your room. Leave your signet*
> *ring on the floor of the lodge. Destroy this afterward.*

"It confirms Wynton's story," observed Cannock. "Rainer *did* go to the lodge. But who gave him this, and why?"

In his mind, Mordecai Tremaine was seeing Rosalind

Marsh as he had seen her in the library earlier in the morning. He was hearing her cool voice telling him without a trace of doubt that Jeremy Rainer had been involved in matters that were on the wrong side of the law and that there had been things in his past about which he had not been anxious for the police to learn. After all, she had said, there *must* have been.

Why had Rosalind Marsh used that expression? What did she know of Jeremy Rainer that had made her so certain?

Tremaine handed the paper back to Superintendent Cannock. He watched him as he returned it to the case. Just what secret meaning lay behind those typewritten sentences? What last strange business had Jeremy Rainer been engaged upon that had taken him out to the lodge in the snow and the darkness and ended in his dead body lying in dreadful fantasy at the foot of the Christmas tree Benedict Grame had been at such pains to prepare?

He sensed that the superintendent was gazing at him expectantly. "There's a typewriter in the library," he said.

"There is," agreed the superintendent. "It's the machine that was used to type that message. Mr. Blaise recognized the lettering when I showed it to him. Apparently it's a machine he uses in carrying out his secretarial duties on Mr. Grame's behalf."

"Does anyone else use it in the ordinary way?"

"No. But Mr. Blaise told me that he couldn't guarantee that no one had ever done so because it's always left out in full view of anyone who might want to type something in a hurry. I asked Miss Arden whether she'd seen anyone at work on it besides Mr. Blaise, and she told me that several mornings ago her guardian was in the library typing."

"All roads," said Mordecai Tremaine softly, "lead to Rainer."

"But Rainer," said the superintendent, "didn't kill himself. Or if he did, it's the strangest suicide I've ever encountered."

"Did Miss Arden know what he was typing?"

"As a matter of fact," returned Cannock, "she did. He was copying out a leading article from the *Financial Times*. It was on the subject of a new plastics combine that's just been formed. I'm working on it, of course, in case it gives us a lead, but I must confess I can't make much of it. As far as I can see, there's nothing in the article beyond a summing up of facts that must be pretty well known in the City, if not to outsiders."

"It's odd," said Tremaine reflectively, "how many of the people here seem to do unaccountable things."

His eyes were bright behind the pince-nez. He looked like a man upon whom knowledge had suddenly broken, but a knowledge so wild and so mixed with surmise that he was half afraid to admit it to his mind. The superintendent saw it.

"Just what," he said, "are you thinking?"

For answer, Mordecai Tremaine turned and raised a hand toward the Christmas tree. He stood looking at its gay tinsel and silver bells. He was thinking of Ernest Lorring, sitting in the half-light, his eyes fixed upon the tree in a steady, baleful stare. He was thinking of Jeremy Rainer, coming into the room when Benedict Grame and Nicholas Blaise had been engaged upon it, and of the intensity of hatred in his face.

And after a moment or two, Tremaine said, "It looks delightful, doesn't it? It's full of the very spirit of Christmas. And yet, somehow, I've a feeling that this is where the solution lies. That if this tree could speak, it would give us both the name of the murderer and the reason why Jeremy Rainer died."

13

The tension was mounting. As yet, there was no open hostility, but the atmosphere was growing steadily more brittle. The strain was a tangible thing. It was possible to feel it in the air, inducing irritation and suspicion, bearing oppressively upon the mind, and fretting at nerves growing ever more ragged.

"There's a crisis on the way. If something doesn't happen soon to clear things up, there's going to be an explosion." Nicholas Blaise spoke with an air of perturbation. His dark face was anxious. Mordecai Tremaine regarded him sympathetically.

"It's a difficult situation for you, Nick, but I'm afraid there's nothing to be done about it. The police are in control, and you can depend upon it that they'll take action quickly enough as soon as they feel they've sufficient evidence."

"But in the meantime," said Blaise, "everybody is looking at everybody else as if they think they're hiding something and ought to go off and confess, or is walking around like a modern Hamlet."

"It's inevitable. When you know that one of your number is a murderer, it doesn't make for a lively gathering. Especially," added Tremaine quietly, "when you're afraid that the police may uncover some of your own secrets during their investigations."

The deep-brown eyes narrowed in inquiry. "Secrets? In *this* galley? You can't be serious!"

"That, Nick, is just what I am."

"But it's absurd," protested Blaise. "I can grant you Delamere, perhaps—and even Lorring. Delamere's a politician, and heaven knows what he's been mixed up in during his career. And I must admit that Lorring's face certainly doesn't exactly inspire confidence. He *looks* as if he might be capable of anything. But the others—no, I just can't believe it. The Napiers, for instance—can you imagine either Harold or his wife having a dark secret in their lives? They just aren't the type. Rosalind Marsh and Lucia Tristam? Each of them is a striking-enough woman in her own way, but that doesn't mean that they're women of mystery. And Charlotte! Poor helpless, ineffectual Charlotte! Can you suspect *her* of having anything to hide?"

"Charlotte," said Mordecai Tremaine, "perhaps most of all. Why was she fully dressed when we came down last night?"

He was watching the younger man as he spoke. He saw the doubt that came onto his face. Then, abruptly, Blaise turned away. "I was afraid," he said over his shoulder, "that you were going to ask that."

"The police are going to ask it, Nick."

"Yes, I know." The words came reluctantly. Blaise looked like a man who was being forced to admit something unpalatable, but which he knew to be the truth and could not avoid.

"*You* know the answer, Nick. What was Charlotte doing?"

"I'm sorry, Mordecai." Nicholas Blaise shrugged his shoulders in a gesture of helplessness. "I can't tell you that. I haven't the right."

Tremaine did not press the point. Instead he went on, as if talking more to himself than to his companion. "I feel sorry for Charlotte Grame. She must have led a very restricted life. I've seen very little of her, of course, but I've found myself wondering whether there was any tragedy in her past."

"Tragedy?" Blaise asked doubtfully.

"Yes. She doesn't strike me as being the kind of woman who remains a spinster from choice. She ought to be married and have a home and children. And yet she seems somehow shut in upon herself, as though she's afraid to show her real feelings. I'll admit that I'm only guessing, but my theory is that she was engaged to be married at one time and was either jilted or something else happened that prevented her going on with the wedding."

There was sudden respect in Nicholas Blaise's dark eyes.

"If you haven't been talking to Charlotte," he said slowly, "you've managed to guess very near the truth. She *was* engaged. It was a long time ago…before I knew her. I don't know exactly what happened, but I believe she was the one who broke off the affair. She's never given any sign of interest in marriage since."

"I wonder," said Mordecai Tremaine. "I wonder."

It was clear from the look Nicholas Blaise gave him that the other wanted to ask questions, but he pretended not to notice it. Blaise knew a great deal more about Charlotte Grame than he had so far admitted. Tremaine suspected that he was uncomfortable over it, and he knew that if he was prepared to wait, Blaise would sooner or later decide that confession was the wisest policy.

"I hear you've been able to give Superintendent Cannock a good deal of help, Nick," Tremaine said, changing the subject, perhaps too obviously.

Blaise shrugged. "It's little enough real help I was able to give. I told him what I could and showed him the layout of the house. After all, I suppose I was the natural choice for the job."

"What you did was appreciated anyway," said Tremaine. "Did you know that Jeremy Rainer had used your typewriter?"

"No," Blaise said quickly, "I didn't know that. *Did* he use it?" And then he said, with a return to his casual air, "I don't suppose it means very much. The typewriter is always easy to find if anyone happens to want it. Benedict often types his own letters, and I believe Denys has used it once or twice. There's nothing significant about Rainer having used it as far as I can see."

"It's a standard model, isn't it?"

"Yes. There must be thousands of them in the country." Blaise seemed to be devoting only half his mind to the conversation. He said, "I don't suppose I've any business asking this, but have the police any definite clues yet? Do they—do they suspect any particular person?"

"Meaning," said Tremaine, "do they suspect Benedict Grame? I can answer that quite easily, Nick. I haven't the faintest idea."

"I still can't believe it," said Blaise slowly. "It seems so horribly disloyal even to think about it. Has Benedict offered any explanation of why it took so long to arouse him?"

"He may have spoken to the superintendent. Have you raised the question with him?"

"I daren't," said Blaise frankly. "I tried to mention it tactfully, but somehow I couldn't get around to it. It was as though I was telling him I thought he was guilty. I believe he suspected what I was driving at as it was. He didn't make any comment, but the look in his face made me feel like a worm and I just had to evade the issue."

Tremaine nodded. "Do you know anything about Denys Arden's parents?"

Blaise looked a little startled at the abrupt change of subject. "Only secondhand. Her mother died when she was a baby and her father when she was still quite young. Rainer was his partner, and he more or less appointed himself as her guardian."

"What about money?"

"As far as I understand," said Blaise, "there wasn't any money. Arden was caught in a financial crash. He was penniless when he died. Indirectly, it was the cause of his death. He contracted pneumonia and just flickered out as though there was no stamina left in him." He eyed his companion curiously. "What are you after? Do you think there's any connection between Rainer's death and what happened to Arden?"

"Thinking," Tremaine said with a smile, "is one of the curses of civilization!"

He left his companion gazing after him with a puzzled stare. It was obvious that there were times when Nicholas Blaise was not at all certain how to take him.

Gerald Beechley had not been seen very much during the day. Tremaine had looked for him on several occasions, for he had come to the conclusion that Beechley would repay a closer study, but the big man was apparently keeping himself out of the public gaze. It was unexpected, therefore, when he came face-to-face with him in the hall. It was even more unexpected when, instead of brushing hastily past him, Beechley hesitated and showed every sign of wanting to talk to him.

The big man's red face was streaked with blue veins. His cheeks were puffy, and he had lost all resemblance to the jovial countryman. His eyes were bloodshot, and although he still possessed his high coloring, it was due to an unhealthy flush that contrasted grotesquely with the yellow pullover he still wore. Hogarth, thought Mordecai Tremaine, would have regarded him as a natural subject for his brush. The other was swaying slightly, and as he drew nearer, he brought with him the odor of spirits.

"I suppose all those policemen of yours are still going around measuring things, eh?"

There was something repellant in Beechley's attitude, in his overobvious anxiety to appear lightheartedly at ease when it was so clear that he was not.

"They're still busy," agreed Mordecai Tremaine.

Gerald Beechley looked down at him. As plainly as he could without using words, he betrayed a man consumed by the desire to ask questions and yet desperately afraid of being caught asking them.

Tremaine waited. Beechley shifted his weight uneasily from one foot to the other. At last, he could keep silent no longer. "Have they…have they found out?" he asked.

"Found out?" echoed Mordecai Tremaine.

"Do they know who did it?" explained Beechley carefully. "Are they going to arrest anybody?"

"I don't know," said Tremaine. "After all, how should I?"

He saw exasperation creep into the other's manner. Beechley was not drunk, but the alcohol had dulled his wits to the dangerous stage where he imagined that he was superior in cunning to the rest of the world. His eyes narrowed. He said, with a transparently artificial casualness, "Is there anything missing?"

Mordecai Tremaine gave him an intent look. There was something positive behind that question. Gerald Beechley was asking it for a reason. "I'm afraid I don't understand," he said.

He was doubtful whether Beechley's state of befuddlement had reached the point where he would give himself away, but in any case, the matter was not put to the test. The sound of voices came from just beyond the hall, and the big man looked around quickly, a startled expression on his face. His fingers went nervously to the collar of his pullover.

"It doesn't matter," he said thickly. "It was nothing."

He did not wait to learn the identity of the newcomers, leaving Mordecai Tremaine in a thoughtful mood. Benedict Grame's not oversubtle hint and Gerald Beechley's own behavior seemed to be adding up to a highly interesting result.

He turned slowly to find himself facing the Napiers. "Hullo," he said. "Were you thinking of going for a stroll in the grounds?"

Harold Napier shook his head. "We've just been wandering through the house."

"It's a fascinating old place," Tremaine said. "I hardly think the superintendent will want us to stay caged much longer. But under the circumstances, I suppose we must make the best of it."

"It was a terrible thing to have happened," said Evelyn Napier. "Poor Mr. Rainer…"

The hall was growing dark. Mordecai Tremaine found it difficult to see them clearly, but he thought that they were both revealing traces of anxiety. Harold Napier's slightly embarrassed air had become more noticeable. His wife's timidity seemed to have become emphasized by a nervous fear that showed itself in a voice not quite under control.

"It's a dreadful situation for Miss Arden," said Tremaine. "And it's placed Mr. Grame in a very difficult position. He can hardly go on with his plans for entertaining us."

"Oh no," said Harold Napier quickly. He seemed anxious to vindicate Grame, as though he felt that he had accused their host of inattention to their welfare by his manner when he had come into the hall. "I'm sure he's doing everything he can, though, to make things easier for us. Of course, his hands are tied by the police being here."

A thought probed itself into Mordecai Tremaine's mind. "Did you know Mr. Grame before you came to this part of the country, Mrs. Napier?" he asked.

He heard the little sound of her gasp as he put the question to her. She looked toward her husband, inquiringly, pleadingly. Tremaine saw the other give a slight worried nod in reply. "Yes," she told him. "We did know him."

They had come into the hall in the aimless manner of people who were in no hurry and who had no definite purpose in mind. But now they were clearly anxious to be gone. And Mordecai Tremaine felt certain that it was his question that had been responsible.

He watched them go with a frown. There was nothing obviously incriminating in a confession that they had known Benedict Grame before they had come to Sherbroome. Why, then, betray so much anxiety? Was it because that in admitting that fact, they realized that they had also admitted something else? That they had, for instance, known Jeremy Rainer, too?

He had mentally written off the Napiers. He had labeled them as a couple of middle-aged lovers of the country life who were unlikely to provide either complications or sensations. Could it be that he had been wrong? Had he been deceived by an appearance of harmlessness deliberately assumed for just such a purpose?

He recalled his first conversation with Evelyn Napier, and it came back to him that there had been the same hesitancy, the same reluctance to answer questions that had seemed innocent enough. It occurred to him then that they had been the same *sort* of questions. Questions about how long they had been in Sherbroome and whether they had known Benedict Grame before they had come to the village.

What did Harold and Evelyn Napier have to hide? Were they the vague, innocuous pair they seemed, or was that merely cunning camouflage to conceal a deep-rooted villainy?

Tremaine thoughtfully pushed open the door of an adjoining lounge and found himself confronting two suspicious faces. One of them was the plump, somewhat pallid countenance of Austin Delamere; the other possessed the gauntly forbidding features of Ernest Lorring.

They presented the appearance of a pair of strange bed-fellows. Tremaine did not think he had intruded upon any confidential discussion; they had the air of men who were prepared to tolerate each other's presence but who had no desire to achieve a deeper intimacy.

Each of them looked from the newcomer back to his companion. Tremaine found himself wondering what either of them would have said had he been alone. For it was clear enough that each was carefully choosing his words, trying to gauge what the effect would be before he spoke.

"Is there—any news?" said Delamere at last. He tried to keep the note of excitement out of his voice and almost succeeded.

"Not," said Mordecai Tremaine, "as far as I know."

"And if anybody does get to know," said Lorring, "it will certainly be *you*."

His antagonism was unashamed. Tremaine was a little surprised that he was revealing his feelings so openly, but his attitude was not unexpected. Lorring had not forgotten that incident when he had been accused—by inference, if not in actual words—of having taken the last present from the Christmas tree.

Delamere did not appear to notice the scientist's manner. He was too concerned with his own thoughts. "Why don't the police do something?" he said petulantly. "They've turned the house upside down. Why haven't they arrested someone?"

"They'll have to find their man first," Lorring remarked sardonically. "You can't expect these country policemen to solve a crime in five minutes."

Tremaine observed mildly, "Superintendent Cannock strikes me as being a very capable man. I don't think anything is likely to escape him. Or *anyone*."

He looked at Lorring as he accented the last word and had the satisfaction of seeing an angry glare come into the other's eyes. He added, "I wonder why those presents were stolen from the tree? Particularly the last one. I've a feeling that if we knew *that*, we'd know a great deal about why Jeremy Rainer died."

There was a mixture of rage and fear on Lorring's craggy face. He looked, thought Tremaine, willing to wound and yet afraid to strike. He said thickly, "If I were you I'd leave the police to ask their own questions."

His glance went to Delamere, as if daring him to make a comment, and then, heaving himself from his chair, he went abruptly from the room, brushing ostentatiously past Mordecai Tremaine in his passage.

The strain in Austin Delamere's plump cheeks softened into relief. "I'm glad that fellow's gone. I never could stand him. I didn't know Benedict had asked him down."

"You've met Professor Lorring before?" probed Mordecai Tremaine gently.

"Yes, I've met him. Heard about him, too."

"Heard about him?"

"There've been rumors. Ugly ones. He was lucky to escape finding himself in the dock. There was talk of his having sold government secrets."

"There often is that kind of talk about people engaged in special work," said Tremaine. "Usually there's nothing behind it."

"This wasn't just talk," persisted Delamere. He seemed unduly anxious to make his point. "It was only because there wasn't sufficient evidence that Lorring got away with it. I've been…" He hesitated and glanced at Tremaine in a furtive fashion, as though trying to find out what the reaction would be before committing himself. "I've been wondering whether he knew Rainer. Whether there was anything between them."

Behind the pince-nez, Mordecai Tremaine's eyes were bright. The witches' cauldron was beginning to bubble. Delamere was anxious to throw suspicion on Lorring. And when people tried to incriminate other people, that usually meant they were frightened and trying to distract attention from themselves.

The pot, he told himself, was trying to blacken the kettle. It was a measure of Delamere's state of nerves that he was making such an open attack upon Lorring.

He did not betray it, but secretly he was grimly amused at the irony of Delamere's attitude. The politician's own past was hardly blameless. There had been whispers enough concerning him. If Ernest Lorring had been lucky not to find himself facing an awkward situation, then so, undoubtedly, had Austin Delamere—and on more than one occasion.

But no one could have told the way Mordecai Tremaine's thoughts were running. He observed, "I daresay the police are making inquiries to find out whether Mr. Rainer had associations with anyone in the house. I expect they're ferreting out all there is to know about *all* of us."

Austin Delamere's plump face went a shade greener. "I suppose they are," he said unhappily.

He no longer seemed disposed to continue his discourse on Lorring's character. Mordecai Tremaine left with the knowledge that he was leaving a badly frightened man.

A few moments later, as he was staring pensively out the library windows, he saw Charlotte Grame. She was making her way down the drive, moving furtively in the shelter of the laurels. He watched her until a bend in the drive concealed her from his sight. It was obvious from her manner that she intended to go farther than the grounds of the house, and he wondered what desperate emotion was driving her.

Momentarily, he considered going after her, but realizing that she had too long a start, he went instead in search of Superintendent Cannock.

"Gone out, has she?" the superintendent murmured, as Tremaine told him what he had seen. "Miss Grame, who seldom leaves the house even when the weather's fine. Now I wonder what can be taking her out at this uninviting time."

"Breaking your instructions," remarked Mordecai Tremaine.

The superintendent shook his head. "Mr. Blaise probably hasn't had time to get around to everybody yet. I told him a little while back that there wasn't any objection to people going out now. Of course, I was a little high-handed in trying to confine them to the house for so long. I thought one or two of them might be anxious to get out by this time."

His tone was significant. Tremaine said, "You mean…"

The superintendent nodded. "Two of the birds have flown. Miss Grame and Mr. Beechley. But I daresay we shall manage to find out where they're gone. And after that, we'll try and find out why they went."

Tremaine was very glad he had disregarded that first impulse to go in pursuit of Charlotte Grame. If the superintendent's men were already engaged upon the task of shadowing her, he had been saved what would have proved to be both an uncomfortable and a fruitless journey.

Cannock was looking at him curiously. "You're not… busy?"

"Oh no," Tremaine said hastily, and the superintendent smiled.

"Then perhaps you'd like to come along," he said.

He led the way up the stairs. He had evidently made himself thoroughly familiar with the house. He went without hesitation to Charlotte Grame's room. The door was not locked, and he pushed it open and went inside.

"We've been here once," he said, "but you never know."

In a few moments, the superintendent had subjected the room to a systematic and thorough search. Tremaine admired the quick certainty of his movements and the manner in which he examined every article and yet, when he had finished, left no trace of his presence.

"What do you expect to find?" he asked.

"I make it a rule," said the superintendent, "not to *expect* to find anything. I'm merely taking routine precautions."

It was a neat room. It was, thought Tremaine, an unpretentious, colorless room that was rather like Charlotte Grame herself. He watched Cannock as the other opened the wardrobe and looked inside. It was not a very extensive wardrobe, and the coats and dresses it contained were not the newest of fashions. Standing at the side of it was a medium-sized suitcase. The superintendent snapped back the catch and rummaged expertly through the clothing and toiletry items that were inside.

He replaced the lid of the case and rose to his feet. He gave a last glance about the room. "Seems innocent enough," he remarked. "Don't you think?"

"Appearances," said Mordecai Tremaine, "are often deceptive." The superintendent's lifted eyebrow invited elaboration. Tremaine said: "I'd like to know what took Charlotte Grame downstairs in the middle of the night. And I'd like to know what took her out of the house this afternoon."

"She doesn't *look* capable of killing anybody," said Cannock.

Mordecai Tremaine pretended to be shocked. "I wasn't suggesting," he said, "that she killed Mr. Rainer. After all, there's no real evidence against her."

"There's no real evidence against anybody," the superintendent said drily.

He led the way out of the room and along the corridor. He stopped outside a door Tremaine knew to be Gerald Beechley's. It was locked. Cannock produced a bunch of keys from his pocket, selected and tried one, and pushed open the door with a murmur of satisfaction.

The room was the antithesis of Charlotte Grame's. Clothes were flung untidily around. A pipe had been left on the dressing table, and tobacco ash had trailed from the bowl. A pair of shoes rested reproachfully in the middle of the carpet, and the door of the wardrobe was half open.

"If he's done all this since the room was tidied this morning," observed the superintendent, "I'd hate to see it if the servants went on strike for a week!"

There was a smell of burning in the air and it was to the fire grate that Cannock turned. It was the open type, and it was choked with a charred mass that revealed an attempt to burn something bulky that had not been disposed of easily.

Cannock poked the blackened embers thoughtfully. "Looks like cloth of some sort. We'll get what's left of it analyzed and see where that takes us."

He looked up at Mordecai Tremaine. The brown eyes were shadowed with thought. "Is Gerald Beechley likely to be short of money?" he asked.

Tremaine's mind went back to the telephone call he had overheard the big man making and to what Denys Arden had told him of Beechley's dependence upon Benedict Grame. "Very likely from all I've heard." And added, "Why?"

"I saw Mr. Grame half an hour ago," said the superintendent. "When I raised the possibility of burglary as a motive the first time I saw him and suggested that Mr. Rainer might have been shot more or less accidentally because he'd surprised someone breaking into the house, he was inclined to be skeptical of the theory and told me that nothing had been taken. But it now appears that there *was* a burglary. A valuable diamond necklace has disappeared from a safe in Mr. Grame's room."

"Miss Arden's!" said Mordecai Tremaine involuntarily, and the superintendent nodded.

"So I understand," he observed. "Intended as her wedding present, wasn't it? I gather that most of the people in the house knew about it."

Tremaine nodded. "When does Mr. Grame think it was stolen?"

"It was there late last night. Apparently, he had occasion to go to the safe to give the rector a donation to the church restoration fund when the carol singers were here. He's positive the necklace was still there at that time. According to his story, his mind was so full of the murder that it never occurred to him to look again until early this afternoon. And that was when he discovered the theft."

"And yet," said Mordecai Tremaine, "he told you that he didn't think anything was missing without even checking on the necklace."

"He says," the superintendent remarked, "that he didn't give a thought to the possibility of the necklace having been stolen because he's a light sleeper and he was assuming that he'd certainly have heard anyone trying to get into his room, let alone trying to open the safe. And then—so he says," Cannock added, "he remembered that he'd been downstairs putting the presents on the tree after everyone else had gone to bed, and that it would have been possible for someone to have entered his room before he went up. He also pointed out that his room was left empty when he was awakened and told about the murder and went downstairs again with the rest of you."

"On the surface," said Mordecai Tremaine, "that means someone in the house is definitely responsible…unless an outsider either took the risk of breaking in at an early hour when there must still have been plenty of lights showing and was lucky enough to find that the one room that mattered was empty, or took the even bigger risk of staying in the house after the discovery of the murder and slipped into Grame's room just after he'd left it and managed to make his escape without being spotted although everybody was up and about by that time."

"That's the way *I* see it," said the superintendent. "The odds are on its being an inside job. That's why I asked you about Mr. Gerald Beechley."

Mordecai Tremaine saw the big man's puffy, lined face and his frightened, bloodshot eyes. The question Beechley had put to him had suddenly acquired a damaging significance.

"*Is there anything missing?*"

It had been the question of a man who knew something, and who was desperately anxious to find out whether the police also knew.

14

Mordecai Tremaine was trying to analyze Benedict Grame's attitude and finding the exercise extraordinarily difficult. But for the background of murder and suspicion, he would have said that the other was in high good spirits. With the dead man's shadow lying oppressively over this Christmas night party, there was something of the macabre in Grame's apparent lightheartedness, something that gave him the air of a painted clown frolicking in a graveyard.

Superficially, the explanation was simple enough. Grame was trying to act up to his responsibilities as host. He was struggling to relieve the atmosphere of depression, and perhaps struggling a little too hard so that his efforts were bringing unreality in their train.

And yet…

Tremaine found himself trying to define something that was eluding him. There was more in Benedict Grame's manner than the desire to put his guests at ease. His assurance was too spontaneous in origin to be merely a cloak he was painstakingly assuming. At times, indeed, he seemed almost exultant.

And why should Benedict Grame be exultant when his best friend had been murdered under his roof? Unless…the thought followed naturally…unless he was exultant *because* Jeremy Rainer was dead.

For the moment there was no conversation. Charlotte Grame was playing Chopin. She was an accomplished pianist, and the others were listening with more than the usual casual attention. Benedict Grame was sitting in a straight-backed chair at the top end of the room. It gave him the appearance of being on a different level from his guests. He seemed, thought Tremaine, to be looking down upon them, somehow as though he felt himself to be the master of their destinies.

When Charlotte Grame finished playing, Tremaine took advantage of the buzz of congratulatory talk to cross to his host's side. Grame saw him coming, and a look of expectancy came into the blue eyes.

"How are the investigations going?" he asked. "I'm afraid that so far I've had very little opportunity of talking to you."

"I believe Superintendent Cannock feels that he's making progress," returned Mordecai Tremaine carefully.

"I don't mean his," said Grame. "I mean *yours*." He did not wait for a reply. He made a gesture that embraced the other occupants of the room. "They seem to be enjoying them-selves reasonably well in view of what's happened."

"You've been having rather a difficult time," said Mordecai Tremaine, "trying to keep things together."

Benedict Grame looked at him from beneath his bushy eyebrows. The blue eyes were amused. "It might have been worse," he said. Before Tremaine could frame a suitably prob-ing question, he added, "The man I envy is yourself."

"Why me?" said Mordecai Tremaine, surprised.

Benedict Grame gave a quick glance about him to make sure that there was no one within earshot. He lowered his voice. "Someone here killed Jeremy," he said, and despite his whispered tones, the vibrant note of intensity was plainly audible. "That someone knows you're after him. What he *doesn't* know is just how much you've found out. Maybe you haven't got very far yet, but even so, what a sense of power it must give you! Another person's life is in your hands. Steadily, strand by strand, you're preparing the rope that one day may hang him. Perhaps you even know the name of the killer already, and you've only to gather the last shreds of proof."

For an instant, Mordecai Tremaine had the impression that Grame had forgotten that he was there. He was staring straight in front of himself. His face had the intent expres-sion of a man utterly engrossed in his own thoughts.

"The greatest power there is," he breathed, in a kind

of taut whisper. "The power of life and death. It must be fascinating—fascinating. You can look at a man and say, 'You only go free because *I* permit it. I need only lift my finger, and the law will reach out to you and hold you until they take you out of your cell on that last morning and the hangman sets your feet against the chalk mark on the trap.' It's like keeping a puppet dancing on the end of a string. Whenever you choose, you can take away the thing that makes it play at being alive."

"And you think," said Mordecai Tremaine quietly, "that it's an enviable power to possess?"

"Of course," said Benedict Grame. "Of course! Without power, what purpose is there in life? Fame? Money? Of what real value are they except for the power they bring with them? It's the sense of mastery that lifts a man and makes him forget that he came from dust!"

Excitement was glittering now in the blue eyes staring into Tremaine's own. They had acquired a hard quality. They were not quite normal in their stony brilliance.

Momentarily, Mordecai Tremaine experienced the sensation that he was on the verge of making a discovery of tremendous significance. And then, regretfully, he became aware that someone was standing at his side. It was Lucia Tristam. She said, "You two seem to be acting like a couple of conspirators!"

She was smiling, but there was no smile to illumine the green depths in the wide eyes and bring out those vital tints. They were dark with anxiety. She searched Mordecai Tremaine's face as though she was trying to draw the thoughts out of him.

Benedict Grame suddenly realized that she was there. The glitter went from his eyes. He seemed disconcerted, as though he felt that she had caught him off his guard.

Mordecai Tremaine studied them both. It was odd, he ruminated, how Lucia Tristam always seemed to appear when he was talking to Grame. Almost as if she feared what the other might say if he allowed his tongue to operate too freely.

"We've been discussing crime and punishment," he said. "At least, one aspect of it."

She shivered. He did not know whether it was assumed or whether he really had laid a chill finger across her soul. "Have you—have you discovered who did it?"

She caught her breath on the last word. Tremaine guessed that she had been driven to ask the question in spite of herself. Her desire to find out what he knew had been stronger than her anxiety not to appear too interested in the progress of the police investigation in case it brought suspicion upon her.

"You mean, have the police found out who killed Mr. Rainer? They probably have their theories, of course, but we're not likely to hear of them until they decide they've enough evidence to justify an arrest."

Did she flash a quick glance at Benedict Grame? Was there a trace of fear on her face? She turned away from him so that he could not see her eyes. It was a natural enough movement, but it might have been intended to prevent betraying herself to him.

"It's much too morbid a topic for conversation anyway," she said. "Can't we dance, Benedict?"

"Of course, my dear," he told her, rising. "It's an excellent plan!"

It gave Mordecai Tremaine an excuse for doing what he had been wanting to do—speak to Charlotte Grame. She saw him coming and looked desperately about her, but this time there was no way out. Lucia Tristam was on the point of dancing with Benedict Grame, and Gerald Beechley was in conversation with the Napiers.

As he put his arm about her, he felt her tremble. It was like holding a frightened, fluttering bird. He said: "I admired your playing, Miss Grame. You have a beautiful touch."

"Thank you," she said breathlessly.

For a few moments, they danced without speaking. And then: "There's no need for you to be frightened of me, you know," said Mordecai Tremaine gently. "After all, I might be able to help you."

She stiffened. Her lips had difficulty in framing the words. "I don't know what you mean."

"I think you do," he corrected her. "You also know that I *did* see you in Calnford the other day."

She lost the rhythm of her movements, stumbled into him. He waited for her to recover. He said, "Shall we go outside? We can talk more easily."

She offered no resistance as he guided her toward the door. Their exit was unobserved except by Ernest Lorring. He gave them a curious, suspicious glance but made no comment.

No one saw them go into the library. Tremaine shut the door and turned toward her. "Now, Miss Grame, suppose you tell me all the things you haven't told the police."

"I don't understand," she said. "I've told them everything."

"Including," he said, "why you screamed?"

The color had flown from her face. Her eyes, frightened and desperate, would not meet his own. "It was horrible. I-I couldn't control myself."

She waited for him to make some comment, but he was silent. His very silence fretted at her self-control. Her voice went up raggedly. "You don't think…you don't think *I* killed Jeremy?"

"Can you," he countered, "think of a reason why anyone else should have killed him? Mr. Wynton, for instance? After all, he was in the neighborhood of the house at the time of the murder—rather unexpectedly, to say the least—and he and Mr. Rainer were known to be on bad terms."

Relief that he had apparently abandoned his direct attack upon her struggled with reluctance to incriminate Roger Wynton. Her voice was troubled. "No," she said. "No. He didn't do it. I'm sure he didn't."

"The police," said Mordecai Tremaine, "can't be so sure. Not in view of Mr. Rainer's attitude toward him wanting to marry Miss Arden."

Charlotte Grame looked up at him suddenly. She spoke hurriedly, like a person who had hesitated a long time before deciding to speak and who felt even now that she must say what she had to say quickly before she lost her resolution.

"I don't believe he did mind Roger marrying Denys," she said. "I think he *wanted* it to happen."

Mordecai Tremaine stared at her. Over the pince-nez, the gray eyes were sharp with inquiry. "You mean," he said, "that what everybody thought was his dislike of Mr. Wynton was merely a pretense?"

"Yes, that's it," she told him. "A pretense. He made out that he wouldn't allow Denys to marry Roger, but underneath I'm sure he liked him."

"But why?" he pressed her. "*Why* should he act like that?"

Charlotte Grame shook her head helplessly. She looked frightened and uncertain. "I don't know," she said. "I don't know. But it's true. I-I could *feel* it. And he told me one day that he was making plans that would surprise us. He said that things would be…different. He used to talk to me like that sometimes. He used to tell me things he wouldn't speak about to anyone else."

"Not even to Miss Arden?"

"Oh no," she said. "Not Denys. He couldn't tell Denys."

"Do you know what he meant by saying that things would be different?"

"No," she murmured almost inaudibly, and this time he knew that she was lying.

But it would gain him nothing if he tried to force her. That much was evident from the manner in which her hands were tightly clenched against her sides and the stiffness of her body. She had reached her last defenses and would give way no further.

Mordecai Tremaine weighed up the situation shrewdly and tried another line of approach. "You'd like to help the police, wouldn't you? You'd like to help them find out who killed Mr. Rainer?"

She nodded—reluctantly, he thought. "Of course. But how can I? What is there I can do?"

"You may possess items of knowledge that seem unimportant to you but that would become highly significant if the police knew them." His eyes searched her face, compelling her to look at him. "Did you see Mr. Beechley when you came downstairs and found Mr. Rainer's body?"

"Gerald?" She was genuinely puzzled. "I don't understand. There was no one there."

"He bought a Father Christmas outfit in Calnford yesterday," Mordecai Tremaine said deliberately. "He was wearing it last night. I happened to see him from my window."

"I didn't know," she said. "I didn't see him—"

"I was wondering," said Tremaine, "whether it was anything to do with one of Mr. Beechley's practical jokes. I believe he has a reputation for doing rather…unusual…things. I thought perhaps his love of a joke was leading him to play some trick or other on the rest of us. Although," he added, "it was rather a cold night for wandering about on the terrace."

Momentarily, Charlotte Grame's eyes were blank. He had the impression that she was trying to assess the significance of what he had told her in relation to knowledge she already possessed. "Are you sure it was Gerald?" she asked.

"I didn't see his face clearly," Tremaine admitted, "but I thought that it must be Mr. Beechley. From what I'd heard about him, it seemed to be the kind of thing he might do."

She did not, as he had half expected, make the obvious reply that the most likely reaction on seeing the figure in red would have been to assume—as he had in fact done at the time—that it was Benedict Grame. It revealed, thought

Tremaine, that she had reason to believe that it *might* have been Beechley.

"A lot of people have the wrong idea about Gerald," she told him. "He isn't as…as irresponsible as he sometimes appears."

Mordecai Tremaine expressed concern. "Dear me," he said. "I'm afraid I've been rather flippant on occasion. I quite thought he had a very strongly developed sense of humor and often indulged in the…er…schoolboy type of prank. Do you mean he doesn't like these jokes after all?"

"I'm quite certain he doesn't. He only does it because—" She stopped suddenly, and her hand went to her mouth as though to prevent any more words being uttered. She had the frightened look of someone who had said more than she had intended.

Mordecai Tremaine was going to press his advantage, but she anticipated him. She said quickly, "Benedict will be wondering what's happened to us. I think we should go back to the others."

She did not wait for him to answer. She crossed to the door, pulled it open hurriedly, and went out without meeting his eyes again.

Mordecai Tremaine waited discreetly for a moment or two. He did not wish to lend the appearance of flight and pursuit to Charlotte Grame's sudden exit.

When, at last, he did open the door, he almost collided

with Fleming, who was just passing. The other murmured an apology and stepped aside. Tremaine gave him a sharp look. He thought for an instant that the other was going to speak to him, and he waited instinctively. But despite the uncertainty on his face, Fleming made no comment. His broad figure moved sedately on down the corridor.

Tremaine heard the music start as he went to rejoin his fellow guests, and as he entered the room, he saw that Charlotte Grame had already found sanctuary and was dancing with Gerald Beechley. He wondered what she was saying to him. He had a feeling that Beechley was not going to receive her tidings any too happily.

Benedict Grame had evidently carried out a highly successful cutting-in expedition and was dancing with Denys Arden. As Mordecai Tremaine was moving unobtrusively to a chair, he heard Roger Wynton say quietly at his elbow, "Have you been grilling Charlotte?"

"*Grilling* her?"

He put pained emphasis on the word, but Wynton was unimpressed by his guileless air. "You went out together. A few moments ago, she came in alone looking as though you'd been raising the family ghost and went straight over to Gerald. What's brewing?"

"As far as I can see," said Mordecai Tremaine, "it looks like quite a pleasant party. Considering the circumstances."

"Do you think that it was either Charlotte or Gerald who killed Rainer?" said Wynton. "Or *both* of them? I'm interested," he added, "because I'm well aware that our mutual friend the superintendent has his eye on me, and as far as I'm concerned, the sooner this business comes home to roost, the better. Not that I've anything against either of them. I've always felt rather sorry for Charlotte, and Gerald's simple enough. Take away his whiskey and his horses, and there's nothing very complicated left of him."

Mordecai Tremaine raised his eyebrows. Wynton said, "Oh, yes, that's where Gerald's pocket money goes. The bottle and the bookmakers. Nobody talks about it, of course, but it's a pretty open secret."

The big man and his partner were momentarily under the full brilliance of one of the electric globes, and the light was not flattering to him. Beechley's puffy, blue-veined face was haggard and strained. All firmness seemed to have gone from his features, leaving them without form and with an unhealthy gray color.

Tremaine admitted to himself that it might well have been some trick of the harsh light that gave him his unprepossessing appearance and that made the hand resting upon his partner's shoulder seem to tremble. He admitted also that because Gerald Beechley might be an alcoholic and a man who gambled on horses—and probably usually lost—it did not make him a murderer. Nothing had so far emerged to equip him with a motive for having killed Jeremy Rainer.

But if the motive was obscure, what of the opportunity? Beechley had gone to bed when the others had gone, and he had only come from his room a moment or two before he himself had reached the door. On the face of it, therefore, the big man could not have been the killer, but there was nothing to prove that he had not left his room at some period during the night, committed the murder, and returned before Charlotte Grame's screams had aroused the household. There was, in fact, more than a suggestion that he *had* left it.

That red-robed figure on the terrace, for instance… Mordecai Tremaine was certain that it had been neither Jeremy Rainer nor Benedict Grame. For there had been puffs of cotton wool over the cap worn by the Father Christmas he had seen from his window, and both the cap on the dead man and the cap belonging to the outfit Grame had produced had been completely red, apart from the white trimming at the edges.

Whether it *had* been Beechley remained to be proved, but two facts at least seemed plain enough. Gerald Beechley had brought a Father Christmas outfit back to the house, and he had burned a quantity of cloth in the grate in his bedroom. Which certainly brought him well and truly into the list of suspects.

Mordecai Tremaine watched the dancing couples. Rosalind Marsh swirled by him in the arms of Nicholas Blaise. He caught a breath of her perfume and inhaled it appreciatively. He thought they made a handsome couple. He wondered whether Nick realized it and whether he realized how beautiful she was.

But this was no time to allow one's mind to be clouded by thoughts of sentiment. Murder was the subject at issue, and so far Rosalind Marsh was as much under suspicion as any of the others. Had *she* left her room? No one had claimed to have seen her, but that did not mean that she had not done so.

He studied the others thoughtfully, his eyes resting briefly upon each dancing couple as they passed him. Lucia Tristam glanced at him as she went by with Austin Delamere. He met her gaze for an instant, and she looked quickly away.

He followed her superb figure as Delamere led her down the room, recalled her as he had seen her, breathless and shaken, looking at Jeremy Rainer's body. She had been one of the last to reach the room. It was true that her bedroom was situated in one of the farthest parts of the house, but had she made her appearance as quickly as might reasonably have been expected? And had there been something of the actress in the manner in which she had reacted to the sight of the body?

Mordecai Tremaine reached out a figurative hand after his thoughts and set them on a less imaginative track. Upon such a basis, it would be possible to build a case against everyone in the house. From Austin Delamere, who seemed to have been first on the scene, to Benedict Grame, who had made such a suspiciously belated appearance.

Analyzing his own thoughts, he found that despite the trails of footprints leading across the lawn, his mind was centered on the people in the house, rather than the possibility of an intruder from outside. The murderer was somewhere within the walls. That was the belief that was slowly growing within him, illuminated by the first faint glimmerings of an incredible truth.

As yet it was too vague even to attempt to define it. He found himself wishing that he could have Superintendent Cannock's access to the life histories of the actors in the drama. Given that, he might find the essential clue. Without it, he could only grope in frustrating darkness, hoping that luck might send him stumbling along the right path.

He looked at Nicholas Blaise. Nick knew a great deal about Benedict Grame's guests and about Grame himself. He would have to talk to Nick. He would have to find out all about the connection between Grame and Jeremy Rainer. He would have to find out what their association had been in the days when they had played active parts in business life.

Nick would talk. That was why he had asked him down. He *wanted* him to know those things.

It was growing rather warm in the room. Mordecai Tremaine got up slowly and went toward the door. Just outside, he met Fleming again. This time, the butler quite evidently wished to speak. His eyes held an appeal. He was a man who had something to say and wished to be encouraged to say it.

Mordecai Tremaine administered the necessary stimulus. "It's been a difficult day," he remarked. "You've dealt with a trying situation remarkably well."

Fleming's impassivity melted into a smile of gratification. The human gossip showed for a moment in his round face. "Thank you, sir," he said. "I've endeavored to do my duty. I think I may speak for the rest of the staff as well, sir."

"I'm sure you can," said Mordecai Tremaine. He observed the signs, and added, "I suppose you knew Mr. Rainer well? It must have been a great shock to you this morning."

"Yes, indeed, sir," said Fleming. "Although I did have what you might call a premonition."

"A premonition?"

"It was last night, sir. When the carol singers were here. I don't know what made me do it, but I counted them as they were leaving."

He paused. He had the air of a man about to deliver

himself of a fact of frightening significance. He said, "*There were thirteen!*"

Mordecai Tremaine tried not to smile. Fleming, the grave, the imperturbable, was superstitious! Here indeed was the heel of Achilles!

And then memory stirred, and there was no laughter in his mind. He pushed back the pince-nez. He said sharply, "*Thirteen?* Are you *sure*?"

"Perfectly certain, sir," said Fleming. His voice was suddenly a trifle chilly. He displayed the dignity of a man who is hurt that his word has been doubted but who preserves his self-control. He said reprovingly, "I was so disturbed that I counted them twice."

Mordecai Tremaine did not make any further comment. His thoughts were whirling chaotically. Thirteen carolers had left the house. But he himself had counted them earlier as they had been singing. And he had made their number *fourteen*.

Which meant that if both he and Fleming were right, that one of them had remained behind.

15

At first, Nicholas Blaise had been reluctant to accompany him, but Mordecai Tremaine would not accept a refusal.

"I need your help, Nick," he had said. "You know the people in the village. You'll be able to pick out any strangers. And it's the strangers I'm anxious to look over."

Blaise had stood hesitantly, a look of doubt in his dark face, and Tremaine had gone on. "I'm sure Benedict can spare you for an hour or two, Nick. Besides," he added shrewdly, "you may be doing him a service. We may discover something that will enable the police to turn their attention in a different direction."

The last remark had carried the day. Blaise had seemed relieved and had said, "All right, Mordecai. I'll just have a word with Benedict before we leave."

And now, twenty minutes later, as they walked briskly over the hard-packed snow toward the village, Nicholas Blaise seemed considerably more interested in the expedition. "You look as though you're on the track of something, Mordecai."

Mordecai Tremaine smiled. "Did you know you have a superstitious butler?"

Nicholas Blaise was taken aback. "You don't mean Fleming?" he said.

"I mean Fleming," agreed Tremaine.

It amused him to see the bewilderment struggling on his companion's face with the desire to display no more than a natural interest. He said, "When the carolers left last night, he counted thirteen of them. He told me that he thought it was a bad omen."

"Oh." Blaise's tone was flat with disappointment. "Is that all?"

"No," said Mordecai Tremaine. "Because *I* counted them, too. When they were in the house. And *I* counted fourteen."

This time Nicholas Blaise was quite evidently interested. He stopped abruptly in the roadway. He said: "You mean— *one of them stayed behind?*"

Mordecai Tremaine nodded. "Yes, Nick. One of them stayed behind. What I'm anxious to find out is which one and why."

"So there was someone there all the time," said Blaise slowly. He seemed to be speaking more to himself than to his companion. There was a high, strained note in his voice. He caught at Tremaine's arm. "Mordecai, you see what that means! It *wasn't* anyone in the house. So it couldn't have been—"

He broke off hastily, but Mordecai Tremaine finished the sentence for him. "Benedict," he said. And shook his head. "Maybe it isn't quite as simple as that, Nick."

"But it *must* be," said Blaise. "It's the only explanation that fits. Don't you see what must have happened? Rainer knew someone in the village. That someone managed to get into the house when the carol singers came. He stayed behind when the others left and waited in hiding until the time he met Rainer. Probably they'd met earlier and fixed up a rendezvous. There was a quarrel, and in the course of it, Rainer was killed. The murderer was scared at what he'd done and dashed out of the house and across the lawn."

Excitement crept into his face. "Yes…that's it! That explains the footprints! There were *three* trails…Wynton's, Rainer's, and the killer's. Two of them leading *toward* the house and the third—the murderer's—*away* from it!"

"It sounds as though you think our old friend the stranger from the past is involved," said Mordecai Tremaine. "And I thought," he added with a shrewd glance at his companion, "that you didn't believe in *that* theory."

"I didn't," admitted Blaise. "But that was before the murder. Besides, what you've just told me puts a different complexion on the whole thing. Find whoever it was who didn't leave the house when the rector and the others went, and you've found your murderer. *You* think so, too, Mordecai.

That's why you're so anxious to get down to the village. Isn't that the truth?"

"It will be interesting," said Mordecai Tremaine evasively, "to find out whether the person who stayed behind *did* know Rainer. If we can get as far as that, we'll have a good jumping-off place for further investigations. We can't assume too much all at once, Nick."

His companion gave a wry smile. "No, I suppose not," he remarked. "I'm too anxious to find a solution that won't involve anybody in the house."

They walked on down the road, Mordecai Tremaine swinging his arms vigorously and reveling in the frost-laden air. "What do you know about Professor Lorring, Nick?"

Blaise shrugged. "Not a great deal. It's the first time I've met him. I believe Benedict ran across him somewhere and asked him down. It's the sort of thing he does."

"He seems a queer choice for Mr. Grame to have made. He doesn't fit into the picture somehow. For instance, even before the murder upset the whole atmosphere, he didn't make much effort to acquire the Christmas spirit."

"If," said Nicholas Blaise, "you mean you think he was behaving like a miserable old curmudgeon without a drop of warm blood in him, I'm ready to agree with you. Maybe Benedict asked him here in the hope that he'd soften him up before Christmas was over. You know what a great schoolboy he can be."

"Do you think he and Jeremy Rainer knew each other?"

"If they did, they didn't give themselves away." Blaise looked curiously at his companion. "Have you anything against Lorring? I'll confess I don't like the fellow, but at the same time I must admit that I haven't noticed anything to make me suspect him."

"I'm only guessing," said Tremaine, "but I think it was Lorring who took the last present from the tree. I'd like to know why."

"*If* he took it," said Blaise, "he might have done so on the spur of the moment. These scientific fellows do some queer things, and there's just a chance that he was doing a bit of investigating on his own account. He may have intended to put it back later, but there were so many people around that the thing became too dangerous and he couldn't manage it."

"So you don't think there's any special significance attached to it?"

"I can't honestly say I do," returned Blaise.

"But what about the other presents? Why should *they* have disappeared?"

Blaise pursed his lips. "The true explanation may be the simplest one after all. Just plain robbery."

"Do you think that's feasible?"

"Why not? If this fellow was really up against it, he'd have been inclined to take whatever he could lay hands on. He may have thought that in such a big house, the presents on the tree were sure to be valuable enough to make it worth stealing them."

"It's possible, Nick. But it doesn't cover two points. It doesn't explain what Rainer was doing dressed as Father Christmas, and it doesn't explain how his gun came to be in his room."

"That's because we don't know the identity of X, the unknown intruder," said Blaise. "Once we've discovered that, the rest may follow."

"Including the explanation of what happened to the necklace?" said Mordecai Tremaine, and Nicholas Blaise was sobered.

"That's a part of the story I don't like," he said quietly. "I'm afraid, Mordecai, that it looks as though someone in the house *was* responsible for that. I've been trying not to think so ever since Benedict told me that the necklace was missing, but it's obvious that the person who stole it knew exactly where to find it and was able to get into Benedict's room at a time when he wasn't here."

"You suspect someone, Nick," said Mordecai Tremaine. "Who is it?"

But Nicholas Blaise shook his head. "I'm sorry, Mordecai. I can't mention names."

He was clearly ill at ease, and Tremaine did not press him.

He thought that he had, in any case, a shrewd idea of what was in his companion's mind.

They turned a corner of the winding road and came within sight of the village. It lay tranquilly before their eyes, with only the thin wreaths of smoke from the cottage chimneys revealing that it was inhabited. With the snow banked up against the hills behind it and lying thick upon the surrounding fields and along the outstretched limbs of the leafless trees fringing the hedgerows, it provided a study in black and white that recalled to Mordecai Tremaine that first impression, gained when he had driven through the straggling main street in the gloom of a failing day, that it was not a place where mortals dwelt. It belonged to the regions of elves, and gnomes, and fantasy.

And fantasy…

The thought crept across his mind like a whisper of warning. If fantasy lay before him, what greater fantasy had he not left behind! What more incredible scene was he likely to find than that which had confronted him when he had found that red-robed Father Christmas sprawled in dreadful irony beneath a decorated Christmas tree that had been despoiled of its gifts!

Nicholas Blaise was studying him thoughtfully. He said, after a moment or two, "It's a picturesque little place…especially now, with all this snow about. It's queer to think that at this very moment, it may be giving shelter to a murderer."

"Strange indeed, Nick," said Mordecai Tremaine slowly.

There was a sense of oppression in his soul. All the deep love of sentiment that was a part of him was stirring in helpless revolt. It was all wrong that greed and hatred, fear and violence should find their way into the lovely places of the earth. It was all wrong that the cold winter beauty upon which he was gazing should be marred by man's inability to live in charity with his neighbors and that murder should lie like an evil smudge across perfection.

He liked to feel that the sun shone always upon lovers. He liked to feel that God was in His Heaven and that all was right with a world in which there was no false note. Perhaps it was a sign of weakness in him. Perhaps it was a shrinking from reality, a refusal to face the bitter truths of existence. But it was an integral part of him, and he could not change it.

They walked on over snow that received them silently, and as they came near the village church, the rector came out of the gate set in the gray stone wall bordering the roadway. He recognized Nicholas Blaise and nodded a greeting.

"Good morning," he said. He hesitated, and then, a little awkwardly, he added, "I've heard the terrible news. I would have come up to the house to see whether there was anything I could do, but it might have seemed like interference on my part and I didn't wish to intrude."

"It was very good of you to have thought of us," said Blaise.

"But the police have taken charge now, of course. There's not much any of us can do."

"Ah, yes," said the rector. "The police. Naturally they will be busy carrying out their investigations." He shook his head sadly. "Poor Mr. Rainer! It was a dreadful thing to have happened. And at such a season when we should all be thinking of peace on earth and goodwill to men. It makes it seem doubly tragic."

"I suppose you saw a great deal of Mr. Rainer?" said Mordecai Tremaine.

The rector shook his head. "I knew him by sight, of course, but I'm afraid we seldom saw him in our congregation here." For an instant or two, the man revealed himself behind the garb of the priest. He said, "Have the police any theories as to who might have been responsible?"

"If they have, they haven't made them public," said Nicholas Blaise.

Mordecai Tremaine said, "We enjoyed the carolers. Their voices were excellently balanced."

The rector did not seem disconcerted by the sudden change of subject. He appeared, in fact, rather relieved, as though he regretted having put his question to Blaise and was anxious to seize any opportunity of distracting attention from it. "I'm so glad," he said. "I'm sure everyone appreciated being able to sing to you. It was the highlight of the evening, you know."

"Were they all local people?"

It might easily have been imagination that he detected a slight hesitation in the rector's manner. "They're all known to me, of course," he returned, and Mordecai Tremaine said quietly: "But were they all *local* people?"

"They all live in the village or the near neighborhood," said the rector. "Except Desmond Latimer. And I suppose you might describe him as being one of us, although I believe his home is somewhere in the Midlands."

The deceptively casual look that concealed an ulterior motive was on Mordecai Tremaine's face. "Latimer?" he said. "Is he rather tall, well-built, and on the dark side?"

"The description certainly could fit him," said the rector. Most of his attention had so far been given to Nicholas Blaise, but now he studied the mild-looking man with the pince-nez who was Blaise's companion with a keener interest. "Do you know him?"

"We haven't been introduced," said Tremaine. "I saw him among the carol singers, and I noticed him particularly because I happened to see him just outside the house on my arrival. As a matter of fact, I was rather afraid of missing my way as darkness was closing in and I asked him if he could direct me."

He waited. The rector's kindly face was thoughtful and a little perplexed. Tremaine saw that he was wavering, and said, "I must confess that he rather intrigued me. He has a striking-looking head. He looks like the kind of man who has a story to tell."

The rector said uncomfortably, "He's staying in the village. You may meet him."

"I'd very much like to," Tremaine said with his most innocent air. And he added in the same casual tone, "I suppose all your—er—flock left the house with you the other night, rector?"

The rector's surprise at the question was genuine enough. At first, indeed, he did not understand what Tremaine meant. "Oh—after the carols? Is that when you mean? Yes. Of course. We all came away together."

"There's no doubt of that? There's no chance of your being mistaken? After all, it was quite a big party. Fourteen people, you know. I imagine that it would have been quite easy for someone to be missing and for it not to be noticed. Especially in the dark."

"Was it fourteen? I'm really not sure. Yes, I suppose it would have been possible for someone to slip away. We were in several small parties—" The rector broke off suddenly, a look of concern in his face. It was obvious that he had become aware of the significance of what he was saying. "You don't mean that someone *was* missing?"

"I just wondered," said Tremaine evasively, "whether you

could be certain that all the members of your party were with you the whole time. Just supposing you were asked that very question, for instance. You couldn't definitely state that everybody left the house with you?"

The rector shook his head. "No," he said. "No, I'm afraid I couldn't." He was looking like a very worried man now. And he was clearly unwilling to be drawn any further into conversation. He said, "I'm sorry I can't spend longer with you, gentlemen. The call of duty, you know. Will you excuse me?"

"Of course," said Mordecai Tremaine. "Forgive me for detaining you with so many trivial questions. I'm afraid I'm rather an inquisitive sort of person!"

They watched the rector's benign form go hurrying up the path and disappear from sight as he entered the stone porch of the church. After a moment or two they walked on toward the village. Nicholas Blaise said, "You rattled the old boy, Mordecai. There's something on his mind. Something about that chap Latimer."

"I think there is, Nick," said Mordecai Tremaine. "When I asked him whether he would have noticed if anyone had stayed behind, it was plain enough that he hadn't given it a thought until that moment. But it was also plain that as soon as the thought *was* in his mind, it was Latimer he suspected at once. Which means that he knows of a reason why that particular member of the carol party might have wanted to stay in the house."

"I feel inclined to go back and put the question to him point-blank," said Blaise. "But I suppose it's no use doing that."

"Don't worry, Nick," said Mordecai Tremaine. "The rector isn't likely to hold back vital evidence. He won't betray confidences by talking to *us*, but he'll talk to the police frankly enough when the time comes."

There were more signs of life in the village now. An excited group of small boys and girls went whooping past pulling toboggans, and Mordecai Tremaine gazed after them enviously. Two men who were obviously not natives of the place came out of the yard adjoining an inn halfway along the main street. Their clothes bore the mark of the town, and they gave Tremaine and his companion appraising stares that inquired who they were and what their purpose was in Sherbroome.

A prickle of anticipation teased its way along Mordecai Tremaine's spine. Reporters, he surmised. The press had arrived.

So far, publicity had been absent. The murder, having taken place in the early hours of Christmas morning, had inconsiderately missed the last editions before Christmas. Both Christmas Day and Boxing Day were blank days in the newspaper world as far as publication was concerned. Only north of the border, where the Scotsmen waited for Hogmanay, could the world's news be found in print.

But tomorrow—ah, tomorrow! Then would the headlines leap in black sensation from the page. Then would the special correspondents be able to enthrall their readers with vivid accounts of the way in which death had come to Sherbroome and made a mockery of the Christmas scene.

Mordecai Tremaine's eyes were glistening. "Let's go in for a drink, Nick," he said. They were within a few yards of the inn door when he stopped, clutching his companion's arm. "Talk of the devil!" he said in a low voice.

A man was coming out of the inn. A tall, dark man whose bulk momentarily blocked the entrance. Recognition flickered in his eyes, and he seemed to hesitate. But it was only for an instant or two. Before Mordecai Tremaine could address him, he had stepped quickly past them and was striding up the street.

"Not," said Nicholas Blaise, "in a chatty mood. I can't say I'm surprised."

Mordecai Tremaine's hand strayed to the pince-nez. He settled them more firmly on his nose. "If I were in *his* shoes," he observed, "I don't think *I'd* be very eager to talk."

They went into the inn. The low-ceilinged bar was vibrating to the hum of conversation from many voices. Tobacco smoke wavered in a blue curtain. There was a pleasant smell of Christmas cigars.

Mordecai Tremaine threaded his way to the counter and ordered their drinks. Tankard in hand, he studied his neighbors. The majority of them were locals. He heard the mellow burr of the county and saw hands calloused by long years of work in the fields. At one end of the bar, a darts match was in progress. He heard a mock groan and a laugh from the spectators and saw that someone had thrown awry. The dart was a good two inches off the board.

Through the drifting haze, he saw the man who had thrown. He was taking aim again. This time the dart went hard and straight to double top.

The other's face was in profile. It was outlined against the light that came through the leaded panes of the bay window looking out upon the street. It was a face he had seen before—in a mirror when he had sat in a tea shop in Calnford.

Mordecai Tremaine's eyes were shadowed with thought. Had the other seen him when he had entered the bar with Nicholas Blaise? Was there any connection between that fact and that badly aimed dart?

He nudged his companion's arm. "D'you know him, Nick?"

Blaise nodded. His voice had acquired a wariness that had not been in evidence before. "Yes. His name's Brett. He's staying here."

"Stranger?"

"In a way. He doesn't live in the district."

"I've seen him before," said Mordecai Tremaine. "With Charlotte Grame. Does that surprise you?"

Blaise did not give him a direct reply. "Does Charlotte know you saw her?" he asked.

"Yes. Because she denied that she was there."

Tremaine was not looking at his companion. He was still studying the man who stood in the little group around the dartboard. So far, Brett had given no sign of being aware he was under observation.

He was not quite as tall as Tremaine had imagined him to be, so his gauntness did not now seem as noticeable as it had been under the hard light of the tea shop. But there was about him still that air of intense, nervous vitality. The eyes beneath the high forehead still burned with that visionary fire. The face was still characterized by the lean and hungry expression that had brought the Shakespearean quotation into Tremaine's mind.

Certainly Brett did not have the appearance of a man who would be easily scared. Could that badly thrown dart have been merely coincidence after all?

Mordecai Tremaine pondered the matter carefully and found that the theory of coincidence was not one he could accept. If Brett had not actually observed his entrance with Blaise, he had undoubtedly noticed him at some subsequent moment and the discovery had shaken his self-control.

But why should Brett have been unnerved by the sight of a man whom he had seen only once before, and that under circumstances when it was reasonable to suppose that he would not even remember the encounter?

To that, there could be only one answer. At some time during the intervening period, Brett had learned something. Something that caused him to regard Mordecai Tremaine as a man to be feared.

The pattern was taking shape. Charlotte Grame had left the house on a hurried and mysterious errand on the previous afternoon, and Charlotte Grame was the only other person, with the possible exception of Lucia Tristam, who knew of that tea-shop encounter. She had seen Brett. She had told him that Mordecai Tremaine had seen them together in Calnford. And she had told him that Tremaine was working with the police officer who was investigating the murder of Jeremy Rainer.

Her sole reason for going out in the gloom of that bitter day had been to find Brett and to warn him. Which meant, Mordecai Tremaine told himself, that she must have considered she had good cause to do so.

His eyes had become more accustomed to the haze, and he was able to discern Brett's gaunt features more clearly. He saw the hard line of the jutting chin. He saw the dark bruise and the long, uneven scratch that marked it.

He caught his breath suddenly as he realized its significance. It was as though a picture that had been dark and obscure had become animated all in an instant so that every detail of it was clear.

Carefully he traced its outlines. If he could impress them upon his mind now while the image was still sharp, he would never again have to grope his way blindly, trying to evolve truth out of the murky shadows.

Across the bar, he caught sight of a face. It was an alert, shrewdly thoughtful face. It was vaguely familiar. It caused him to search in the depths of his mind for the reason for the sensation that he had seen it before.

Memory brought the clue. Reporter. The face turned speculatively toward his own belonged to a newspaperman who believed that he knew Mordecai Tremaine and was trying to recall his identity.

Tremaine set his empty glass on the bar counter. He turned to Nicholas Blaise. "Shall we go, Nick?"

He was relieved when they stood outside the door of the inn and no one had spoken to them. It had not occurred to him that the presence of so many reporters in the village might constitute a personal danger, but he was on his guard now. If one of them connected him with the Mordecai Tremaine who had achieved such a blaze of publicity over another murder case not so long ago, his relationship with Superintendent Cannock would be jeopardized. For while the superintendent might be willing to admit him to an unofficial confidence, it was highly probable that he would shrink from being linked with him in the newspapers. He was, after all, answerable to his superiors, and those superiors would undoubtedly take a poor view of amateurs being allowed to play a part in what should be purely police business.

Nicholas Blaise was in a silent mood on the way back to the house, and Tremaine, busy with his own thoughts, did not try to draw him into conversation. They were within sight of the lodge gates when Blaise said hesitantly, "I don't want you to think that I'm holding out on you, Mordecai. Especially after having been responsible for bringing you here. But there are some things that…well, that I don't feel justified in talking about."

Mordecai Tremaine looked quizzically at him over the pince-nez. "Meaning our friend Mr. Brett?"

"Yes," admitted Blaise. "Meaning Brett."

His companion gave him a slow smile. There was warmth and understanding in it, but Blaise was too preoccupied to notice it. "Maybe I know the reason, Nick."

They were passing the old lodge now. Blaise gave a glance toward it. Tremaine said, "I wonder what took Jeremy Rainer there so late at night."

Blaise swung back to him. "*Did* he go there?" he queried sharply.

"Yes. It must have been just before he was killed. Any

ideas, Nick? Why do you suppose he went trudging through the snow to the lodge after everybody else had gone to bed?"

"I imagine that whatever his motive was," Blaise said slowly, "it must have been a pretty strong one. What do the police think? I presume they know all about it."

"They know he went to the lodge," Tremaine replied. "But they don't know *why* he went. At least, they didn't the last time I saw the superintendent. You don't suppose," he added, "that Benedict could tell us?"

Nicholas Blaise did not reply for a moment or two. And then he said, "Benedict seems to be in your thoughts a great deal, Mordecai. You know the way I feel about that."

"It does you credit, Nick, but it doesn't answer the question. If Jeremy Rainer went to the lodge, it's obvious that there can be only two explanations. Either he went there of his own accord, or someone told him to go. If he went for his own reasons, we've a wide field to cover, but if he went because someone else wanted him to, then the only person, so far as we know, who was close enough to him to have had that much influence is Benedict Grame."

"But why on earth should *Benedict* want him to go to the lodge? The place is never used, and in any case, why choose such a time?"

"I thought," said Mordecai Tremaine, "*you* might be able to suggest a reason."

Nicholas Blaise's face was grave and intent. "Listen, Mordecai," he said earnestly. "If you suspect Benedict, you're making a terrible mistake. I *know* he isn't guilty. I don't doubt that they had their differences at times, but he and Jeremy were too close, too much a part of each other's lives."

"Can you *prove* he isn't guilty, Nick?" persisted Mordecai Tremaine. "Can you prove, for instance, that he didn't leave his room again when he went upstairs after decorating the tree?"

Blaise hesitated. "Well, no," he admitted. "I can't *prove* he didn't. But I know Benedict, and I know that he couldn't have killed Jeremy!"

His sincerity revealed itself in a note that was desperately anxious. Mordecai Tremaine said quietly, "All right, Nick. There isn't a case against him yet. And I promise you I'll let you know if anything else comes to light."

Lunch was the usual macabre affair that meals had become. There were moments when everyone tried to be gay at once, punctuated by long intervals of silence. The ghost of Jeremy Rainer sat behind every chair.

Except two. Glancing around the table, Mordecai Tremaine reflected that he and Benedict Grame were the only people who seemed free of the dead man's influence. Grame was talking animatedly, trying to include them all in his gestures and working with all the intensity of the captain of a side spending his last energies in an effort to keep his flagging team together.

In the hours that had passed since the discovery of the murder, Grame had grown in stature. While the others had become steadily more subdued and anxious, he had been developing confidence. He gave Mordecai Tremaine the impression now that he was even enjoying the situation. And not merely enjoying but somehow controlling it.

He looked toward the head of the table and met the amused glance of the blue eyes. The bushy eyebrows lifted a trifle. Grame might have been inviting him to share a joke that he knew only the two of them could appreciate.

Gerald Beechley was not present. His vacant chair was a question mark that invited comment and yet did not receive it. There might have been a tacit understanding among them not to mention the big man's absence.

Only Mordecai Tremaine, untroubled by scruples in such a matter, presumed to probe openly. "I wonder what's happened to Mr. Beechley," he said to Rosalind Marsh, who was once again his neighbor.

She gave him a glance in which there was a faint hint of surprise. "I thought," she said coolly, "you would have known. Gerald's been hitting the bottle again."

"Again?"

"It isn't an entirely new phenomenon," she told him.

It was evident that she believed him to be feigning ignorance in order to draw her out. Mordecai Tremaine considered for a moment or two whether he should press the subject, then decided against it.

His brief exchange with Rosalind Marsh had already attracted attention. He did not think that their actual words had been overheard, but both Delamere and Lorring were looking in their direction, and the predominant expression on each of their faces was suspicion.

The situation had reached the point where each member of the party was furtively watching the others, anxious to miss nothing that might have a bearing on the tragedy that overshadowed them. And above all, Mordecai Tremaine knew, they were watching him. Every action he performed, every word he spoke was being analyzed to see whether it would give an indication of his thoughts, and whether it would reveal the direction in which the suspicions of the police were trending.

It was, he thought, not so much like sitting on the proverbial barrel of gunpowder as being the fuse to the barrel. It only needed someone to believe that he or she had struck a spark, and the whole thing would explode.

After lunch, Benedict Grame took charge of his guests. He was clearly determined to prevent any morose brooding in lonely rooms until suspicion and irritation produced the inevitable crisis. The afternoon was spent in games of the old-fashioned variety that required everyone to take part.

Even Lorring allowed himself to be blindfolded with no more than a brief, halfhearted snort of protest.

The main brunt of the program fell upon Nicholas Blaise. Time after time, Grame called him to his aid, and time after time, Blaise submitted himself to be the butt of some new piece of entertainment. He bore it all with a smile, although it was clear that he must have been feeling the strain. There was a kind of dogged devotion about him that Mordecai Tremaine found almost pathetic.

So close a watch did Grame keep upon the party that it was difficult to slip away. When at last even his host's energies began to slacken, Tremaine managed to efface himself unnoticed, and he experienced a sense of relief when he was outside the door. The atmosphere was unhealthily near hysteria. The sight of a number of people whom he knew to be obsessed by dark fears all trying to behave as though they had nothing in their minds but a desire to outdo each other in gaiety of manner possessed a grotesque quality that verged upon the indecent.

The door of Gerald Beechley's room was locked. Tremaine rapped upon it in the peremptory manner of a person who did not intend to be refused admittance, and in a few moments there were fumbling movements inside the room and the door was opened.

Beechley, unnaturally flushed, stood swaying on the threshold, peering at him.

Mordecai Tremaine said, "I want to talk to you." There was an unaccustomed edge to his voice. It penetrated even Beechley's alcohol-sodden mind. He made no protest as Mordecai Tremaine stepped past him. He shut the door again and huddled himself into an armchair pulled in front of the fire blazing in the wide grate.

Tremaine looked at it. He said: "Have you been burning any evidence today?"

An expression of fear sharpened Gerald Beechley's features. "What do you mean?" Although he had undoubtedly been drinking heavily, he was still in possession of his senses. His eyes were red-rimmed buttons of defensive cunning.

"I mean that Superintendent Cannock is well aware that you burned a Father Christmas outfit in here yesterday. You didn't make a very successful job of it. There was enough of it left for the police experts to find out what it was."

Beechley half rose from his chair. "You interfering little snake," he said thickly. "Let me get my hands on you…"

Mordecai Tremaine tried not to betray his alarm. He faced the big man, apparently unmoved by his threatening manner. "Violence won't do you any good," he said quietly. "But frankness might."

Something in his voice sobered Beechley. The malevolence drained out of him. He relapsed into the armchair and sat there hunched. "What are you getting at?" he said shakily.

"You bought a Father Christmas outfit in Calnford," said Mordecai Tremaine. "An outfit you later burned because you were afraid it might be found in your possession. You were wearing it on the night Jeremy Rainer died."

"You've been spying on me," said Beechley. His voice contained an odd mixture of savagery and petulance. "Ever since you came here, you've been watching and prying. But you've got to have proof to make a case against anyone, and you can't prove anything against *me*."

"Perhaps," said Mordecai Tremaine, "I can. Suppose someone informed the police that you bought that outfit. Things wouldn't look too good for you."

"Maybe not," said Beechley, something approaching a sneer in his tone. "But they didn't."

"But," said Mordecai Tremaine, "they did. It was Benedict Grame."

Mentally he justified the statement as he made it. Even if Grame had not spoken directly to the police, he had been well aware when he had been talking on the terrace that he was doing the next best thing, and that his words would reach the ears of Superintendent Cannock.

The effect on Gerald Beechley was greater than he had expected. The big man's breath came hissingly. He huddled back in the chair as though he had been dealt a physical blow. "Benedict?" he said. "*He* told them?"

Mordecai Tremaine nodded. "It was Mr. Grame," he said.

Beechley seemed to be struggling to adjust his thoughts to meet a new and unpleasant situation for which he had not been prepared. He passed his tongue over his lips. Watching him intently, Mordecai Tremaine saw his expression lose its mixture of fear and dismay and harden into vindictiveness.

At last, the other leaned forward. His eyes had a glitter in them. He reached out to clutch Mordecai Tremaine's sleeve. He said hoarsely, "Here's something else for the police to know since they're so anxious to find out things. *Where was Benedict when Jeremy was killed?*"

Tremaine carefully held back the excitement from his voice. "In his room, one presumes."

"That's just it," said Beechley. There was a savage bitterness in the words. "He *wasn't*. His room was empty."

"How," said Mordecai Tremaine, "do *you* know that?"

This time, despite his care, he could not keep his tone level, and Beechley seemed abruptly to realize where his emotions were leading him. He sat back again in the chair, and it was as if he were retreating into a shell. A shell from which his eyes peered suspiciously.

"I was joking," he said shortly. "I'm not myself. I didn't know what I was saying."

There was a look on his puffy face that warned Mordecai Tremaine that he had reached the flash point. Beechley was a badly frightened man. So frightened that he would become ugly if he decided to tell himself that he had been irretrievably cornered. And looking at the big frame and the powerful hands, Tremaine knew that the time had come to make his exit. "Very well," he said. "Any time you feel you'd like to change your mind, let me know."

Beechley did not try to stop him from leaving, and when he was outside the room once more, he metaphorically wiped his brow. That interview had been a little too much like a visit to the tiger's cage.

But it had undoubtedly been fruitful. If Gerald Beechley knew that Benedict Grame's room had been empty on the night of the murder, he could only have gained his knowledge because he himself had been there. Which promptly connected him with the missing necklace.

No doubt it had been the realization that he was betraying his own guilt that had caused him to change his attitude. In his vindictive desire to accuse Benedict Grame, he had momentarily overlooked the fact that he was incriminating himself. For it was obvious that if he had gone to Grame's room at such a time, it had not been with any intention of paying a social visit. Taken in conjunction with his known financial difficulties and the strangeness of his manner when he had asked whether there was anything missing, it provided a damning indictment.

But it was not the fate of the necklace with which Mordecai Tremaine was concerned. Benedict Grame, who had taken such an unreasonable time to be aroused and who had apparently been the last person to hear the disturbance taking place immediately beneath him, had been missing from his room at some time on the night of the murder.

That was the damaging fact that Gerald Beechley had thrust into prominence. Grame's alibi, unsupported though it might have been, had at least possessed the merit of being as valid as that of any of the others. Now it was indeed a sorry thing of shreds and patches.

16

The newspapers had seized upon their opportunity with an enthusiasm that seemed to have been intensified by their two days' inability to burst into print. The setting and circumstances of the murder were bizarre enough to have entitled it to a prominent display in any event, and as it happened, it reaped the benefit of a post-Christmas dearth of news. The bitter irony of the red-robed Father Christmas lying dead beneath a decorated Christmas tree, the missing presents, and the snow-covered countryside providing such a seasonable background to the crime had all fired the editorial imaginations. And a liberal allowance of space had permitted said imaginations to indulge in passages of the purest purple.

Mordecai Tremaine spent the morning searching for and reading copies of each newspaper. He was relieved to find that his own name did not appear. None of the reporters, apparently, had yet discovered his identity and turned the spotlight on him.

So far, in fact, and stripped of the colorful trimmings,

no report contained more in the way of basic facts than
that the dead man had been found in the early hours of the
morning lying beneath a Christmas tree from which the
gifts placed there by the host of the party had mysteriously
vanished. Tremaine sensed the hand of Superintendent
Cannock. That gentleman had presented the press with
the bare bones of the murder and had discouraged more
detailed inquiries. He had not been anxious for too much
information to find its way into print before his investigation could get fairly started.

It was unlikely, of course, that such a state of things would
last much longer. These were the first editions, and the
reporters had been told enough to enable them to give the
story a good send-off. It had not, therefore, mattered a great
deal that Superintendent Cannock had kept them away from
Sherbroome House and that since the majority of the guests
had stayed indoors, there had been little opportunity to add
to the official details.

But now London would be demanding follow-up accounts.
Which meant that the reporters on the spot would be a great
deal more persistent. Each of the occupants of the house
would have to face a polite but determined questioning.

At present, Austin Delamere was receiving the most
attention. As he was a public figure, it was, of course, to be
expected. The newspapers had their files concerning him

ready to hand, and they had briefly outlined his career for the benefit of their readers.

Delamere clearly did not relish it. His plump face was clouded with sullen anger. He was avidly reading as many accounts as he could, and yet each newspaper he obtained served merely to upset him further. He turned their pages with a kind of savage resentment, as if he wished he had the persons responsible for their publication at his mercy.

No accusations had been made against him. There was not a suggestion anywhere that he had had a hand in the death of Jeremy Rainer or that he knew why the other had died. But his name had been linked with murder, and it was plain that he was fearful of its effect upon his career.

To Mordecai Tremaine, that was not without significance. It meant that Delamere knew that his reputation was not above reproach. It meant that he dared not risk a hint of scandal now, lest it revived old suspicions and placed him in a position where resignation would be the only course.

"I see," he remarked to Delamere, deliberately drawing him, "that it didn't take the newspapers long to make a talking point out of *your* being here. It's one of the penalties for being in the public eye, I suppose."

The politician rustled the newspaper he was holding aggressively. "Damn lot of prying ghouls," he grunted. "Why can't they leave a man's private life alone!" He tried to speak angrily, but there was a quaver in his voice that betrayed him. Mordecai Tremaine knew that Austin Delamere wasn't indignant. He was frightened.

He left the plump man still torturing himself and, wrapping himself warmly, went out to the terrace. Lucia Tristam was already there. He had, in fact, seen her from the window, and her presence had led to his own decision to go out. Her fur coat pulled tightly around her, she was pacing to and fro in front of the french doors of the room in which Jeremy Rainer had died.

Mordecai Tremaine said: "Would you like a stroll as far as the village before lunch?"

There was a momentary hesitation before she replied. It might have been because she had only become aware of him when he had spoken to her. "No, thank you," she said. "It's too cold to go far."

"I think you're wise," said Mordecai Tremaine meaningfully. "After all, there are sure to be dozens of inquisitive newspaper reporters about."

The green tints flashed in her eyes. It might have been either anger or fear that was alive in them. Her lips moved stiffly. "Is that important?"

"*Isn't* it?" said Mordecai Tremaine gently. He looked over the pince-nez. He said: "They're a very persistent race, you know. They ask all sorts of questions. They *might* ask questions you would find embarrassing."

She took a sudden, instinctive step toward him. Color had come into her face. She looked very lovely—and very dangerous. "I don't know where to place you," she said in a low, tense voice. "You don't *look* as though there's any warm blood in you. I didn't think I needed to worry about you at first. I thought you were just a harmless, talkative busybody. But now…" Her hand came down upon his sleeve. He felt the warm, generous life in her, even through the glove and the cloth. "Now I'm not so sure," she said. "How much do you really know?"

"I know," said Mordecai Tremaine, "that Jeremy Rainer was in love with you. And that Benedict Grame is in love with you."

She turned abruptly away from him to stare out across the lawn. Despite the partly concealing fur, he could discern the quick rise and fall of her breasts.

"Supposition," she said, "isn't proof."

"I don't suppose," said Mordecai Tremaine, "that anyone could prove now that Rainer loved you. But what about Benedict Grame?"

"*What* about Benedict?" she said quickly.

"You must be aware," he said, "that things are looking black for him at the moment."

"No," she told him, "I'm not aware of it." She turned to face him again, and there was an urgent note in her voice. "What are you trying to say? What has happened?"

Mordecai Tremaine pushed back his pince-nez. "Benedict

Grame," he observed levelly, "was out of his room at the time of the murder. Jeremy Rainer was in love with you. And Jeremy Rainer is now dead. You realize the construction the police will place on those simple facts?"

There was no doubt that he had shaken her. The bright flush of color came and went in her face. "It isn't true," she said. "It isn't true! Benedict didn't kill Jeremy! I *know* he didn't. He *couldn't* have killed him. Because—" She broke off. Fear was in naked command of her eyes.

"Because?" prompted Mordecai Tremaine.

But she would not respond. He did not think, in fact, that she had even heard him. She gave a little choking sound and brushed hastily past him.

A moment or two later Mordecai Tremaine heard a dry, deliberate cough. He turned. Ernest Lorring had come out on to the terrace and was regarding him sardonically. "You appear to have a gift for upsetting people," Lorring said.

"Only," said Mordecai Tremaine, "those people who have cause to be upset."

The wiry eyebrows bristled. Lorring stalked past with a snort. Tremaine said quietly, "I presume you're no longer so interested in the Christmas tree."

The other spun round, his heel scrunching upon the snow. His gaunt face was black with anger. "Be careful, Tremaine," he snarled. "I'm warning you! Don't try me too far!"

For a moment or two he stood motionless, his expression menacing. Tremaine was glad that their encounter was taking place on the terrace, and that it was unlikely that Lorring would risk a display of physical violence in public. For he knew that the other's mood was ugly enough to have impelled him to strike out viciously if they had been unobserved.

Slowly, Lorring regained control of his temper. He turned away at last. Mordecai Tremaine allowed him a moment or two to leave the terrace and then pushed open the french doors and went into the house himself.

He found himself facing Benedict Grame, and behind his host were Denys Arden and Roger Wynton. It was clear from their faces that they had witnessed that brief scene. Grame cleared his throat self-consciously. "I'm sorry, Tremaine," he said awkwardly. "I'm afraid Lorring's a little difficult sometimes. He isn't an easy man to understand. But he doesn't mean all he says, you know."

Tremaine looked at the other reflectively. Benedict Grame seemed anxious to give his guest a good character. He wondered whether Grame had observed his conversation with Lucia Tristam, and whether there was any connection. He did not doubt that Grame really was in love with her.

His gaze went slowly around the room. It was very much as it had been when Jeremy Rainer had been lying dead and the tragedy had been raw in its impact. Although the police had finished their investigation, there had been an understandable reluctance on the part of the members of the household to make use of it. Even the servants had so far made no attempt to touch it.

Tremaine's eyes came to rest on the Christmas tree. A thought came into his mind, and he said to Benedict Grame, "Isn't there something a little odd about that bracket? I mean the one with Mr. Rainer's name on it. I wonder if you'd mind getting it down for me."

Grame gave him a puzzled stare, but he made no objection. He glanced at the tree, hesitated a moment or two, and then fetched the pair of wooden steps still standing against the wall. Roger Wynton and the girl watched him curiously as he climbed up and removed the bracket from the tree.

It took him only a moment or two. He descended the steps and handed it to Mordecai Tremaine. That gentleman turned it over, studying it intently. His eyes were bright with excitement.

"Well," said Grame, "what does it tell you?"

Mordecai Tremaine put the bracket carefully into his pocket. "A great deal," he said softly. "A very great deal."

It seemed that Benedict Grame was on the point of putting another question, and then gave a quick glance toward Denys Arden and Roger Wynton and changed his mind.

He said, "If you three people will excuse me, I've one or two things to discuss with Nick this morning. He insists on keeping me to the grindstone!"

When the door had closed behind him, Tremaine said to Roger Wynton, "Well, young man, so they haven't put the handcuffs on you yet?"

"Thanks to you," returned Wynton. "If it hadn't been for your intervention, I'm pretty sure the superintendent would have had me behind bars by now."

"I don't know how to repay you for what you've done," said Denys Arden. "I know he wouldn't have believed Roger's story if you hadn't spoken to him."

She was so prettily serious that Mordecai Tremaine was embarrassed. He felt as though he had been mistaken for a hero and presented with a medal for a deed he had not performed. He said hastily, "Did you know that your guardian didn't really object to you marrying Mr. Wynton?"

Denys Arden stared at him. "But he *did* object," she told him. "That was what we couldn't understand."

"What," said Roger Wynton suddenly, "made you say that?"

"Never mind why for the moment," said Mordecai Tremaine. "Are you quite sure that he disliked you so much?"

Wynton frowned. "No," he said. "I'm not. When I first knew Denys, we were on good terms. It was a complete surprise when he suddenly changed. And sometimes I've had an odd feeling that there was something behind it and that he was saying things he didn't really mean—almost as though he was playing a part. I thought that it was just my imagination and that it was just because I was trying to find a ray of hope. But now *you've* mentioned it, so perhaps it wasn't merely my imagination after all."

"Perhaps it wasn't," said Mordecai Tremaine.

His mind returned often to Denys Arden and Roger Wynton during the day. They were so obviously in love that it was a source of comfort to his sentimental soul.

It was a difficult day. The unspoken fear of the reporters they might meet was sufficient to confine them all uneasily to the house. It was clear that everyone was anxious to leave and equally clear that no one dared to go.

The inquest and the funeral still remained. To be missing from either of those necessary functions would be to invite unwelcome comment, and neither was due to take place before the morrow.

Mordecai Tremaine was relieved when the day was over and he was able to retire to the shelter of his room. Even his intense interest in all that took place had shown signs of wilting under the oppressive atmosphere and the dark suspicion that met him in nearly all their eyes. He was tired and a little sick at heart. His faith in humanity was burning dim.

He pushed open his window and gazed out over the snow-covered fields shining under a clear moon. He drew the cold air into his lungs and felt it caressing his forehead.

He knew his own symptoms. He was nearing the end of the road. So far, he had been sustained by the excitement of the chase. He had been savoring the keenness of matching his intellect with a fascinating problem that had been largely of the mind.

But now that problem had been reduced to a human equation. He had become more intimately aware of the actors in the drama, and instead of shadowy creatures whom he could study dispassionately and whose emotions he could analyze without feeling, they were beings of flesh and blood among whom he moved and talked. And above all, he now knew which one of them it was by whose hand Jeremy Rainer had died.

The murder had suddenly resolved itself into a sharply personal thing. Something that meant tragedy and horror and the judicial destruction of someone with whom he had lived for days that now seemed an eternity.

He shivered, and went over again in his mind all the things that had led him at last to this inescapable conclusion, testing them for flaws, searching for some little sign that would tell him that, after all, his theories were wrong.

But they were not wrong. He did not know the whole

story. There were some things it would be necessary for Superintendent Cannock to explain, things at which he could only guess. But the truth was there, terrible and incontestable.

He closed the window and climbed into bed. He started to read *Romantic Stories*, but it was a gesture that had no heart in it, and after a moment or two he put the magazine aside and lay staring into the darkness.

When he awoke, after a troubled, dream-filled sleep, it was to a household fearful with expectancy, fretting to learn what the inquest might have to tell and yet afraid of what the knowledge might bring. The frost had broken. The snow had begun to melt, and already a dreary sludge had broken the beauty the frozen whiteness had lent to the land. It was a cheerless morning, breathing depression and from which all hint of Christmas had gone.

Before he went down to the village, Tremaine slipped in for a last glance at the Christmas tree. He thought the gray morning light was unkind to it. The branches were sagging dejectedly, and its decorations hung limply, their sparkle dulled.

The funeral was not the ordeal that had been expected. The service was conducted in the village church, and Jeremy Rainer was laid to rest in the little churchyard adjoining it. There was nothing to show that there was anything different between this solemn occasion and the others the ancient gray building had seen.

The inquest was held in the village schoolroom in the early afternoon. Mordecai Tremaine gazed at the wooden desks, the blackboard, and the colored maps pinned along the wall, and tried to keep his mind centered on the pleasant scenes the room must have witnessed. But despite the innocence of its setting, the grimness of the task for which they had gathered was too pronounced to be dismissed into the background of one's thoughts.

The coroner was a brisk, efficient personage with military crispness, who evidently believed in leaving the conduct of affairs in the hands of the police and who did not intend to allow matters to drag on discursively. He handled the witnesses swiftly and expertly, kept them to the point, and in a very short time had established the fact that Jeremy Rainer had been murdered by some person or persons at present unknown.

Mordecai Tremaine was not called upon to give evidence. Benedict Grame, Denys Arden, and Nicholas Blaise were the only persons from the house who were required. The remainder of the witnesses were technical—the police surgeon and the superintendent among them, the superintendent briefly official and quite obviously in possession of more information than he was yet prepared to divulge, and the surgeon casually precise and firing a battery of medical terms.

During the cross-examinations, Tremaine studied the occupants of the schoolroom. Besides the party from the house and the reporters, a number of local people had managed to squeeze themselves into the building. At the back of the room, plainly very interested in what was taking place, he saw Desmond Latimer and the man Nicholas Blaise had called Brett.

Of the two, Latimer was undoubtedly the more ill at ease. His face wore a nervous, furtive look. He might have been expecting the hand of the constable who stood at the door to fall upon his shoulder in dread summons. When he realized that Tremaine's eyes were upon him, he glanced hastily away.

Brett, on the other hand, gave back a challenging stare. A wintry smile curled his mouth. Tremaine thought he could detect a hint of sardonic laughter in his lean face.

It was not an easy matter to contact Superintendent Cannock when the inquest was over. Too many people seemed to be intent upon surrounding him. He managed at last, however, to catch his eye, and the superintendent divined the urgency behind his manner. He made a meaningful gesture and Tremaine nodded understandingly. He picked his way slowly through the trampled slush and walked along the road in the direction of Calnford.

Only the Napiers seemed interested in his departure. They were standing together just outside the schoolhouse, a short distance apart from the others. Against the dreary background of gray stone, leaden skies, and melting snow, they seemed more drably unimportant than ever.

He saw Evelyn Napier clutch her husband's arm. He could not hear what she said, but he knew that their eyes were fixed upon him with dread expectancy. He did not allow them to see that he had noticed them, but the incident gave him further cause for reflection.

He turned a corner in the road that hid him from the village and waited by a convenient stile. Ten minutes later, Superintendent Cannock's car, snow and water flurrying from its wheels, stopped alongside. The superintendent opened the door. He said: "You look as though you've got the murderer in your pocket!"

"Perhaps," said Mordecai Tremaine gravely, "I have."

Cannock's jocular manner left him. He stepped from the car. His weather-beaten face had an eager look. "Well," he said. "Well. Who is it?"

"Not yet," said Mordecai Tremaine. "The proof isn't complete. There are things I must know first."

"What things?" said Cannock.

"For instance, why did Charlotte Grame go out? Was it to see a man called Brett who's staying in the village?"

The superintendent nodded. "Yes. She went straight to the inn and asked for him."

"Anything known against him?"

"Not so far. I'm having it followed up, of course."

"What about Beechley?"

Cannock pulled at his chin thoughtfully. "I'm not at all sure about Beechley," he said. "He realized that he was being followed and tried to throw my man off the scent. He's hiding something all right."

"Did he see anyone in the village?"

"No. But he put through a telephone call. Evidently he didn't want it to go from the house. I've had it traced. It was to the private address of a gentleman named Rubens. He's the senior partner in MacAnstey and Brenlow, a Calnford firm of Turf Commission agents."

"A bookmaker," said Mordecai Tremaine.

"A bookmaker," agreed the superintendent.

Tremaine digested the information he had been given. His eyes were speculative. He said at last, "What have you been able to find out about the people at the house? Lorring and the others."

The superintendent did not betray any impatience at the cross-examination. He said, "Lorring I'm still working on. It takes time to check everything. But I've been able to get details about some of them. Maybe you won't be surprised to hear that Delamere's been mixed up in one or two shady affairs. A bit more proof, and he wouldn't have been able to bluff his way out of the last one. It was about five or six years ago. A nasty business about the placing of government contracts. If a certain letter he wrote hadn't disappeared, he would have been finished. I don't doubt," added Cannock drily, "that *he* realized it too and took good care to see that the letter was destroyed."

"What about his financial position now?"

"Fairly sound. At least as far as I've been able to discover."

"Any connection between Delamere and Rainer—or with Grame?"

"Nothing suspicious. He seems to have known Grame for some years. Comes regularly to these Christmas house parties."

"Anything significant in Rainer's past?"

Cannock pursed his lips. "We-ell," he said slowly, "it's murky. I haven't been able to get at all of it yet. It's going to be a job to go back that far. I understand that Rainer was Miss Arden's guardian…paid for her education and so on. The odd thing is that it looks very much as though it was Rainer who ruined her father. Arden lost every penny in some clever gold-share swindle and went down with pneumonia shortly afterward.

"Denys Arden was only a child at the time. Rainer seems to have had an attack of conscience and made himself responsible for her upbringing. From what I've been able to find out so far," the superintendent added grimly, "I'd say he needed a few more twinges. He had to leave South Africa in a hurry with the police only a move or two behind him. It was an illicit diamond-buying affair. There might have been a murder charge on the end of it if they could have brought it home to him."

Mordecai Tremaine nodded approvingly. "You've moved fast, Superintendent."

"Crime doesn't stop for Christmas!" said Cannock. There was a sparkle in the depths of his brown eyes as he looked at his companion. "There's another item of news for you," he said. "It concerns our friends the Napiers."

"Ah," said Mordecai Tremaine softly, "the Napiers."

"Harold Napier hasn't always called himself Napier," the superintendent went on. "Once upon a time, his name was Newton. *Dr*. Newton. He was struck off for supplying drugs to his patients. He was lucky that was *all* that happened to him. There was an element of doubt, and he escaped a criminal charge. You wouldn't think so to look at him now, but he was quite the man about town. Always seen in the West End nightclubs. Spent money like water. He was certainly not the type to bury himself in the country. His nerve seems to have broken completely."

Mordecai Tremaine was displaying the satisfaction of a man who finds his theories vindicated. He beamed over the pince-nez.

"You've given me a good deal of information, Superintendent. Maybe now I can give some to you. Do you happen to know the name of the man from whom Benedict Grame bought Sherbroome House?"

"Not offhand. Melvin, I believe. Wasn't it the Melvin family who owned it?"

"Originally," agreed Tremaine. "But the estate passed to a distant branch when all the Melvins died out. Benedict Grame bought the house from a man named Latimer. Do you appreciate what that means, superintendent? A man named Latimer. There is a man named Latimer staying in the village at this moment. *And he was in the house on the night of the murder!*"

The superintendent was staring at him, gripped by the note of drama in his voice. "What have you found out?" he said sharply.

"I will tell you," said Mordecai Tremaine gravely. He spoke earnestly to his companion for almost half an hour, and when he had finished, Superintendent Cannock agreed without question to the request he made.

17

Ahead of him in the roadway, Mordecai Tremaine saw a woman's figure. He hurried forward through the slush, and as he drew level with her, he saw that it was Rosalind Marsh.

"At least that's one ordeal over," he remarked.

She turned to look at him. "*Is* it?" she said tonelessly.

He saw then that her face was drawn and tired. She had lost her cold, impassive beauty. She looked a great deal older. Shadowy ghosts were in her eyes. Tremaine said, "What was it *you* did?"

There was bitterness in her reply. "So it's come out at last, has it?"

"It was bound to," said Mordecai Tremaine. "Once the police had been called in, it was inevitable."

Rosalind Marsh laughed. It was a harsh sound that had despair in it. "What a fool I was," she said. "What a stupid, unthinking fool. I believed that you were in it, too. I even thought that you might help."

"Did you speak to Lorring?"

"No. He isn't the kind of man you can speak to."

"What about the others?"

"The others?" Her lip curled. "It was hopeless. It's been going on too long. They're all afraid."

"Even Delamere?"

"Delamere most of all. There was only Jeremy. Only Jeremy I could depend upon. And you know what happened to Jeremy."

"Yes," Mordecai Tremaine said quietly, "I know what happened to Jeremy."

They did not speak again during the remainder of the journey back to the house. When they reached it, Rosalind Marsh went up to her room and he did not attempt to detain her.

The inquest seemed to have broken the tension under which the house party had been living and had replaced it with feverish relief. Since no one had been directly accused, they had all acquired a brittle gaiety. The conversation was inclined to be unnaturally bright.

Behind the facade, Mordecai Tremaine reflected, there was one thought dominating their minds. The desire to get away. There was nothing to keep them now. They would make their excuses to their host and depart, nursing their secret fears, but hugging also the sense of security that distance would bring them.

As soon as he was able, he took Nicholas Blaise to one side. "Can you spare a few moments, Nick?"

"Of course." Blaise followed him as he led the way into the room where Jeremy Rainer had died and closed the door behind them. His dark face was curious. He said, "You're on to something?"

"Yes, Nick, I'm on to something," Mordecai Tremaine said. "There's an entrance to the secret hide in this room. Do you know how to operate it?"

Nicholas Blaise nodded. "Why, yes. It's simple enough when you know where to look."

"The other day," said Tremaine, "Denys Arden told me about the hide. We were going to explore it more fully, but when we got back to it, Benedict Grame and yourself were decorating the Christmas tree in here so we didn't do it after all. I take it that no one else would have been likely to have used it?"

"I shouldn't think so. It's only a curiosity now. It doesn't lead anywhere."

"Open it, Nick," Mordecai Tremaine said urgently.

Obediently, Blaise moved across to the wall. His hands searched familiarly over the panels. There was a click. Mordecai Tremaine took a flashlight from his pocket and flashed the beam into the darkness behind the wall.

"There," he said. "*There!*"

In the hide, the dust and cobwebs were thick. But just within the entrance, on the topmost step of a flight of stairs leading down below the house, it was patterned and disturbed.

There were no definite footprints, but it was clear enough that someone had been standing there, and very recently.

Nicholas Blaise gave an exclamation. "You're right, Mordecai! There *was* someone here!" His eyes had a sudden burning eagerness in them. "Who was it? Do you know *that*?"

Mordecai Tremaine nodded. "I think I do," he said. "But there's more yet, Nick."

Blaise closed the panel that formed the entrance to the hide. He followed his companion once more, and this time Tremaine led him to the long, gloomy corridor running along the top floor of the house where the storage rooms were situated. Portraits of forgotten generations of Melvins peered down at them from the walls. Mordecai Tremaine switched on the electric light. He stopped before the painting of a man in the dress of a cavalier. "Sir Rupert Melvin…about the middle of the sixteenth century. Notice anything, Nick?"

Nicholas Blaise said, puzzled, "No…what *should* I notice?"

For reply, Mordecai Tremaine reached up his hand. His palm covered the lower part of the face of the man in the painting, hiding his beard. "Do you see it *now*?" he asked.

A wrinkle of perplexity appeared on Nicholas Blaise's

forehead. "There's *something*," he said. "I've a queer feeling that I've seen him before."

"You have," said Mordecai Tremaine. "Here. On the night Jeremy Rainer was murdered."

Blaise stared at him, clearly unable to comprehend. Tremaine said, peering over the pince-nez: "It isn't quite as crazy as it sounds. When Benedict Grame bought this house, did he actually meet the previous owner?"

Blaise thought for a moment. "No," he said. "No, I don't think he did. The solicitors handled all the details."

"I imagined," said Tremaine, "that was probably what happened. All Grame or yourself knew was his name—Latimer."

He pushed open the door of the room opposite where they were standing. It was the room from which the unhappy Lady Isabel was reputed to have flung herself to her death long before even the time of the cavalier in the portrait. He went slowly to the window. Just outside was a low stone balustrade, and beyond he could see the ragged patchwork of fields stretching away from the house. They looked surprisingly far off. Here at the very top of the building there was an uninterrupted view for many miles.

"It must be a dreadful thing," he said, "to be faced as Latimer was faced with the necessity for selling the heritage that had been held by his family for centuries. He held out as long as he could. Even although he could not afford to live in the house, he refused to sell. He used to come here during the summer and camp on the grounds."

Blaise nodded. "That's true," he said. "I remember it now. Of course we never saw him. He didn't come after Benedict had bought it."

"How he must have hated it," said Tremaine. "At one time, all the land we can see from this window must have belonged to his ancestors, and now circumstances had forced him to relinquish even the house itself into alien hands. It must have made him bitter. It *did* make him bitter. I think he felt he was entitled to revenge himself on the people whom he considered had usurped his rights."

"You mean," said Nicholas Blaise, "that it was Latimer who was in the hide?"

"Yes. He came with the rector's carol party. The rector knows him, of course, and when Latimer heard that the carol singers intended to come up here on Christmas Eve, he asked if he could join them. No doubt the rector thought that it was a case of sentiment, and that he wanted to get inside the house again without drawing attention to himself, so he naturally agreed. He didn't dream that Latimer had any other reason or that he had stayed behind after the rest of the party had gone. That's why he was so obviously startled when we spoke to him the other morning.

"Latimer's real purpose wasn't so innocent. He probably

knew all about Benedict Grame's Christmas parties and came down here a few days ago with the deliberate intention of getting inside the house somehow and seeing what he could lay his hands on. The visit of the carol singers offered him the ideal opportunity, and once he was inside, the rest was easy. He merely had to slip away from the others and wait for a chance to get into the hide. He knew that he could stay there undetected for hours if necessary. It's obvious that whoever made use of the hide must have known all about it and how to operate it."

"What put you on to him?" said Blaise.

"At first it was mere chance. When I arrived here, Latimer was standing outside the gates. It was plain from his face that he wasn't just an ordinary passerby. He was looking toward the house as though he had some terrible personal animosity for the people living here. I suppose that made me pay more than usual attention to him, and when Denys Arden brought me up here and we saw the portraits, I noticed the resemblance. I didn't connect the two straight away, but the thing stayed in my mind, and when I saw Latimer again among the carol singers, I began to think about him seriously. I'd already heard the name of the man who used to own the house, and when the rector told me that this fellow had the same name, it was obviously more than coincidence."

Nicholas Blaise was staring out the window. His dark,

nervous features bore a look of concentration. He turned around suddenly. He said, "The necklace! That's the motive, Mordecai! He came here after the necklace!"

"He may have come with that intention, but he *didn't* steal it," said Mordecai Tremaine. The big oak chest he had noticed on his former visit to the room was still against the wall. He seated himself upon it. "Latimer's story isn't the only one in this case, Nick. When you start looking for the main thread in a murder inquiry, you find yourself getting involved with all sorts of other odd things. That's where I want you to help me. You can probably fill in some of the details I've only been able to guess at. You can tell me, for instance, about Charlotte Grame. She wants to get married. And Benedict Grame doesn't approve. Am I right?"

Nicholas Blaise looked uncomfortable. But he said at last, "I don't suppose there's much point in trying to hide it any longer. She's in love with that fellow Brett. The chap who was at the inn. They were planning to run away together."

"Ah!" Mordecai Tremaine gave a sigh. He said: "I saw them in Calnford. I knew there must be something between them when Charlotte denied it. Mrs. Tristam's in it, too, isn't she?"

"She's been trying to persuade Benedict to change his mind. She's on Charlotte's side. When you spoke to me before, I felt that I couldn't say too much in case it got back to Benedict's ears and made things even more difficult for Charlotte."

"When I heard her scream on the night of the murder," said Tremaine, "she gave herself away. She was screaming so frantically, not because she was unnerved at having discovered Jeremy Rainer's body, *but because she wanted to warn someone*. She said she couldn't sleep and went downstairs to investigate strange noises she'd heard. But she wasn't in her dressing gown as you might have expected. *She was fully dressed*.

"She was fully dressed because she was running away with Brett. He was waiting for her outside the house. She screamed so desperately because she was warning him to get away. Brett was the man Roger Wynton tackled. When we saw him in the inn, he still carried the marks on him. It was because she had to see him, because she had to tell him what was happening and to find out whether the police suspected him, that she went down to the village so furtively that afternoon."

There was respect in Nicholas Blaise's eyes. "Yes," he said, "that *is* what happened. Charlotte told me. I suppose she felt she had to tell someone, and she's always given me her confidences. She made me promise not to reveal it to a soul. She came to my room that night to tell me she was running away. I knew the reason why she was fully dressed, but you see, I couldn't—I didn't have the right to explain to you."

"I don't think it matters now," said Tremaine slowly. "Neither Brett nor Charlotte Grame had any hand in the murder. The fact that their elopement was planned to take place on the night Rainer was killed helped to confuse the issue, but the parts they played are clear enough."

He paused. He pushed the pince-nez back into position. He said: "That's two people accounted for. Now let's try to deal with the rest of the house party. If we eliminate everyone who *wasn't* guilty, it will make the murderer stand out more plainly."

"I take it," observed Blaise, "that we can discount Roger Wynton and Denys? *They're* not among the suspects. Who's next on your list?"

"The man who stole the necklace," said Tremaine. "Gerald Beechley."

"*Gerald?*" Shocked surprise was in Blaise's voice. "Are you *sure?*"

"As sure as I can be without definite proof. He's been losing money, and his bookmaker's been pressing him for settlement."

"But he's been hard up plenty of times before this. He had only to go to Benedict."

"He did. And Grame refused to help him. I saw Beechley's face just after their interview, and it was plain what had happened. Beechley was desperate. He had to get money from somewhere, and he thought of the necklace. Perhaps he told himself that even if he was suspected, Grame wouldn't risk a scandal. He went to Grame's room, and luck was with him because Grame wasn't there. Taking the necklace was easy.

"And then his luck wasn't so good. The murder was discovered. He realized that if it became known that he'd been out of his room and that he'd stolen the necklace, there was every possibility of him being accused of having killed Jeremy Rainer. And he'd have no alibi.

"Besides, he'd bought a Father Christmas outfit in Calnford and was wearing it that night. He knew that if *that* fact came out, he'd really be up against it. That's why he's been shutting himself in his room and soaking himself in whiskey. He's been scared to death of finding himself under arrest for murder."

"Gerald was wearing a Father Christmas outfit?" said Blaise. His voice was mystified. "But why? Why on earth should he want to do that?"

"I don't think," said Mordecai Tremaine, "he did want to. He did it because Benedict Grame told him to do it and because he was afraid to refuse."

Nicholas Blaise lifted his hands in a helpless gesture. "This is getting too deep for me, Mordecai. *Why* should Benedict want Gerald to go wandering about the house wearing a Father Christmas outfit?"

"Think back, Nick," said Tremaine. "Why did it take Benedict Grame so long to make his appearance, despite the fact that Charlotte was screaming at the top of her voice right underneath his room? *It was because he wasn't there.* He waited until everybody had gone downstairs and he could get back without being seen, and then he deliberately stayed in his room until you went up for him to make it appear that he'd been there all the time.

"Telling Gerald Beechley to wear a Father Christmas outfit was done with the object of safeguarding himself if anyone had happened to find out that his room was empty and started asking questions. Beechley was intended to be mistaken for him—I did it myself, as a matter of fact, when I happened to look out my window and see a Father Christmas on the terrace—so that if it *was* discovered that his room was empty, he wouldn't have to betray where he *really* was. I daresay Beechley suspected something of the sort, and that was why he chose that particular time to go after the necklace."

Blaise was making an obvious effort to absorb the significance of what his companion was saying, despite his undoubted bewilderment. "Where *was* Benedict?"

"With Lucia Tristam," said Mordecai Tremaine, and Blaise stared at him almost openmouthed.

"With…with Lucia?"

"Yes. With Lucia. He could hardly admit that. Nor," added Tremaine drily, "could she. No wonder she's been on edge all the time. It was a distinctly awkward situation for her, wasn't it? Jeremy Rainer murdered and Benedict Grame missing from his room at the vital time, and both of them in love with her and known to be jealous of each other. Once the police began to suspect Grame's alibi, she knew that she'd be forced to confess in order to save his neck."

"So *that* was why it was," said Blaise. "*That* was why Benedict didn't come down straight away."

His long fingers were intertwining. He was evidently laboring under suppressed excitement, like a man who had at last seen a clear path through the darkness encompassing him.

"I've got it, Mordecai!" he said. "I can see all of it now. Latimer came here as you said, breathing revenge and out to take what he could. He waited in the hide until Benedict had placed all the presents on the tree, and then he came out and stripped them off. He'd almost finished when Jeremy came in from the lodge through the french doors. He was wearing a Father Christmas outfit—we'll have to find the reason for that—and Latimer thought it was Benedict come back. You see, Mordecai! *He thought it was Benedict!*

"He'd been caught in the act of robbery by the very man he hated most, the man who'd bought the house that had been his. It must have been the last bitter dregs in his cup. He saw red for a moment, grappled with Benedict, and killed him. And then he realized what he'd done and rushed out across the lawn, blindly trying to get away!"

A little breathlessly, Nicholas Blaise finished. Tremaine adjusted the pince-nez that had all but reached the end of his nose. His air of harmless benevolence had never been more marked.

"You're getting near the truth," he said. "It's quite true that Jeremy Rainer was killed by mistake, and that it was Benedict Grame who should have died. But it wasn't Latimer who killed him."

The look of elation faded slowly from the other's face. "Not...not Latimer?" he said. "Then who did kill him?"

"*You* did, Nick," Mordecai Tremaine said quietly.

18

There was a moment's silence. An incredible, painful silence. And then Blaise said unsteadily, "I don't think that remark was in very good taste, Mordecai."

Tremaine rose slowly from the big chest upon which he had been seated. "Murder," he observed, "isn't in very good taste either."

He lifted the heavy lid of the chest. He rummaged through the items it contained—an assortment of household goods that had evidently been pushed inside and forgotten over the course of the years. At the bottom, where it had been hidden from sight, was a small sack. With a murmur of satisfaction he took it up and tipped out its contents—colored twine, decorated paper, and a collection of articles that included a wristlet watch, a fountain pen, a jeweled brooch, and a leather toiletry case.

Nicholas Blaise was breathing more quickly now. His dark eyes held a furtive uncertainty and a dreadful, dawning fear. "What are those things?"

Mordecai Tremaine closed the lid of the chest. "You should know. You put them there after you'd taken them from the Christmas tree. They were too dangerous to keep in your possession, and yet you couldn't destroy them and daren't take them out of the house in case you were seen. It occurred to me that you might have thought of the old chest in this room and decided to use it to hide them until it was safe to get them away. You reasoned that even if anyone did find them, there would be nothing to connect them with you."

Blaise's tongue passed over his lips. "You're crazy," he said. "Why should I want to kill Benedict?"

"For a very ancient reason," said Tremaine. "For money."

Blaise tried to infuse a sneer into his voice. "Does it sound likely? By killing Benedict, I'd be putting myself out of a job. I don't suppose he's left me any great sum in his will. Certainly nothing large enough to make me want to kill him."

"You laid your plans very cleverly. I don't doubt that you even made sure that Benedict *didn't* make a suspiciously large provision for you in his will. You wanted the police to believe that you had nothing to gain by his death. You wanted them to believe, in fact, that you stood to lose by it, since your relationship was a good deal closer than that of master and servant. But you weren't interested in legacies. You knew that by killing Benedict Grame you could provide yourself with a source of income that you could go on drawing upon for years."

"And just what was this remarkable gold mine?"

"Blackmail," said Mordecai Tremaine icily, and this time Nicholas Blaise did not sneer.

"Almost from the moment I arrived," Tremaine went on, "I noticed how everybody seemed to be interested in one thing—the Christmas tree. It wasn't just an ordinary interest. It was as if they were fascinated by it. There was Jeremy Rainer, who came into the room when Benedict Grame and yourself were attending to the decorations and stared at it so intently that he had no eyes for anything else. There was Professor Lorring, whom I found sitting in front of the tree when it was all but dark, looking as though he wanted to shrivel it where it stood. And there was Austin Delamere, whom I happened to see just as he arrived. Almost his first thought was about the tree.

"I began to ask myself what there was about it that should cause it to have such an attraction for Benedict Grame's guests…and an attraction that wasn't, apparently, a very pleasant one. It seemed such an ordinary tree. In fact, I thought that it was quite a happy idea of Grame's, a pleasantly seasonal touch, to provide a gaily decorated Christmas tree with a present for each of the members of his house party.

"But that simple explanation didn't fit in with what seemed to be happening. There was a definite attitude of fear and dislike toward that tree, something that wasn't at all simple. And when I tried to find out why, I discovered a number of curious things.

"I discovered that each year the same people were in the house party. I discovered that they seemed to regard it as highly important that they should spend Christmas with Benedict Grame. For instance, Austin Delamere must be a busy man, but he came this year just as he's come before. Jeremy Rainer was going to America, but he canceled his passage. It could be, of course, that being fond of Grame and knowing his delight in his Christmas gatherings, they didn't want to disappoint him. But somehow I couldn't bring myself to accept that as the truth.

"You see, there was Lorring. It was his first visit, so obviously *he* couldn't be feeling the pull of tradition and friendship. It seemed odd to find him in the house party at all. He's been disinclined to talk to anyone, and he's certainly shown no signs of possessing the Christmas spirit. He gave me the impression that far from being a willing visitor, he was here against his will. And there was Jeremy Rainer's visit to America. Not even Denys Arden knew why he suddenly decided not to go. If it had been because he didn't want to disappoint Benedict Grame, there was surely no reason why he shouldn't have said as much."

Nicholas Blaise did not make any comment. His eyes were fixed upon Mordecai Tremaine in a baleful glare.

Tremaine said: "There were other curious things. There was Rainer's attitude toward Roger Wynton. At first, he and Wynton were on friendly terms, and then, without warning, Rainer changed. For no apparent reason—just as unexpectedly as he later canceled his American trip—he developed a violent dislike for him and wouldn't hear of Denys marrying him. At least, that was what the situation appeared to be, but Charlotte Grame told me that it wasn't true. She said that Rainer *didn't* dislike Wynton.

"There was Charlotte's own peculiar behavior. She was afraid to admit that I'd seen her in Calnford. She dreaded her association with Brett becoming known, although you'd imagine she was old enough to choose her own course of action. It was Charlotte, incidentally, who gave me another interesting item of information. She told me that Gerald Beechley wasn't really fond of practical jokes, despite his reputation for indulging in schoolboy pranks.

"And then there were the Napiers. They didn't look the kind of people to enjoy being buried in the country. They seemed out of their element, and whenever I questioned them casually about how long they'd been in the neighborhood, and whether they'd known Benedict Grame before coming to Sherbroome, they were evasive and ill at ease."

Mordecai Tremaine paused. Through the open window, he could see light clouds drifting across the sky. The room was very quiet. They might have been in a secluded world of their own, completely cut off from every other human being.

"It seemed to me," he went on after a moment or two, "that there could be only one solution. If so many individuals were doing things they didn't really want to do, it could only be because they had no option. Because they were being made to do them. And that led me to Benedict Grame. For the one thing common to all of them was the fact that they all attended Grame's Christmas parties—*and that they all received a present from his Christmas tree.*

"It was the tree that dominated the situation. It was fear of the tree that was in all their minds and was responsible for the atmosphere of strain that you could always feel despite the apparent gaiety. It was not, of course, the tree itself but what it stood for. The knowledge that Benedict Grame was their master, and that no matter what he might require, they would be compelled to do his bidding.

"It wasn't the old, crude type of blackmail, the obvious demand for money and yet more money. It was more devilish to the spirit than that. Benedict Grame isn't interested in money. Maybe only because he already has sufficient for his needs, but it's true that money holds little attraction for him. His craving is for something less tangible, perhaps, but infinitely more terrible…for power!

"That's the real motive behind these outwardly merry

Christmas parties. They aren't given by Benedict Grame, the immortal Pickwick, delighting in spreading happiness and goodwill. They're given by Benedict Grame the tyrant, cracking his whip over his slaves, reveling in his sense of power."

Mordecai Tremaine's eyes had lost their mildness and their benevolence. They were cold with an anger that was the more potent because it was so seldom there. "Under the pretense of spreading the Christmas spirit," he said stonily, "he's been making a mockery of it. He's been deliberately encouraging a belief in his generosity and his goodwill and his real enjoyment of the Christmas season in order to inflict added torture upon his victims.

"He knew they wouldn't dare reveal the truth. He knew they'd have to aid him to keep up the pretense of a gay house party celebrating in the old-fashioned way. It amused him to make them suffer. It amused him to act the benevolent host and watch them reacting to the tunes he called, knowing all the time that they hated the whole thing and that for them it was a ghastly, empty farce."

Nicholas Blaise crooked a finger into his collar. He loosened it, as though he found it difficult to breathe. "Even if this incredible story of yours were true, what is there in it to prove that *I* had a hand in the murder?" he asked.

"Enough," said Mordecai Tremaine, "to hang you. I imagine that you learned the truth about Benedict Grame in a gradual fashion as you gained more and more of his confidence. I don't suppose he actually told you, but you must have seen and heard enough to make you suspect, and once you realized that there was something queer going on, you set to work to find out what that something was. I don't doubt that when you did find out, you told yourself that Benedict Grame was wasting his opportunities. If *you* possessed the knowledge Grame had, you could make far better use of it. You aren't a rich man, and if money doesn't mean anything to Benedict Grame, it means a great deal to you.

"You didn't dare try blackmail on your own account, even when you'd discovered the secrets of Grame's annual guests. It would have been too dangerous. One of them might have told him, or he might have found out himself, and that would have uncovered you—something no blackmailer relishes. So you decided that Benedict Grame would have to die.

"Naturally, you didn't want to find yourself in the dock on a murder charge. You had to kill Grame in such a manner that the crime wouldn't be brought home to you. I don't know how long you were working out your plans, but you certainly didn't want to leave anything to chance. That was why you persuaded Grame to invite *me* here for Christmas.

"A friend of mine once told me," Tremaine added reflectively, "that I was a murder magnet. He said that no matter where I went, murder seemed to follow me. I thought of that when Jeremy Rainer died. It seemed almost as though it was true, and that in some strange way, murder *did* follow me.

"But the explanation is a very simple one. *This* murder was premeditated, and it was part of the murderer's plan—*your* plan—that I should be here when it happened. You wanted me here because you thought that I would have the confidence of the police, and you intended to put the right ideas into my head before the murder so that I could pass them on *after* it. That was why you added that postscript to your invitation. You wanted to plant the belief in my mind that there was something out of the ordinary going on even *before* I arrived.

"And when I did get here, you carefully hinted that Jeremy Rainer was responsible for what you described as Benedict Grame's uneasiness. Rainer was the man you intended to be accused of the crime you were going to commit, and you wanted to throw suspicion upon him from the very beginning.

"Christmas Eve was the time you planned for the murder. You knew that Benedict Grame would keep to his usual program of placing the presents on the tree after the rest of the household had gone to bed. That was the fact upon which you were counting.

"You stole Jeremy Rainer's revolver from his room, taking care not to remove his fingerprints, and when the others had gone to bed and before Grame arrived as Father Christmas, you fixed the gun in position in the earth under the Christmas tree. The trigger needed only a slight pressure to bring the hammer down, and you ran a length of thin cord up through the center of the tree, over the top branch and down to the bracket with Rainer's name upon it, so that it ran taut from the trigger to the bracket. If the branch bearing the bracket was pulled down it would have the effect of tightening the cord still further and causing the gun to fire.

"You helped with the decorating of the tree, and you took care to see that it was placed in the best position to aid your plan. You must have made very careful calculations to find out the exact angle at which the gun needed to be set, but you'd had plenty of opportunity to study Benedict Grame, and it was only a matter of perseverance.

"As part of your plan, you'd given Jeremy Rainer instructions, purporting to come from Grame, that he was to go to the lodge late on Christmas Eve and leave his signet ring there. It was the kind of thing Grame might have been expected to demand in order to show his power—just as he compelled Gerald Beechley to play those practical jokes everyone thought he enjoyed—and you knew that Rainer would obey. Your object was to incriminate him by making it plain that he was out of his room at the time of the murder.

"Leaving that one present on the tree was intended to provide a further piece of evidence against him. Benedict

Grame's orders to his victims were given in the form of type-written slips included in their Christmas presents. Rainer's present was to be left for the police to find. They would examine it and would promptly discover that Grame had been blackmailing him.

"The motive for the crime would then appear to be plain, and together with the gun you'd left in his room in a place where it was certain to be found and the fact that he was not where he was supposed to be at the time of the murder, he'd find it difficult to prove his innocence. You had to get rid of all the other presents, of course, otherwise the police would have realized that Rainer wasn't the only person who was being blackmailed, and that would have weakened the case against him."

Nicholas Blaise seemed to be trying to force himself to speak. He said at last: "You make it sound so ingenious that I can't understand how it came to go wrong."

"It went wrong," said Mordecai Tremaine, "like the plans of a murderer always do go wrong—because it's impossible to foresee just what is going to happen. You may have suspected that Jeremy Rainer was trying to find a way of breaking Benedict Grame's hold over him—and after all, that was excellent from your point of view because it strengthened the evidence against him. *But it certainly didn't occur to you that Benedict Grame would use a stepladder.*

"That was the simple little fact that destroyed all your careful calculations. Grame was in a hurry. He was going to Lucia Tristam, and he didn't want to waste too much time. The steps he'd had during the morning was still in the room, so he carried it over and used it to put the presents on the tree. It meant that he didn't have to stretch up to that top branch, and consequently he didn't exert the necessary pressure on the cord that would have pulled the trigger of the gun and killed him.

"Still, even that needn't have mattered. All you would have had to do was to take the gun away, and you would have been back where you were. No one would ever have suspected what you had planned to do.

"But two more unforeseen developments went against you. Charlotte Grame was going to run away, and she came to your room to tell you about it. You were later than you had intended in going downstairs to find out what had happened, and in the meantime, the second unexpected thing had taken place. Jeremy Rainer had come back from the lodge.

"You had given Rainer a part in your little drama, but you hadn't allowed for the fact that he might decide to play a part of his own as well. He'd gotten hold of a Father Christmas outfit—no doubt so that he'd be mistaken for Grame if anyone saw him—and he came back into the house and began to cut the presents off the tree.

"Exactly what he was going to do I don't suppose we'll ever find out, but he probably had some idea of checking the names of the others who were being blackmailed and forming an alliance against Grame. Charlotte told me that he'd said that things were going to change, and I don't think there's much doubt over what 'things' she meant. The ends of the cords were still on the tree, but I daresay he was going to examine the presents in his room and replace them later when the household should have been soundly asleep and there wouldn't be so much risk of being disturbed. The last present he touched was his own. He reached up to it...and pulled down the branch.

"When you eventually came down, you saw Father Christmas lying on his face in front of the tree *and you assumed that everything had gone according to plan and that it was Benedict Grame*. In the darkness, you didn't notice the remnants of cord on the tree, and for obvious reasons, you weren't anxious to linger any longer than was necessary.

"You saw the sack at the side of the body and one present in position, and you took it for granted that Grame had started at the top of the tree with the vital branch and had been killed before he'd had time to attend to any of the others. You cut the cord and took away the sack of presents and the gun. There was plenty of opportunity for you to plant it in Rainer's room later.

"It was the very extent of the evidence against Rainer that first made me suspect that he might have been killed by mistake. It seemed so much as though he should have been the murderer and not the victim that it started me wondering whether it *was* Rainer who had been intended to die after all. He'd been wearing a Father Christmas outfit, just as Benedict Grame was known to do, and the angle at which the bullet had been fired was decidedly curious. It looked as though the murderer must have lain on the floor and fired upward.

"I examined the tree carefully and found the remains of the cord that had been over the top branch. It wasn't the same color as the other pieces. It was green, obviously so that it wouldn't easily be noticed. There was also a mark in the soil that might have been made by a gun butt, and one of the decorations had been shattered. It was directly in the path the bullet might have taken if it had been fired from a position at the foot of the tree at a man stretching upward. This suggested that the murderer had not actually been present when the shot was fired, and *that* gave added weight to the theory that the wrong man had been killed."

Mordecai Tremaine's eyes, bright and watchful, peered over the pince-nez at his companion. He said, "Do you remember what happened when Charlotte Grame screamed? You were one of the last people to arrive. No one paid any attention to it at the time, and a little later on, it was Benedict Grame's failure to appear that was in the limelight.

"Looking back, it seemed to me that it was curious that you'd taken so long—almost as though you knew what to expect and hung back deliberately. And you didn't look like a man who'd been roughly aroused from sleep. Your hair was as neatly brushed as if you'd just performed a careful toilet—*or as if you hadn't been to bed.*

"And do you remember what else happened? You didn't give more than a glance at the body. You turned straight to me and asked me to find Benedict Grame's murderer. There wasn't a doubt in your mind that it *was* Grame who was lying there.

"In itself, that might not have been significant. You weren't the only person to jump to the conclusion that it was Grame who was dead. Ernest Lorring undoubtedly did, and I'm pretty sure that so did most of the others. In fact, apart from Lucia Tristam—we know now that she had her own reasons for it—the only person who didn't assume that it was Benedict Grame and who saw at once that it was Jeremy Rainer was Denys Arden.

"The explanation, of course, is that Denys Arden's mind, unlike the minds of the other people in the room, was unclouded by previous knowledge. She did not know anything of the blackmail that was going on. She did not know, as the others did, that there was a very good reason why Benedict Grame might have been murdered.

"I imagine that it was that knowledge that made Lorring take the risk of stealing the last present. The blackmail in his case was only just beginning. It was his first visit, and although he knew that it was connected in some way with the tree, he didn't know exactly how, and he took that present because he wanted to find out before the police arrived.

"Incidentally, another little point that gave you away was the manner in which you drew attention to the fact that there was one present on the tree. Everyone else was too concerned with the fact of the murder itself to notice it. But *you* weren't. You weren't because you knew it was there and because it was part of your plan that it should be seen.

"They were only small things individually, but taken together, they became significant. And once I was certain that it was Benedict Grame who should have died, they began to fall into place. There were four marks on the wooden flooring in front of the tree that might have been made by the steps. I asked Grame to hand me the bracket with Rainer's name on it, and he used the steps to reach it. I was sure then that my theory was the right one, and that he'd done the same thing on Christmas Eve and so saved himself from death."

Mordecai Tremaine's voice was remorseless now. There was no trace about him of the kindly sentimentalist. "It must have been a ghastly moment for you when you saw that the dead man was Jeremy Rainer. You knew that your plans had gone awry in some terrible fashion, but you couldn't tell why or how. You knew that your neck was in peril and that you had to think of a way out. You had to adjust yourself to the new situation without betraying yourself.

"But you *did* betray yourself. It was because your mind had become accustomed to the thought that Benedict Grame would be dead that you didn't do the obvious thing and look for him at once. It was a suspiciously long time before you seemed to realize that he hadn't come down. You didn't miss him because the part you'd so carefully mapped out for yourself was based upon the assumption that he would be already there in the person of the victim.

"What a feeling of panic you must have known. You'd prepared every move in advance, and now the whole careful edifice had been endangered because something you hadn't foreseen and hadn't guarded against had undermined it. That was why you tried to question Charlotte so urgently about what had happened. That was why you appeared to give up all interest in whether I tried to find the murderer or not, despite your rather extravagant exhibition when you came into the room.

"Then you began to recover your nerve. You saw that if you hadn't been able to get rid of Benedict Grame in one way, you might be able to do it in another—*by accusing him of the murder.* You pretended to be shocked at the idea that Grame might be guilty, but all your protestations had one object—to keep drawing attention to all the things that made it appear that he *was*.

"You protested so much that you gave away your real intentions. As a matter of fact, it was your own attitude that convinced me that you knew all about Benedict Grame's blackmailing activities. When we were talking about possible suspects, you affected to laugh at the suggestion that any of the people in the house might possess secrets they wouldn't be anxious to have revealed—but you proceeded to name the very persons I was already confident *did* have such secrets.

"Just recently, you've changed again. You've been genuinely doing your best to convince me of Grame's innocence. I suppose the truth is that he's realized that *you* must have killed Rainer in mistake for himself, and he's been making you dance to his tune. It's ironic, isn't it? You tried to murder Benedict Grame in order to take over the power of blackmail he exercised, and instead you found yourself among his victims. And you delivered into his hands the greatest power of all—the power of life and death, the power to send you to the gallows!"

Nicholas Blaise had moved gradually nearer so that now he was standing close up against Mordecai Tremaine. His dark eyes had a madness in them.

"You're quite right," he said. "He did find out. He's been cracking the whip over me. Just as he did over Jeremy when he was alive, and just as he's been doing over Beechley and Delamere and Lorring. Benedict loves power. It amused him to make Gerald do all those stupid things, and to prevent Charlotte getting married, and to compel Jeremy to adopt an unreasonable attitude toward Roger Wynton.

"All that was Benedict's doing, of course. Jeremy liked Wynton, and he knew that he was hurting Denys by behaving objectionably toward him. But he daren't disobey because Benedict could have gotten him hanged. It was over something that happened in South Africa. Besides, he couldn't risk Benedict's telling Denys that he'd been responsible for ruining her father and had caused his death. He really did love her as though she was his own child.

"I found it all out gradually—just as you said. All about the Christmas parties and about the Christmas tree. I found out that Benedict wasn't a lovable character at all, but just a sadistic, leering devil who liked playing with people. So I decided to kill him and run things *my* way. Of course, I wasn't an altruist. I was after the money all right. But it would have been better for the victims themselves in the long run. They'd have known where they stood. They'd have known how much they had to pay, and there'd have been none of the refinements of torture Benedict liked to inflict."

A note of hatred crept into his voice. It vibrated harshly. "He knows how to put the screw on," he said viciously. "All those damned parlor games the other afternoon. They were for *my* benefit. He knew I was helpless, and he wanted to watch me squirm.

"I thought it all out—the best time to choose, the way to do it. I went over it a thousand times. I even practiced on Jeremy beforehand to make sure he'd obey any instructions I gave him in Benedict's name. I left the notes in his room like Benedict himself would have done. I got him to type out a whole lot of stuff from the *Financial Times* and send it to an address in London. He did it without a murmur.

"I thought that nothing could go wrong. Especially when I hit upon the idea of getting *you* down and using you to influence the police and to act as my eyes and ears so that I'd learn all that was going on."

Blaise's hands went out to grip Mordecai Tremaine's shoulders. They moved slowly toward his throat. "You've been clever," he said softly. "So very, very clever. You've reasoned it all out just as it happened. But you must realize that I wouldn't have admitted it if I hadn't a reason. This is the room where they kept the Lady Isabel. She flung herself out of the window and was killed on the terrace down below. I shall say that you climbed out to the balustrade to examine something on the roof and that you slipped on the melting snow. I tried to save you, but I was too late. I shall be distracted with grief, of course. Everybody will say that it was a tragic accident—*and no one will ever know what you've just said to me.*"

Mordecai Tremaine swallowed hard. His heart was hammering, and he felt himself succumbing to the hypnotic glare in the dark eyes staring into his own. But he said shakily, "You're wrong. Someone *will* know. You see, there was a witness."

The pressure of the hands relaxed. Nicholas Blaise said sharply, suspiciously, "You're lying! You're trying to trick me! There couldn't have been!"

"But there was. It was Latimer. He was in the hide. He saw you put the gun in the tree. He waited, not daring to come out because there were still people about, and he saw you come back after the murder and take the gun away."

Mordecai Tremaine's voice was steadier now. He knew from Nicholas Blaise's face that he had shaken his assurance. He added, "I wasn't foolish enough to come up here alone."

There was a sudden sound from beyond the door. Nicholas Blaise drew back. His hands fell away. A snarling exclamation broke from his lips, and then, like an animal, he made a leap for the window. He forced himself through the opening and crouched against the stone balustrade, facing back into the room, and now there was a gun in his hand.

Superintendent Cannock said, "The game's up. Better

come without making a fuss. This won't do you any good, you know."

Blaise was still breathing heavily after his exertion. But now that the crisis was upon him, he had regained his self-control. "A very pretty little plot, Superintendent. So you were listening outside all the time. Stupid of me not to have guessed it."

Cannock moved a pace nearer. "You needn't say anything," he said. "Not unless you want to."

Nicholas Blaise smiled sardonically. "Is this where you give the official warning? You needn't trouble, Superintendent. I'm afraid I've left you a rather unpleasant mess to clear up, although I daresay you'll be able to prevent quite a lot of it from getting into the newspapers. Gerald will be able to return the necklace, and I don't suppose Benedict will want the scandal of prosecuting him. As for Benedict himself, he'll have to cry a halt to his blackmailing, but I doubt if you'll be able to prove anything against him. The victims will be too scared to talk.

"He might even marry Lucia. He's been using a hold over her, of course, but now he's really in love with her. That's why he made the Napiers take her for so long. It's odd, isn't it! The magnificent Lucia, falling in love like a schoolgirl!"

"Come down," said Mordecai Tremaine. "Put that gun away and come down."

"And be hanged by the neck until I'm dead?" There was a smile twisting Blaise's lips. "I don't think I'd care for it somehow. Give my love to Denys," he added. "Tell her I hope she'll be happy with that young man of hers."

Before they realized what he intended, he had climbed up on to the balustrade. He stood looking down at them, his tall figure dark against the hard blue sky with its drifting clouds.

"What a pity I didn't provide myself with one of those fashionable cyanide vials. It would have been so much neater. Goodbye, Mordecai. I was a fool to ask you here."

With a sudden gesture, he flung the gun from him and laughed softly at their instinctive defensive movements. "It's all right," he said. "It isn't loaded. I'm not desperate enough to make a good murderer!"

Superintendent Cannock divined what was going to happen. He flung himself desperately forward. But his outflung hand closed upon air. Nicholas Blaise had stepped backward.

ABOUT THE AUTHOR

Francis Duncan knows how to write a good murder mystery, and from the 1930s through the 1950s, his whodunits captivated readers. His character, Mordecai Tremaine, was the best at unraveling a narrative. However, there was one mystery that went unsolved: Who exactly *was* Francis Duncan?

When Vintage Books, an imprint of Random House UK, decided to bring back Duncan's *Murder for Christmas* in December 2015, questions still loomed around the author's unknown identity. In fact, there wasn't a trace of biographical information about the author to be found, and Vintage republished the book without solving the puzzle. Francis Duncan remained a man of mystery.

That is until January 2016 when, after seeing *Murder for Christmas* on shelf at a Waterstones bookstore, Duncan's daughter came forward to the publishers, revealing that Francis Duncan is actually a pseudonym for her own father, William Underhill, who was born in 1918. He lived virtually all his life in Bristol and was a "scholarship boy" boarder at

Queen Elizabeth's Hospital school. Due to family circumstances he was unable to go to university and started work in the Housing Department of Bristol City Council. Writing was always important to him, and very early on he published articles in newspapers and magazines. His first detective story was published in 1936.

In 1938 he married Sylvia Henly. Although a conscientious objector, he served in the Royal Army Medical Corps in World War II, landing in France shortly after D-Day. After the war, he trained as a teacher and spent the rest of his life in education, first as a primary school teacher and then as a lecturer in a college of further education. In the 1950s he studied for an external economics degree from London University. No mean feat with a family to support; his daughter, Kathryn, was born in 1943, and his son, Derek, in 1949.

Throughout much of this time he continued to write detective fiction from "sheer inner necessity," but also to supplement a modest income. He enjoyed foreign travel, particularly to France, and took up golf on retirement. He died of a heart attack shortly after celebrating his fiftieth wedding anniversary in 1988.

Look for the next book in Francis Duncan's classic Mordecai Tremaine mystery series

A MORDECAI TREMAINE MYSTERY

MURDER Has a MOTIVE

FRANCIS DUNCAN

"How do any of us know what strange creatures our neighbors become when they go into their houses and shut their doors upon the world? How do we know what people are thinking and saying behind all those innocent-looking facades?"